OF LAST RESORT
PRINCES OF THE BLOOD

Of Last Resort
Princes of the Blood
By Megan Derr

All rights reserved. No part of this book may be used or reproduced in any manner without written permission of the publisher, except for the purpose of reviews.

Edited by Samantha M. Derr
Cover designed by Aisha Akeju

This book is a work of fiction and all names, characters, places, and incidents are fictional or used fictitiously. Any resemblance to actual people, places, or events is coincidental.

Second Edition November 2019
Copyright © 2019 by Megan Derr
Printed in the United States of America

*Dedicated to my sister Brandie,
Who shares my love of blood, violence, and horror*

OF LAST RESORT
Princes of the Blood

MEGAN DERR

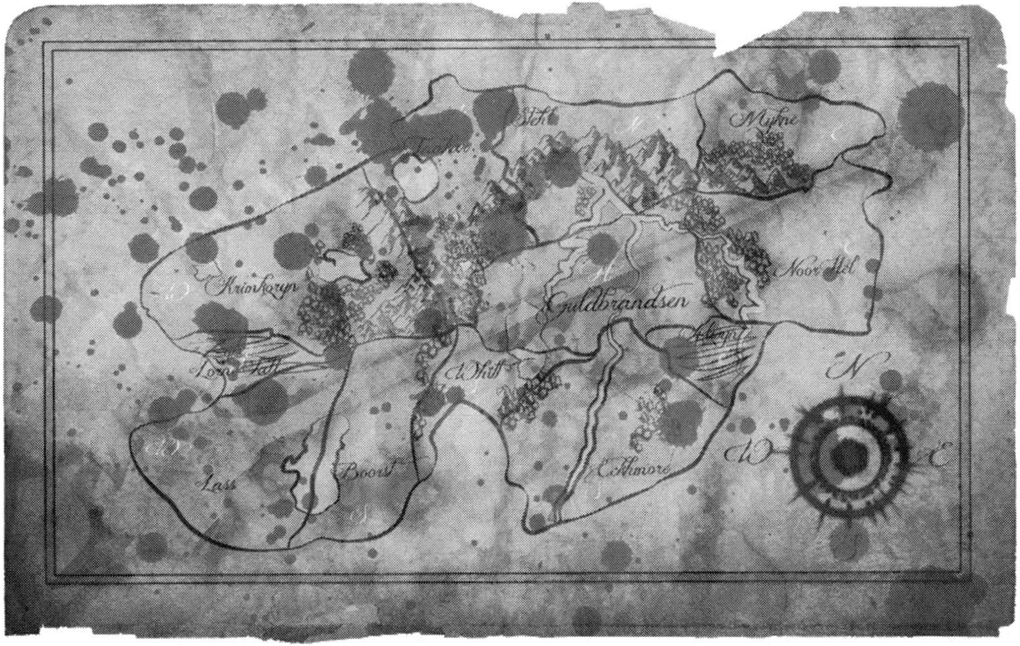
Myfne
Noor Hel
Guldbrandsen
Whiff
Boort
Lass
N
W
E

Part One
Blooding

CAMBORD

"What do you mean he ran away?" King Waldemar demanded, his tone making everyone around him recoil, save Crown Prince Birgir, standing beside him, and the Princes of the Blood, standing in a line behind the throne that reached from one end of dais to the other.

In front of Raffé, his parents cowered. He wasn't sure why. Showing that sort of weakness would not encourage King Waldemar to be kinder. "I—" His father swallowed, tried again. "I beg your forgiveness, Majesty. We went to rouse Tallas for dinner and found his room empty, his belongings gone, and only a note saying farewell pinned to his pillow. I don't know why—"

"You can spare me your whining and pleading," Waldemar said. "Your children bear the proper ratio of demon blood; by law you are required to provide one son for Blooding. Those suited to the Blooding are few, and we need all that we can get. Refusing to undergo the Blooding is not just breaking the law, it is treason."

"Take me," Raffé said before his parents could speak, stepping in front of them to drop to his knees before the throne. He placed his fisted hands in front of him, knuckles to the floor, and bowed his head low. "My blood is the same. Take me in his place, Majesty."

Silence met his words, and Raffé's cheeks flushed as he braced himself for the shame of rejection. He could all but feel his parents' mortification, hear the amused derision of the assembled court in their tittering, poorly muffled laughs, the disapproval of his fiancé in his soft sigh. He cringed when the silence stretched on but said, "I am not my brother, Majesty, I know. We are the same blood, however, and I have not run away. I will not run away." He dared to look up, meet the king's gaze, hoping he understood what Raffé was not saying: that he would die if his Majesty would spare his parents.

Because he wasn't Tallas, who was tall, broad, all muscle and agility. He wielded sword, lance, and bow as though they were toys. He was handsome, with his sun-dark skin and brown-red hair, and more people than Raffé could count loved to say how charming Tallas could be. Without ever seeming to try, Tallas was everything desired of those who underwent the Blooding. Raffé could not understand why Tallas had run. If he had remained, he would have had a place of honor. He would have been royalty, possessed of rare abilities, capable of recovering from practically any injury ... and that was only what Raffé knew from rumors.

Raffé resembled his aunt, his mother's ill-favored little sister. He was average in height but less than average in everything else. His form, appearance, martial abilities, and strength were all unremarkable. He was plain, with pasty skin and flat black hair and a quiet, soft-spoken manner. He was better off shunted into an office than let onto the battlefield with his peers. He had always excelled at numbers and failed at everything else. In a month, he would marry an affluent merchant who would bring money and connections to his family and settle him neatly in a handsome townhouse with his husband's two wives.

That he could join the ranks of the Princes of the Blood was absurd. So he said nothing when the court laughed and jested and King Waldemar and the Princes of Blood around him remained coldly silent. Finally, King Waldemar demanded silence with a sharp cut of his hand and regarded Raffé pensively.

If Raffé undertook the Blooding, and died trying, then the bargain was kept, honor satisfied, and though his parents would suffer for the broken promise, they would not lose their lives or their livelihood. The situation worked out neatly for everyone—except Raffé, but it was his duty to assume the burdens his brother had abandoned. If he wished his vain, vapid brother had stopped and realized his behavior would forfeit the lives of his parents and brother ... Raffé wished for a lot of things. That did not mean he was stupid enough to think he would ever get them.

Two of the Princes stepped forward at King Waldemar's bidding, bending low to converse with him and the crown prince. Raffé tried not to stare, but he did not dare risk looking somewhere else and appearing disinterested. His chest felt as though it was seizing when the king dismissed them and once more regarded Raffé. "So be it," King Waldemar pronounced, and dread and depression churned in Raffé's gut. "You are dismissed for tonight. The Blooding will take place at dawn as originally planned."

That gave him eight hours left to live. Raffé could not imagine that he would survive—if he had the potential to take, and survive, the Blooding, they would have chosen him. He could not even really comprehend it. They had been at the castle for a month, and that after a long three month journey from the southernmost corner of the kingdom where his family's holdings were located. He had loved the traveling, seeing Castle Guldbrandsen, which was the source of so much notoriety, and the colorful inhabitants who had been little more than stories to him until their arrival. He had spent his days exploring as much as he could, memorizing it so he could feed off the memories the rest of his dreary life.

He'd envied his brother the chance to live a larger, brighter life. Had long ago resigned himself to a miserable one. Raffé had spent most of the evening making plans about his quiet, simple wedding with his fiancé. He'd thought he'd had all the time in the world to be miserable.

A long stretch of life reduced to eight hours. Raffé felt something should be said, done. Such a moment should not pass in silence. No one spoke, however, so he only bowed his head again and murmured his gratitude before he rose and followed his parents out of the throne room and back to their suite.

"You're a fool," his mother said when the doors were closed and the servants dismissed.

Normally, Raffé said whatever was necessary to calm his mother and move on. Anything was better than enduring the razor edge of her temper for the hours or days it lasted. But he only had eight hours left—what did her anger matter to him? He was losing his life because of his stupid brother, and as was typical, she blamed him instead. "Tallas is the fool," Raffé said. "I'll do my best to survive the ceremony, but if I hadn't volunteered, we would all be going to the noose right now."

"Whether you live or not, our lives are ruined. Your brother is gone, you will be gone—we're disgraced and now the alliance with Hilto will never happen," his father said, looking tired. "We will have to give back all that betrothal money, and you know how sorely we needed it."

Raffé shoved back the hurt. What had he expected, words of love? Words of gratitude? His parents had never had enough of either to spare for their tepid son. "Blame Tallas. He is the one who committed treason. At least now you'll live to complain about us both." He turned and walked away before they could reply, refusing to waste his last hours arguing with them.

He wandered the halls of the castle until he reached the maze he had adored from the moment he saw it. He'd heard it whispered that the Shadowmarch used it for training, but it was also open to all who cared to try it, so he did not know if the training rumor was true. The Shadowmarch maze was nothing like the childishly simple hedge maze in his mother's garden. No, the Shadowmarch maze was made of dark stone polished to mirror smoothness and towered nearly twice his height. Since he was largely unnecessary and left to his own devices, he had explored the maze for hours in the month they'd been at Castle Guldbrandsen. So far he had managed to find three different routes to the center. It was unfortunate he would not have the opportunity to find more, silly a thing as it was to be disappointed about hours from his death.

Night had fallen, snow drifting down lazily. It would get worse later, to judge by the feel and the smell, but for the moment it was a beautiful, quiet winter night. Raffé relished it, lingering at the entrance to the maze. He could not read the gold plaque set in the wall beside the entrance in the weak light of the torches, but he knew the words by heart: *The only way to find yourself is to get lost.*

"Raffé?"

He turned at the sound of his name spoken in that smooth, cultured voice, surprised and elated that Almor had sought him out. It sped the beating of his heart, reminded him of what he had hoped to ask Almor. He smiled in greeting and said brightly, "Almor, I was hoping to speak to you tonight. I am sorry for this turn in events. I hope you will forgive me, forgive my family." He stepped in close, reached up to kiss—and was stung when Almor turned so that the kiss glanced off his cheek.

"It is a shame that it has come to this," Almor said briskly.

"It's not over yet," Raffé said, suddenly annoyed. Why did everyone so quickly and easily assume he would die? There was a chance, however slight, that he would survive the Blooding. Did no one have faith in him, or even hope he would defy the odds? Were they all so eager to say goodbye? Maybe they were just putting on a brave front. He would prefer they be encouraging, counter his own terror, but he was fairly certain they really just wanted the whole matter over with.

"Speaking of the Blooding, I did want to speak to you about—about something." Raffé curled his hands around the edges of his cloak, shoulders hunching,

"What was that?" Almor asked warily.

Raffé ignored it because damn everyone, he had the right to a last request. "I'm but hours from dying, and I just wondered—I was hoping—"

"Say it. You know how it drives everyone mad when you fumble and stutter so."

OF LAST RESORT

He wouldn't struggle to speak if everyone did not treat him as if he was some form of torture, but Raffé kept the bitter thought to himself. "I wondered if my honored fiancé would spend my last night with me. I don't want to die without— without knowing—" He stopped, unable to say it and then comprehension filled Almor's face, and Raffé's heart sped up again. They'd never exchanged more than perfunctory kisses, and they were both quite busy. It did not help that Almor lived hours away in a larger city, where he managed his merchant company with his two wives. Raffé had only met them once, but they had seemed nice, and he had hoped he would fit well into the family. He'd heard that such marriages could be enjoyable when all parties got along. Obviously he would never know, but he hoped to have some taste of it before he died.

"I don't think that's a good idea," Almor said, his tone cool.

"What?" Raffé asked, face burning with humiliation. He wasn't his brother, but he wasn't hideous. "Why not? You're still my fiancé, and we were to be married in less than a month. Haven't you been looking forward to ..." He trailed off at the look on Almor's face. His heart giving a painful twist, and it suddenly hurt to breathe.

Almor drew himself up stiffly, looking and sounding decidedly uncomfortable. "It was a business marriage, Raffé. I'm sorry, but ... it's not a good idea. Good luck tomorrow with the ceremony." He gave Raffé's cheek a perfunctory kiss then turned and walked away.

Raffé had cried a lot as a boy, unable to understand why nothing he did was right, why everything about him was wrong when he tried so hard to please. Why everyone gave Tallas everything and would not give him even a single chance. He'd stopped crying when he realized it made matters worse, was one of the things wrong with him. He had refused to cry again. People might hurt him, but they did not need to know it—they did not deserve to have that kind of power over him.

He wanted to cry then, alone at the entrance to a maze, seven hours from a likely death, with no one to bid him farewell, to say they loved him, to ensure his last hours were happy ones.

Was he so terrible a person?

But looking back, he could not remember anything about him that was remarkable. He had always stood in his brother's shadow, always been one face in a thousand. So he was not terrible, no. He was simply ... tepid. Who liked tepid?

He still wished someone ...

Pushing the futile thought away, he plunged into the maze, following the third path to the center that he had discovered. It was nearly impossible to see, but memory and weak torchlight sufficed for him. Letting his feet walk the memorized path, he lost himself in a favorite daydream: A figure walking into Raffé's study, a marriage mark on the back of their right hand, tired but happy to be home. Raffé abandoned his desk to greet the figure, kiss them warmly, laughing when they made it clear a mere kiss would not be enough.

After a few minutes, he pushed the daydream away again, unable to bear the pain. It had always been a slender hope and had quite firmly moved into the realm of impossible. He had learned a long time ago that nothing was gained by dwelling on the impossible. Only a few more hours. Maybe in his next life he would do a better job of living.

He wondered where Tallas had gone and hoped something horrible was happening to the selfish wretch. The stupid bastard deserved to—

Someone grabbed him, and Raffé cried out in panic, but his breath whooshed out of him as he was knocked against the stone wall of the maze, smooth and cold against his back despite all his layers. Black, everything was absolutely black. The torchlight did not extend to the little nook where his captor held him. "What are you doing?" Raffé asked.

The man chuckled, his voice deep, rough, running right down Raffé's spine in a way he'd never felt before. Certainly being shoved around had never affected his cock. "Normally, the first question put to me is, 'Who are you?'. That is followed by, 'What do you think you are doing?' sometimes with a 'How dare you!'. Usually after that comes, 'Do you know who I am?' No one ever simply asks what I am doing."

"I sincerely doubt my identity has anything to do with the matter." Raffé's heart was still pounding madly in his chest, but other than the first scare, the man did not seem inclined to harm him. "As to yours— if you were interested in making yourself known you would have introduced yourself, not grabbed me and thrown me into a wall. Do you often grab people in the dark and throw them into walls?"

"Depends on the reason. I often throw men into things when they prove threatening. But men like you? Not very often at all."

"Men like me?" Raffé asked. "I do not take your meaning. Men like what?"

There was only silence in reply, but Raffé knew silences. Words had too many sharp edges. Silences were simple. Whatever the man had been deliberating, he finally settled on, "I overheard you and your fiancé. Ex-fiancé, strictly speaking."

Raffé cringed, face going hot again, and he was extremely grateful for the dark. Bad enough that his fiancé had rejected him hours before he was to die, had told him in no uncertain terms that Raffé was not worth fucking—why did the gods hate him so much that his humiliation had been overheard?

"You should be feeling relieved, little prince," the man said, startling Raffé by calling him that.

He was a little prince, if only for a few more hours. Some small bit of pride sparked at that. There were currently only fourteen Princes of the Blood. Finding those with the correct amount of demon blood in their veins who would be able to handle the difficult transformation and the brutal life that followed was close to impossible. He might only be a replacement, he might be too weak to survive the Blooding and ill-suited to the life anyway, but for the next seven hours he was a little prince, and no one could take that from him.

"Relieved?" he finally asked.

"Your ex-fiancé proved himself a coward by his actions, and no man wants to be married to a coward."

"He is not the one called coward," Raffé said quietly. He tried to at least look in the direction of the voice, though it was hard to gauge with the way sound echoed around the stone walls. He tilted his head up, sensing the man loomed over him.

The man chuckled, and that sensation trickled up and down Raffé's spine again, made him feel more awake. "You are many things, little prince, but I would not call you a coward. I watched you in the throne room, and I listen to you now. Cowardice is not what comes to mind."

Raffé wanted to know what did but was terrified of the answer. "You still have not explained why you are shoving me into walls."

"I believe there is a last request in want of fulfilling, little prince," the man said, voice going husky, and before Raffé could process the words, his mouth was taken. He-he was being kissed. Really kissed, like a lover.

The man's mouth slid over his, rough and wet, tongue pushing into Raffé's mouth when he parted his lips in surprise. He was being kissed. By a complete stranger, in the dark of the maze. The thought, the press of that insistent mouth, made him shiver, made him ache. Raffé whimpered, clung, tried to return the kiss. When the man eventually drew back, he made a rumbling noise that went straight to Raffé's cock. "You are sweet, little prince. I will gladly take what that coward was stupid enough to reject."

"Is—what should I call you?"

The man stilled, then chuckled, though Raffé had the impression he was laughing at himself. "Call me ... Cambord, little prince."

Raffé laughed, instinctively leaning forward to muffle the noise against the man's broad chest. Cambord—the family name of the most famous architects in the kingdom. They were often called 'wall makers' since that was how they had begun their trade generations ago. Every other person claimed to be related to the family. "Cambord, then."

"Is this what you want, little prince?" Cambord asked, and Raffé shivered again as calloused fingers trailed along his cheek. The gentle touch, somehow far more potent than the kiss, made his eyes sting. Nobody ever touched him, not really. Perfunctory kisses and stiff, expected embraces were not the same.

He swallowed, then said raggedly, "That's— Yes. If you want me, take me."

Cambord made a soft noise and kissed him again, arms sliding around him, a cushion between Raffé and the cold stone wall. Raffé kissed back eagerly, mimicking Cambord's motions, shyly wrapping his hands around shoulders that proved to be wonderfully broad and firm beneath layers of fabric. He broke away with a startled cry when Cambord abruptly lifted him off his feet, arms jerking reflexively to twine around Cambord's neck.

Then the kisses were back, hard, eager, and Raffé could not believe that somebody wanted him, was giving him a chance to feel something he had always so desperately wanted. He refused to think about the fact that Cambord probably just felt sorry for him. For one damn night—his last night—he was going to enjoy feeling like he was wanted. It was the closest he would ever get.

He was panting when they pulled apart, and the rough hairs on Cambord's jaw scraped against his skin in a way that kicked Raffé's awareness ever higher. "It's a little cold out here, isn't it?"

"Do you feel cold, little prince?" Cambord asked against his ear before nipping the lobe.

Raffé shuddered. "N-no." Cambord was wonderfully, almost unbelievably warm, even discounting the heat he'd sparked through Raffé's body.

Cambord chuckled again and kissed him, then began to work on Raffé's clothes. When his fingers brushed against Raffé's cock, he almost came then and there. But Cambord gave another one of those husky, lust-inducing laughs and nipped at his lips. "By all means, spend, little prince. We're just getting started, and a man as young as you can go the whole night."

The words made Raffé hot, rendered him helpless to do anything except feed moans into the mouth that claimed his again as Cambord's hand wrapped firmly around his cock and began to stroke him. It was nothing like his own hand, not even close. Raffé struggled to draw breath when Cambord's mouth tore away. "Come, little prince. Come apart in my arms. Let me feel you shudder against me as you find pleasure. Then I will show you a thousand pleasures more."

Raffé obeyed, happily and eagerly, and wished only that he had a face to put to the beautiful voice, those wonderful hands, the musky leather and wool scent that surrounded him.

But he would take what he had and treasure it, and think of it when he died at dawn.

"Beautiful," Cambord murmured. "The loveliest thing I have seen for an age. I thought you intriguing the few times I've seen you about the castle, especially in the throne room, but I like you best exactly like this." He let go of Raffé's cock, wet, sticky fingers smearing seed across Raffé's skin. Raffé swallowed, shivered, and could not quite hold back a whimper. Cambord chuckled, low and husky, a touch of smug satisfaction to it.

Raffé drew a sharp breath as fingers traced his lips. He licked them, shuddering when he realized he was tasting himself. It seemed like something that should have been filthy, but it only made him ache and burn. When Cambord pushed a thumb into his mouth, Raffé sucked it clean, drunk on the combined taste of himself and Cambord's faintly salty skin.

Withdrawing his fingers, Cambord replaced them with his mouth, sucking at Raffé's lips before licking into his mouth and stealing his breath. Raffé reached up to cling to his shirt, fingers digging into the soft fabric. Cambord pressed down on him, and Raffé gasped at the unmistakable hardness grinding against him. Letting go of one sleeve, fingers skating hesitantly down Cambord's arm, he slowly trailed them over and down. He paused again, shyness winning out, but Cambord pushed against his hands, murmured against his mouth, and Raffé's curiosity took back over. He dipped his hands further down between their bodies to rub his fingers over Cambord's cock, firm and hot beneath layers of fabric.

Cambord made a noise that almost sounded like a genuine growl—not impossible with the various types of beings that roamed the castle—and bit his bottom lip, rubbed against him, pushed into his hand. Sparks raced down Raffé's spine, over his skin, making him feel too warm, too tight. He loosed his other hand, trailing his fingers up to comb through Cambord's hair.

He gave a startled gasp when he was jerked up. Large, heavy hands gripped his ass, smoothed down to his thighs, and settled Raffé across Cambord's lap. He was hard again, bare cock rubbing against the soft fabric of Cambord's clothes. Raffé wrapped his arms around Cambord's shoulders, held on tightly, groaning into the kiss that took his mouth, claimed it, as fingers teased along his skin, pushing fabric out of the way and replacing it with scorching heat.

Raffé wanted to ask if Cambord could see him; he seemed to move so easily in the dark. But then he would only say something stupid about wanting to see Cambord, and being denied that would only ruin the mood. So he drowned the words in Cambord's mouth, buried his fingers in Cambord's soft hair.

"I am increasingly horrified as to how stupid the rest of the world must be," Cambord said, fisting Raffé's cock, mouth sliding wetly along his neck until teeth nipped gently at the edge of Raffé's ear. "I cannot decide if I want to fuck you next, or feel your cock in my throat."

The words made Raffé groan, his cock twitching in Cambord's hold. His eyes stung, breaths lodging in his chest, so much emotion and need and disbelief proving overwhelming. Raffé drove it all back and found his voice, hating that it was not entirely steady when he said, "Fuck me. I want to feel that."

Cambord gave another one of those delicious growls, fingers biting into Raffé's skin where they were still curved around his hip. "As you command." He then pulled away, laughing when Raffé whined in disapproval. "I have to make my little prince more comfortable." Raffé listened to a rustle of fabric, the scrape of boots on stone. A hand curled around his arm and helped him to his feet. His cloak was stolen away with a soft kiss, and a few moments later Raffé was pushed down upon what he realized were their cloaks piled on the ground to make a crude bed.

A breeze cut through the night, carrying a winter chill. The first snows had arrived the previous week, and the royal temple would soon be celebrating the first day of winter. Raffé could only feel the unbelievable heat of Cambord's body, shyly running hands over the skin that met his fingers, surprised that his chest was smooth and hairless—it was not an affectation favored by most men.

"You have every indication of being quite wicked once you know your way, little prince," Cambord murmured, licking at his mouth and giving another drugging kiss before pulling away to lavish attention on Raffé's throat. Teeth nipped hard, sting soothed by that distracting tongue, and Raffé thought he might have a mark there come dawn.

He hoped so.

Cambord's hands trailed further down his body, chased by his mouth, tongue dragging across one patch of skin while his hands teased another until Raffé was a gasping, moaning, writhing mess upon the improvised bed and Cambord's soft, satisfied chuckles washed over him. He moved briefly away but returned after only a moment. Raffé could hear the sound of clinking glass and then the smell of honey roses filled the air briefly. He shivered, nerves returning, as Cambord's heavy hands settled on his thighs, spread them further apart.

Raffé startled as Cambord sucked up a mark on the soft skin of his inner thigh that echoed the one on his throat. He was so distracted by that, he almost missed the fingers that teased at his hole—almost. But it was impossible to completely miss the new, strange sensation of a warm, slick finger gently pushing inside him. His hands fluttered about for a place to rest and finally settled for tangling in the cloak upon which he rested, so soft against his skin it felt like a wicked indulgence all on its own.

Warm lips trailed back up his body as that finger pushed and twisted inside him. Cambord nibbled and licked at Raffé's sore lips, took a deep kiss as he added a second finger to the first. Raffé moaned into his mouth, clung tightly to him, and by the time Cambord slipped a third finger in, he felt as though he were going to shake apart.

Cambord sucked another mark up on his throat until Raffé was trembling, aching, in desperate need of more. "Cam—"

"You beg prettier than the most expensive whore, all the sweeter for the sincerity, little prince," Cambord murmured against his mouth.

Raffé could feel his cheeks burn, the pleasure coursing through him at the warm, even fond tone of the words giving him courage. "If I b-beg so prettily, give me what I want."

Cambord laughed, body shaking against Raffé's, and he nipped sharply at the edge of Raffé's jaw before pulling back and removing his fingers. A moment later Raffé felt the heavy weight of Cambord's cock pushing into him, the stretch making him groan. Cambord hitched his legs up, guided them, and Raffé obediently hooked them around him, clinging to Cambord's shoulders as he kept pushing inside.

They were both panting by the time Cambord was finally all the way inside. It was like nothing Raffé had ever felt—hot and full and consumed. Cambord's skin was slick with sweat beneath his fingers, muscles tight. "Good?" Cambord asked softly.

"Yes," Raffé said, moving his hips slightly, liking the noise Cambord made. He did it again with more certainty, got a wet, clumsy kiss for his efforts—and then Cambord was moving, pulling out and thrusting back in, muscles bunching and rippling beneath Raffé's fingers. Raffé tried to meet his movements, awkward and off-rhythm at first, but eventually he managed it and that just got him more of those delightful noises, Cambord moving faster, harder, pressing deeper, every movement burning pleasure into Raffé's skin from the inside out.

He cried out when Cambord wrapped a hand around his cock, his voice rough and raw in Raffé's ear. "Spill for me, little prince."

Raffé obeyed, too consumed and overwhelmed to do otherwise, shouting Cambord's name as he came apart a second time.

"Beautiful," Cambord said and resumed his determined thrusts until he tensed and shuddered above Raffé, face buried in Raffé's throat.

A few moments later he sat up, and Raffé groaned as his cock slipped free, leaving behind a foreign but pleasant ache. Cambord stretched out alongside him and bundled him close, hands petting lazily, lips moving across Raffé's face. "I think you will do quite well here, little prince."

"Will I—" Raffé stopped as the bells began to toll. So close to the bell tower, it was impossible to be heard. They rang twenty-five times, marking the Hour of the Dragon—two hours to go before a new day officially began, and too few left before dawn.

Cambord sighed. "Damn that clock. Is it so late already? I fear I must go, sweet prince." He kissed Raffé long and slow, and by the time he pulled away,

Raffé could not remember what he'd wanted to say—no longer wanted to say anything, desperate to make the moment last, afraid speaking would break it.

Gentle hands pulled his clothes back on, lingered on his skin, Cambord pressing soft kisses to random bits before covering them up. "Gods favor you, little prince. Welcome to the King's Legion." He cupped Raffé's face and kissed him again, lips moving over Raffé's as though he had every bit of Raffé memorized and was savoring his favorite treat. There was something more to it, something Raffé could not quite name, but it caused a sharp, hot and twisting ache in his gut, caused tears to cloud his eyes. Cambord kissed them away, kissed his mouth one last time ...

And then was gone. Raffé drew several ragged breaths, half-convinced he'd dreamed the entire encounter. But his lips felt swollen and used, and he could feel the bruises already forming on his neck from Cambord's eager attentions. No dream could have left the aches in his body or the wetness between his thighs.

"Thank you," he whispered, then stiffly left the alcove and made his way back through the maze to return to his room.

PRINCELING

Six hundred years ago, twelve countries had fallen into a bitter war that waged for three centuries. By the end of it, two of those countries had been rendered uninhabitable. The many sides were so locked in hate they had resorted to means that still made the world shudder at the memory—means that had left scars that would never fade, wounds that would never close.

Magic had reached to great heights and terrifying lows. Monsters had been called, beasts created, and demons summoned. Chaos reigned for centuries, and when it all finally ended, the world had changed. The remaining ten countries were united under one queen, though it was not a victory she won easily. The remaining population was but a sliver of the masses that had once filled the land, and recovering those lost numbers was a war yet to be won.

The monsters and terrible magic remained, across the land and in the blood. Mere humans could not conquer the nightmare creatures or fight the hellish magic that could not be unlearned, and it was to the very blood they had fought that the people turned for help. In order to maintain her tenuous grip on her fragile new kingdom, the queen built an army of men who were all part human, part something else. They became known as the Queen's Legion, fourteen branches of elite and powerful warriors and mages whose sole purpose was to defend and die for the kingdom: Dragoons, Titans, Summoners, Sorcerers, Priests, Paladins, Geomancers, Gremlins, Dredknights, Shades, Shadowmarch, Tamers, Alchemists, and the Princes of the Blood.

Most notorious of her Legion were the Princes of the Blood, those who carried a measure of demon blood in their veins. Dark, secret magic woke the demon blood, turned them into half-demons of fearsome strength and magical prowess. Their only weakness was a need for the blood of pure humans.

To join the ranks of the Princes of the Blood was the highest honor in the kingdom. Repeating that to himself as he walked down a long flight of worn, slippery, dark stone steps did nothing to reassure Raffé. Men died attempting to become Princes, and those who succeeded eventually died in battle. No Prince of the Blood had ever died of old age.

Guards had escorted him through the castle to the entrance to the lower levels where few were permitted. Then they'd left him there alone, which was surprising. Surely after his brother's behavior they would have wanted to ensure he went the whole way? They had left him, though, and so he'd shrugged and walked on, opening a door painted black and marked with the rune and thorn crest of the Princes.

The stairs were as black as the door, worn from decades of use, and he was halfway down them before he realized they were made of marble and likely once had been smooth and gleaming and beautiful. At the bottom of the stairs was a hallway of more black marble carved with hundreds of thousands of runes that shimmered with red and blue light as he walked past them—protection and warding to keep in something that was too dangerous to be let out. He'd heard stories of Bloodings gone wrong, where the ceremony turned the candidate into a full demon instead of a half-demon. Selecting proper candidates was a difficult matter. Some had too much demon blood, some too little, and some possessed the blood of demons far too dangerous to ever wake. Once, the kingdoms might have kept track of such things better, but nearly all knowledge had been lost in the fighting.

At the end of the black marble hallway, a vaguely familiar figure stood waiting for him in front of a door. Prince Dalibor, the king's nephew and a Prince of the Blood for more than a decade. Rumor had it he'd married one of the elusive and nigh-legendary Wolves of the Moon. "Little prince," he greeted. "You did, indeed, come." He smiled in a way that bared his sharp fangs, eyes a bright yellow.

"I said I would," Raffé replied quietly. "I was surprised nobody escorted me."

Dalibor laughed in a rough but easy way. "The last walk is your own, little prince. Come." He pushed open the door and led the way into what proved to be a wide, circular room at least as big as Raffé's bedroom.

All around the perimeter stood the Princes of the Blood. Each had yellow eyes with that shine peculiar to animals. They varied in shape and size but shared a predator's stillness. Each wore a dark red tunic trimmed in silver, chests emblazoned with the crest of the Princes: a cluster of thorns inside a circle of runes.

On the far end of the room, directly opposite the door through which he'd come, stood the king and two men in dark red robes, deep hoods hiding their faces. Priests of the Blood, their identities hidden for their own safety, for they were the only ones who knew the whole of the ceremony that would wake his demon blood, transforming him forever into something less than demon but far more than human.

Well, that was what would happen if he survived. The Blooding was arduous, dangerous, and Raffé would only be the latest in a long line of men who simply lacked the strength to survive the transformation.

The taller of the two Priests stepped forward, beckoning to Raffé. "Come into the circle, little prince."

To Raffé's surprise, Dalibor gripped his shoulder in a friendly fashion and smiled before he slipped away to take his place along the wall. Raffé obeyed the Priest, stepping further into the room and over a white line that had been chalked onto the slate floor.

"Strip," the Priest ordered.

Raffé started to ask if he was serious but stopped at the last moment. The Blooding was no place to fool around; of course the Priest was serious. He removed his clothes quickly, handing the bundle over to the Priest and trying not to show his discomfort. The room was damp and cold, and it was difficult not to be acutely aware his pale, skinny, unremarkable body was a weak imitation of the warriors around him.

The Priest returned, holding a bowl filled with some dark, shimmering liquid, and said, "Spread your legs, hold out your arms. This will be cold and uncomfortable but try to hold still. I will work quickly, but it must be done correctly." Raffé nodded and the Priest dipped his fingers into the bowl and began to draw runes all over Raffé's skin. The dim, wavering light made it hard to see them in any detail, but he thought there were some for summoning and others for binding and warding. It was cold and uncomfortable, as he'd been warned, but Raffé had been made to hold still for far more difficult things in school. All the same, he hoped warmth was provided before his balls retreated or froze and fell off.

That flippant thought led to memories of Cambord, but Raffé shoved them away. The Blooding required his full attention. Cambord, and all the sweet aches and bruises he'd left before departing, would have to wait until the end.

Finally, the Priest finished painting him with runes. He stepped away, and the other Priest stepped forward holding a smaller bowl filled with a thick, dark liquid that Raffé knew just by the smell and look of it: blood. He had really hoped he wouldn't have to drink blood—not so soon, anyway—but he supposed it was best to begin as he would have to go on, pretending that he had any chance of surviving.

"Drink," the Priest intoned and gave him the bowl. The blood was warm and faintly sweet. Not that it helped. Raffé almost gagged as it filled his mouth but forced himself to relax and drink every drop.

"Good," the Priest said, and Raffé was surprised by the genuine approval in his voice. He took the bowl away and set it aside then turned back to Raffé. "Now, little prince, we are going to seal you inside the circle. After that is done, we'll begin the awakening spell. It will hurt—a lot. You may want to sit down, though certainly you may remain standing if you prefer."

Though he gave serious consideration to sitting down, in the end, Raffé decided to stand. He thought he heard the Priest sigh and mutter something but wasn't certain. The first Priest stepped forward to join the second, and holding out their hands toward Raffé, they began to chant intricate, lyrical words of magic.

OF LAST RESORT

Heat was the first thing Raffé noticed, followed by a faint glow in the chalk circle. Then it burst into bright, blue-white light that forced him to close his eyes. As the light eased, he slowly opened his eyes again. He was surrounded by a hazy wall of dim light, barricaded from the rest of the room. It was as if he were staring at them through a glowing spring mist.

The Priests' chanting grew deeper, slower, began to resonate with a power that made Raffé's skin crawl, made the back of his neck prickle with awareness, and he had to fight the urge to whip around to see who stood behind him.

After a couple of minutes, their words of warning came true and everything began to hurt. Every mark painted on his skin began to burn, and Raffé felt as though he was being struck with a thousand red-hot branding irons at once. He bit the inside of his cheek against a scream, his eyes stinging with tears of pain. He couldn't breathe it hurt so bad, wanted to drop to the floor and curl up in a ball and beg for somebody to make it stop.

The pain dug deeper, all the way to his marrow, and he finally screamed. The pain just kept coming, and now it was chased by whispers, by the feeling of something crawling, creeping through him, twisting through his veins, raking at the inside of his skin.

His vision grayed out, then his awareness, though he was never able to entirely blot out the pain or the sound of his own screams. It was then that he thought of Cambord. The warmth of his mouth, the knowing touches of his calloused hands. For a few hours, Raffé had felt precious, like he mattered to someone. A fantasy, but who begrudged a dying man the delusion that he had been loved?

The happy memories were torn away as the pain got the better of him once more. This time the focus was on his mouth, where it felt as if someone had shoved knives into his jaw and wrenched, twisted, yanked.

After that, Raffé remembered nothing.

~~*

He woke with a scream on his lips, cut short by the rough hand that clapped over his mouth. "Shh, Prince," a vaguely familiar voice said. "The pain will ease with feeding."

Raffé didn't know what that meant, but when his mouth was held against something soft and warm, it seemed the most natural thing in the world to bite down and drink. Hot liquid filled his mouth, sweet with a hint of wine and mulling herbs. A sharper flavor, and after a few moments of fuzzy thought, he realized what it was: blood. The thought snapped through him but immediately slid away again, exhaustion and his own pain and the marvelous taste in his mouth blotting out everything else.

After a couple of minutes, he was pushed away and settled back down on his bedding. He licked traces of blood from his lips and let sleep overtake him once more.

When he woke again, it was to searing sunlight across his face. Raffé grunted in displeasure and dragged his pillow over his face to block it. Soft laughter filled the room, followed by the sound of footsteps, the familiar jangle of a sword belt and armor. The warmth of the offending sunlight vanished, and Raffé slowly removed the pillow. He stared up at the face of Prince Telmé, the king's youngest son and Commander of the Princes of the Blood and the Legion. "Fair morning, Princeling. The sunlight is going to bother you for some time until your over-sensitivity eases."

Raffé stared blankly at him. "Pardon, Highness?"

"Telmé is fine," Telmé replied. "We Princes tend to be informal with each other."

"We ... I don't ... understand."

"No?" Telmé laughed. He cocked his head and stared down at Raffé with gentle amusement. "Generally when one survives a Blooding, one becomes a Prince. Though you're new, and we do like to put our new Princes through their paces, so I'm afraid you're going to be stuck with 'Princeling' for some time."

"Prince ..." Raffé's eyes popped open wide, and he gaped at Telmé. "I'm a— I survived?" But even as he asked, he could remember bits and pieces. He could also feel that his mouth was different, especially the shape and weight of his teeth. "I survived," he said again, more softly.

Telmé laughed again and sat down beside him on the bed as Raffé shoved away his blankets and sat up. "Yes, and you did quite well. Even Dalibor did not stay on his feet the whole time. He is very irate; the others are teasing him mercilessly."

Raffé stared at him, confused and a little lost.

"Are you well?" Telmé asked, laughter fading, replaced by a puzzled look.

"I'm fine, just ... surprised." He also wasn't used to people being so open and friendly with him. "My family?"

"Gone. Left three days ago," Telmé said. "We prefer they leave as soon as possible; it's easier for all parties. This is your life now; you answer only to the King and your fellow princes."

Raffé nodded, thoughts spinning wildly through his head. He was alive. He was not human. His family no longer had any bearing on his life. He was meant to fight the greatest threats and terrors plaguing the kingdom. It was too much to absorb, so he latched onto thoughts he could handle. "How long have I been asleep?"

"Not quite a week. Come on. Acting is better than idling. Now that you're on your feet we'll get you better acquainted with the castle and all. You're probably also hungry, and I could use a bite myself, so we'll head for the temple first." He winked.

Raffé surprised himself by laughing. A bite, indeed. He supposed it was hard not to make a joke of that. He stood up, feeling a little unsteady on his feet but not so bad he wouldn't be able to manage.

Telmé reached out and lightly touched his shoulder where the shadow of a bruise still lingered. He smirked. "Have a bit of fun before your execution, Princeling? There was more than a few of those on you. Be aware, a few of your new brothers have bets going as to who put them there."

Raffé flushed at the teasing words even as sadness washed through him as he realized that most of the marks were gone. Soon no sign would remain of the man who granted his last request, provided comforting thoughts as he stood freezing in a dark room certain he would die. He wondered if he would ever know Cambord's real name.

Chuckling, Telmé said, "Best get used to the teasing, Princeling. We're not a very shy or well-behaved lot."

Whatever Raffé had expected, it wasn't teasing, or so much easy laughter. He hadn't expected the Princes to be nice. They guarded the kingdom from the shadows, fed on the blood of pures; they were regarded with equal parts fear and awe. Looking upon them from afar, they had seemed cool, remote, fierce.

Nobody had ever said they were so normal. Even if he'd known that, Raffé wouldn't have expected to be treated like one of them. He was used to being ignored or tolerated where ignoring him was not possible. No one ever *included* him. He ducked his head, suddenly overcome by it all. He was alive, he was a Prince of the Blood, he wasn't being held in contempt or coldly ignored.

"All right, there?" Telmé asked quietly, and his hand slid over Raffé's shoulder, gripping it firmly. "Let it go, Princeling. Let them go. You'd be surprised to learn what we all thought of you that day, what we thought of your family."

"I—" Raffé choked the words off, afraid he really would embarrass himself by crying. "Everyone assumed I would die. Everyone. Even I did not think I would live."

Telmé squeezed his shoulder again and said, "Not everyone. Come, it's time for your first proper meal. Then you will have to meet the others—well, the ones who are here. A few were sent out shortly after your Blooding to address various problems. Here are some clothes, though the castle tailors issued orders that you were to visit them for proper fits. They're very demanding, tailors. Best to do what they say, but it can wait another day or two."

Raffé took the bundle thrust at him and tried to dress quickly. He was far more used to the clothes of a clerk than those of a soldier. But when he put them on, the leggings, shirt, undertunic, and tunic all fit well enough and were actually easier to move about in. The boots he pulled on were a touch too big, but they would do for the present.

"All set, there?" Telmé asked and then with a brisk nod led the way out of the room and through the halls of the castle.

As a visitor, Raffé had not seen much of it. The heart of the castle was shaped like an octagon—was three, actually, forming an enormous tower, each smaller than the one below. There were three floors to every octagon, and the rest of the enormous castle sprawled out from each side: the Hall of War, the Hall of Magic, the stables, the smithies, barracks, dorms, schools, and dozens more. Large enough to be practically a small city all its own, Castle Guldbrandsen was the heart of the kingdom and the last defense should they ever lose the fragile war against the monsters and magic they constantly fought.

They walked along the outer wall of the second octagon, passing all manner of people: servants, lords, soldiers, visitors, messengers ... Telmé acknowledged all of them but did not stop. He eventually abandoned the walkway and led Raffé inside then down flights of stairs and through more dim-lit halls until they reached the enormous, lavish great hall. It was relatively empty, filled with not more than perhaps a hundred people scattered about in various groups, voices quiet as they talked. Fires were arranged in various pits across it, giving the enormous, echoing room a bit of warmth. Telmé led him to a cluster of important-looking men standing in front of the king's table at the head of the room. "Hail, Legion."

One of them, a brawny man with a shock of curly red hair, lifted a hand in greeting. "Hail, Prince Telmé. I see your Princeling is up and about, and fair morning to you."

"Fair morning," Raffé murmured.

Telmé rested a hand on his shoulder and gestured to each of the four men in turn. "Captain Morré of the Royal Guard," he said, pointing to the handsome, red-haired man. Beside him was a large man with a rough, wild sort of air about him. He had black hair threaded with silver and blood-red eyes. "Ilkay Thrace, though we all call him Moon. He is leader of the Wolves recently come down from the mountains to join the Legion." Telmé waved his hand in the air, looking at Moon. "I thought you and Dalibor were leaving this morning?"

Moon smiled, a bit of tooth in it though mostly he seemed amused. "Our ship suffered some damage in the night—all this damnable hail. We should be leaving within the hour, though."

"You're a Wolf of the Moon?" Raffé asked, surprised.

"Aye, Princeling," Moon said. "My blood heart is right miffed because of you. Not often a slip of a thing like you shows him up." He winked.

Telmé snickered. "Serves him right." He pointed to the third man, the only one to come close to Moon's height and broad build. They all seemed to be about Telmé's forty-odd years, except the man before him, who seemed older than Raffé but younger than the rest.

He was handsome without being pretty, a rough-cut soldier so unlike the soft, well-dressed men Raffé knew better. His hair was the color of wheat, the ends jagged as though only just beginning to recover from being poorly cut. His eyes ... Raffé could not look away. They swirled with colors exactly as he had always heard. At present, they were mostly green. "You're a dragon," he said. "I mean a Dragoon."

The cluster of men laughed, and the blond-haired man bowed. "Aye, Princeling." His words were spoken quietly. There was a note of huskiness to his voice, but Raffé remembered hearing somewhere that Dragoons generally had rough voices. "Captain Alrin Westor of his Majesty's Dragoons," Alrin said and swept a playful bow. He looked up, his eyes mostly green but constantly shifting through other colors. "An honor to make your acquaintance, Princeling."

"You weren't kidding about me hearing that everywhere," Raffé said, making a face, not quite rolling his eyes.

The last man in the group snickered and swept a bow himself, his long, blue-black hair spilling over his shoulder. His eyes were a tawny brown and set in a face that was delicately pretty, his severely thin build in stark contrast to the broader men around him. Telmé gestured. "This is Captain Boris Karr of the Shadowmarch."

The Shadowmarch, one of a very limited set permitted to use dark magic. It was said they could see in the dark as easily as in the day. Was his mysterious Cambord a Shadowmarch?

OF LAST RESORT

He shoved thoughts of Cambord away because if he tried to solve that mystery he would drive himself mad. At any rate, it was foolish to assume that Cambord wanted to be known to him. One night was one night, and yearning for more was just a sign of Raffé's naïveté.

"Come along, Princeling, before this lot starts trying to fill your ears with gossip," Telmé said.

"Have fun, Princeling," Morré said, and the other men laughed and offered their partings, exchanging a look Raffé feared he understood all too well.

Once they were well away, he said, "Surely the Princes of the Blood are too serious an affair for such things as pranks."

Telmé threw his head back and laughed. "Pranks, perhaps, but that does not mean we do not have our fun."

Raffé sighed but could not find it in him to be upset. It was already clear, though he scarce dared believe it, that whatever the Princes did would be nothing like the malicious pranks he'd endured in school. He still wasn't certain he wasn't dreaming. People saw him and spoke to him and acted like it was perfectly normal for him to be there. He was afraid to get his hopes up that he might belong after all, but he always had been a fool.

They walked in silence the rest of the way to the temple that resided behind the castle. The two were divided by a river, actually a branch of the Great River. An enormous bridge of gleaming white stone spanned it, the second bridge to be built after the first had been destroyed in the early days after the war.

At midmorning it bustled with all manner of people making the trek between the two buildings, either returning from the recently concluded prayers or headed to attend the late prayer hour. Raffé winced at the sunlight but resisted an urge to shield his face with his hands. It hurt. He hoped he got used to it sooner rather than later and could walk about as unaffected as Telmé.

"It will get better," Telmé said with a laugh. "You are handling it remarkably well for whatever that is worth, especially since the last one as sensitive as you was Håkon."

"Why the sensitivity?"

Telmé shrugged. "Demons work best at night, when the Goddess of Hell is strongest. The more powerful the demon blood, the more sensitive the Prince. You're lucky you can venture outside during the day at all. I suspect you will also be like Håkon in that you will prefer to avoid the sun and become a true night crawler." Goddesses, thinking of cool dark made Raffé want to whimper. Telmé's mouth ticked up at one corner, eyes crinkling. "Yes, definitely a night crawler. Speaking of demons, the the very moment they're allowed, the mages will hunt you down to begin tracing your blood back to its demon source."

"The Book of Demons," Raffé murmured. "I always wondered if it was true the mages kept such a record."

"They keep many records, and you will become acquainted with most of them—possibly all, depending on where your strengths lie," Telmé said. "I think there is potential in you to be very powerful, but it is hard to say for certain until you are trained up and standing true on your own feet."

Raffé shook his head, wondering when he would really believe all that was happening to him. "I don't care if I'm powerful or not—I'm happy to be alive."

Telmé reached up and ruffled his hair. Raffé stared at him, making Telmé chuckle. "I think you will do quite well, Princeling, and those who doubted you will regret it."

The words echoed Cambord's, and the reminder of him caused a brief, sweet ache that Raffé hated to set aside. "I think they will be happier free of me, of what they consider 'the whole mess'. My parents are very strict adherents to the old ways and were not happy to discover that between them they had managed to sire children with the proper amount of demon blood." They had been positively infuriated to learn of it so late in life, when the required tests done when their sons were children had cleared them, no doubt because of a mistake on the part of the Priest who had tested them.

"They were less pleased to be reminded that the Law of Blood now applies to them."

"What!" Raffé tripped on his own feet he was so startled and only avoided slamming his face into the ground because Telmé grabbed him and held him upright. He shook his head. "You're jok—" He broke off, realizing abruptly that it wouldn't be a joke. Telmé was right: if his parents were capable of providing Blooding candidates, then they were obligated to carry on the line. His mother, however, was too old to give birth. That meant his father would be expected to find additional wives. "That will be hard for them. Our territory clings to the old ways, and multiple spouses is one of the 'new' traditions they abhor the most. They were extremely displeased my fiancé already had two wives, but the offer was too financially generous to refuse."

"If they wanted the luxury of abstaining from the tradition they should have made certain that your brother did not run off so you would be available for providing heirs," Telmé said with a shrug. "What's done is done, however. Perhaps your brother will show sense and return. I've no doubt three wives is a duty your father will learn to manage. Certainly there are worse."

Raffé gave a weak laugh. "My fiancé already had two wives and three children. He was permitted a husband because my brother was going to marry a woman and so the line would have carried. I was not certain at all how it was going to go, but I wanted to try. No wonder my parents were so angry with me—they already knew they'd have to take new wives into the household."

Telmé gripped his shoulder again. "Do not worry upon them, Princeling. They are no longer your responsibility. Your duty now is to serve as a Prince of the Blood. Their problems are theirs, not yours. Believe me, we've plenty enough of our own."

"I'll do my best," Raffé said. "As I said, I am grateful to be alive. I don't intend to throw that away."

"Good," Telmé said, and they continued on the rest of the way in silence.

The midmorning bells began to toll as they reached the temple, and a man appeared at the top of the steps. He had light, yellow-brown skin and shockingly white hair that fell to his shoulders in fine dreadlocks, and was dressed in flowing dark blue robes and a silver circlet set with a sapphire. At Raffé's side, Telmé smiled warmly and quickened his pace to climb the steps, taking the hand that reached out and tugged him close.

OF LAST RESORT

Raffé looked away as Telmé exchanged a brief but immodest kiss with his husband, the High Priest of the Church of the Sacred Three and the Reach of the House. He looked back after a moment, and the High Priest smiled at him in greeting and motioned him forward, though his other hand did not leave where it rested at the small of Telmé's back. "Hail, Princeling. It's good to see you up and about. Come inside and we'll make introductions and get you fed. I would imagine that if you're not feeling hungry now, you will be shortly. My name is Korin."

"An honor to meet you, High Priest," Raffé replied and followed them into the temple.

It was warm inside, surprisingly so, but then Raffé recalled that the oldest temples had magic in the very stones that assisted with such things. It was beautiful, candlelight reflecting and gleaming off the white stone walls, displaying the colorful prayer tapestries that hung along them from one end to the other.

Three Priests stood before the altar on a raised dais chanting hymns. The sanctuary was filled with hundreds of people sitting on whatever they had brought with them. Some were on fat, cushy pillows, others on simple prayer mats, and still others sat only on their cloaks or nothing at all. The smell of incense wafted through, mingling with the scent of the outdoors that followed them inside.

"This way," Korin said over his shoulder with a smile, indicating Raffé should keep following them. He then turned to Telmé, voice going low and soft as they chatted together. They made a handsome pair, the pale, dark-haired prince and the Priest with brown skin and pale hair, and Raffé tried to remember if he had ever heard tales of their marriage.

Princes of the Blood married pure bloods—humans without any sort of extraneous component in their blood, or such a small amount that it was insignificant. They were human, and that made them both rare and powerful. The five pure blood families controlled the Reaches into which the kingdom was divided.

The Reach of the North was controlled by the High Priestess of Temple of the Sacred Heart, the only family with one hundred percent human blood. The Reach of the East was controlled by the Grand Duke of Hel—that was Raffé's Reach. The Reach of the South was controlled by the Grand Duchess of Sēkfar, and the Reach of the West by the Grand Duke of Rannik. The Reach of the House was ruled by the Temple of the Sacred Three and had always stood by the royal family. Priests of the Temple of the Sacred Three often married into the royal family, and it was likely that Telmé's marriage had been arranged right alongside his fate as a Prince of the Blood while he was still wrapped in swaddling.

Watching Telmé and Korin together made Raffé think of Almor, and then of Cambord. Almor would never have kissed him in public like that, or walked hand in hand with him. Cambord ... he knew nothing about Cambord except that he was kind, passionate, and possessed of a wicked mouth, but Raffé still thought Cambord would have kissed him like that wherever they were if they had truly been lovers.

He was pulled from his thoughts when they stopped in front of an open archway. "This way, Princeling," Telmé said with a smile and led him into a room where several Priests milled about. By the profusion of plants, fresh and dry, and the various bottles, boxes, mortars, pestles, and dozens of other items and instruments, it must have been part of the apothecary. The pungent smell of the herbs made his nose itch the same way the sunlight was still aggravating him.

"It does take getting used to," Telmé said wryly. "Even worse is the resistance to substances like medicinal herbs and alcohol. Trust me, the first time you try to get drunk and fail miserably you are going to hate being a Prince."

Raffé made a face, cheeks burning slightly. "I've never been drunk."

Telmé and Korin both looked at him in surprise. Then Telmé laughed and clapped him on the back. "I don't know whether to congratulate you or extend my apologies."

"A little of both, I imagine," Korin said then turned to the Priests pretending not to stare. He cast his eyes around the room, as though searching for someone, then raised a hand and crooked a finger at one of them. "Méo."

Méo, a short, dark-haired Priest who looked a little older than Raffé, abandoned where he had been wrestling with a pile of dried, thorny vines and walked toward them. He bowed low, clasping his hands in front of him. "Prince, High Priest, and Princeling, it is an honor to see you this morning. How may I serve?"

"All pretty manners when my husband is about, aren't you?" Korin drawled. "Come along, Méo. It's time for the Princeling's first feeding."

"Yes, High Priest," Méo said and smiled brightly at Raffé, casually hooking a hand around his elbow as they left the workroom and went further down the hall. When they stopped in front a closed door, Méo looked at Korin, brows raised in silent query. Korin nodded, and Méo smiled. "Come on there, Princeling."

Korin cast Raffé an amused look. "I'll leave you with Méo. He's a brat but good at what he does."

Raffé only nodded, wondering why such a fuss was being made. Was feeding that difficult or dangerous or something? But if so, they wouldn't leave him alone …

He went along when Méo tugged him into what proved to be nothing more than a small sitting room featuring only a chaise and a couple of chairs. Méo moved to the chaise and sat down, patting the space beside him. "You're quite different from the usual sort we get as Bloods."

"I—I wasn't really expected to survive," Raffé said. "I'm only replacing my brother."

Méo smiled crookedly, but he didn't comment, only loosened the high collar of his robe and pulled the fabric open, revealing a long throat marked with more than a few bite scars. Raffé's jaw ached with a need for food. His heart kicked up, and he realized the smell that had been tickling his nose was not lingering herbs, but the smell of suitable blood. Not all Priests were pure, but enough pure sons were given to the Temple of the Sacred Three to sustain the Princes. He started to lean forward, but then caught himself and pulled back, covering his face with one hand.

Blood, he craved blood. He had known he needed it, of course, but to actually hunger for it … hazy memories of feeding returned to him, a soft voice reassuring him. Telmé? A Priest? The memory was not clear, but the ache in his jaw sharpened at the memory. Sacred Three, he really was a blood drinking half-demon. Raffé shivered.

"Starting to feel hungry, there?" Méo asked with a soft laugh and pulled his hand away. Raffé's skin seemed to tingle not quite painfully in the wake of his touch. "You're quiet." His eyes were soft, almost shimmery as the sunlight struck them. A trick of the light? Some element of his holy power? Raffé knew little to nothing of Priests.

Raffé made a face at the too familiar words. "So I'm told. My nurse called me 'mouse' when I was a boy."

Méo snorted at that. "No mouse would survive the Blooding. Did his Highness tell you anything about feeding?"

"No," Raffé said. "But I think that's half the fun for them."

Laughing, Méo stood up then gave Raffé a push, forcing him to shift so that he lay on the chaise in order to avoid falling right off it. To his utter astonishment, Méo straddled him, and then bent down close to him. Raffé's cock twitched, his face burning, and he had absolutely no idea where to put his hands. "They're brats, the lot of them. Terrifying beyond the walls of the castle, make no mistake, but little better than boys when they're here. Now, as to feeding ..." He grinned. "I doubt you need me to tell you how to bite. Your lot knows that part like breathing. But the first feeding is always ... exciting for the Bloods. First few feedings, actually." He laughed harder as Raffé's face flushed anew. "You are different, Princeling. Now, bite."

Raffé had thought he'd be more hesitant about feeding. Goddesses knew his mind fled from thinking about it too hard. It was not something that ordinary people ever saw—that anyone but the Princes and those they fed from ever saw. Whispers were all the rest of the world had, rumors of men who were one step from demons and barely even that much when they feasted on the blood of their fellows.

But there was no hesitation at all. His hands shook, and his face still burned red though the rest of him felt cold with anxiety, but it still seemed the most natural thing in the world to slide his fingers into Méo's soft, dark hair and tilt his head just so, bare that long throat and sink his teeth into the point where his pulse beat.

He moaned as blood filled his mouth, not realizing until then how weak and tired and hungry he'd felt. Holes he had not known were there began to fill, and it brought his body to life. He felt too hot, too tight in his own skin. He drank deep, eager for satiation, growling low at the sweet, potent flavor of Méo's blood.

A soft whimper drew his attention but mostly because it echoed his hunger. Raffé drew back, licked blood from his lips, then moved without thought, pressing his fingers to the wound, feeling magic both foreign and familiar wash over Méo's skin, healing the wound.

Méo whimpered again, licked his own lips. "You're the quiet sort that's dangerous, sure enough," he said, panting slightly, squirming in the most evil ways against Raffé. Drinking had briefly distracted Raffé from all else, but he was abruptly, sharply aware of how hard his cock was and that there was a secondary hunger thrumming through him. Méo pulled off his robe and cast it aside, revealing a slim, trim body that was sun-kissed all over. Raffé swallowed, reaching out to touch without thinking.

All his life he had wanted to touch, to be touched; he had long resigned himself to the fact he would never have it. Had dared to hope that had changed when he'd become engaged. He had been happy with Cambord. How had he wound up with a naked, eager Priest in his lap? Raffé watched his own hands as they mapped Méo's skin, half-thinking they must belong to someone else, though he could feel every fine tremor in Méo's body, hear his breaths, smell sweat and blood and need on the air.

"Mm," Méo murmured, closing his eyes and enjoying for a moment. He slowly opened them again, a teasing smirk curving his pretty mouth. He wiggled away enough to get Raffé's hose open, took his cock in hand, and gave it a few, teasing strokes. Raffé growled—and froze, startled by the sound. Méo laughed and rose up over him, then slowly guided himself down on Raffé's cock.

The sensation whited out Raffé's world, made him forget about everything but the feel of Méo's body around him and the taste of Méo's blood still in his mouth.

No wonder Cambord had left him so sore, if this was how it felt to fuck someone. It was not something he had ever thought he'd know. It was something he desperately wanted to do again and again.

Méo chuckled, the sound warm, fond, and bent to bare his throat once more. "Come on, Princeling. Take all that you want. I'm very good at serving Bloods."

Lost to sensation, slave to his strange new nature, Raffé obeyed, sinking his fangs back into Méo's throat as he began to thrust into his body. Méo grunted at the bite but held fast, took it all like there was nothing else he'd rather do.

Eventually Raffé finished feeding and sealed the wound. He felt full, hot, and eager for a release that was still eluding him. Méo sat up and began to ride him in earnest, rising up and then driving back down. It took minimal effort to find the right rhythm, and Raffé's hands clung tightly to those sharp hips, fucking Méo as hard as he could, guided by lust and hunger.

He barely managed to muffle his cry as he came. Méo leaned down to muffle his own cry against Raffé's throat.

Eventually Méo sat up, looking like a smug little cat. "Quiet is definitely dangerous with you, Princeling."

"I really hope not every feeding is this way," Raffé said, groaning as his softened cock slipped free of Méo's warm body. "How would anyone get anything else done?"

Méo laughed and lay down on top of him, kissing his cheek. "It does ease off. They'll tell you all that. They just get a childish thrill out of seeing new Princes come out all flushed and embarrassed. But mark my word, Prince Telmé did not run off with the High Priest to have tea." Raffé tried not to picture that and failed miserably, face going red—and all the redder when Méo started laughing. "You're nothing at all like the others."

That put Raffé back on even ground a bit, embarrassment and the satisfaction from their recent activities fading as he was reminded how much he really wasn't meant to be a Prince of the Blood.

"Oh, don't look sad again. They could use different." Méo fumbled with his robe, finally pulling out a cloth, which he used to clean them both up, then got dressed again. "Come on. I'm sure Telmé is waiting for you with that smirk of his. But now Korin will be disinclined to punish anyone today. I don't think he realizes we like his Highness because he puts Korin in a better mood, not because he's good looking." He winked.

Raffé laughed as he stood up. He righted his clothes then combed fingers through his mussed hair in a futile effort to tame it.

Méo grinned at him. "The pures will be fighting over you. The king will marry you off quickly just to get some peace."

"I doubt that," Raffé said, remembering the way Almor had rejected him. He had no interest in explaining that his fiancé had not even been willing to bed him on what they had believed was his last night to live. How had Almor reacted when he learned that Raffé had survived the Blooding? Not that it really mattered anymore, but Raffé would have liked to have seen his face.

They left the sitting room, Méo once more casually looping a hand around his arm as he guided Raffé back to the main parts of the temple.

Telmé and Korin stood chatting in front of the altar, and both smirked when they spotted Raffé—which immediately caused him to turn red, which made the other three laugh. "Have fun, Princeling?" Telmé asked. "What do you think of our little Méo?"

"He thinks I'm perfect, same as everyone," Méo interjected. "Always a pleasure to serve the Princes of the Blood. Visit whenever you like, Princeling. Highness, High Priest, I bid you fair day." He swept a bow, hands clasped, and then turned around and walked away.

Korin chuckled, watching him go for a moment, and then turned to Raffé. "He was very close to a

Prince of the Blood. They likely would have married, but he died when Méo was fourteen."

"He's very dear to all of us and devoted to helping the Princes," Telmé said. "His friend was a good man. Killed by a demon."

Raffé flinched. "I'm sorry."

Telmé smiled briefly at him, nodding in thanks. "Come, the others are eager to meet you properly. If we had known your brother was going to prove a coward, we would have spent our energy getting to know you before the Blooding. But what's done is done, and we can move haply forward from here. Korin, I'll see you tonight."

"Of course," Korin said. "Best of luck to you, Princeling."

Raffé nodded to him in parting then walked alongside Telmé out of the temple. "Feeding will get calmer, eventually," Telmé said. "Be thankful Dalibor was not the one to take you; he has absolutely no shame."

Not wanting to know what that meant, Raffé only nodded. "I hope— I hope I am not—" he stopped, not certain what to say or how to say it. He didn't want to be a failure, a disappointment. He'd been that before the Blooding. Being a Prince was a second chance.

He didn't want to waste it, but he had no idea how to be like Telmé or Dalibor or any of the other Princes of the Blood. He was highly skilled with arranging numbers in neat columns and adding them together. His knowledge of magic was worse than his swordsmanship, and that was best described as deplorable.

OF LAST RESORT

As near as he could tell, there was only one word to describe the fact he was a Prince of the Blood: laughable.

Telmé stopped him, made Raffé turn to face him. "If you were not suited to being a Prince of the Blood, you would be dead right now. There are only fifteen of us in total. Remember that, Prince Raffé, and not the words of the ignorant. The first step to proving your worth is recognizing your worth."

Raffé nodded, unable to get words out. He had survived. He was one of fifteen. Telmé was right—that meant something. "Y-yes, Highness."

"Good, you begin truly to get it." He squeezed Raffé's shoulders. "Now, come."

They slipped back into the castle then climbed up a flight of stairs that spilled out onto the mezzanine that overlooked the enormous practice yard at the back of the castle. It was currently filled with a mixture of three different groups. Raffé could see the black uniforms of the Shadowmarch, the dark blue of the Paladins, and the deep green of the Dragoons.

Sunlight on metal caught Raffé's eye, and he barely noticed when he stopped to watch a mock battle ... except it was only mock in the sense that they weren't actually trying to kill each other. A large man in a Shadowmarch uniform lunged at a Dragoon, dual long knives flashing—and he bellowed in outrage as the Dragoon swung his glaive, throwing him aside before he got close enough to be a threat.

The Dragoon spun his glaive with the elegance of a perfected art then gestured with a tilt of his head for the Shadowmarch to try again. "Come along, there, stripling. Your grandmother hit me harder than that last night."

"Yeah, and you probably begged her to do it again and again," the Shadowmarch said with cheer and lunged gain.

On his second try he managed to slip past the Dragoon's defense, knock the glaive out of his hands, and send him to the ground—but again found himself in the dirt when the Dragoon threw him off with a growl. Standing, the Dragoon beckoned him again, this time with an arm that gleamed with bright green scales from the elbow down, the fingers replaced by claws. He spoke with a faint, rumbling hiss as he said, "At least now you're hitting harder than your grandmother."

Laughing, the Shadowmarch picked himself up and went in again.

Telmé chuckled at Raffé's side, reclaiming his attention. "A rowdy lot but damned good at their job. They don't get enough credit for what they do. The Paladins and the Dragoons are the main arm of the Legion. The Shadowmarch rarely get credit for the things they do, but without them a number of small problems would become large problems."

"So much skill. I don't quite see what I can offer," Raffé admitted. "Everyone knows the Princes of the Blood are invaluable, but I guess I never really appreciated how beyond what little the rumors say."

"Don't worry, you'll learn more than you ever wanted, Princeling. Today is your last day of freedom; tomorrow the hard work begins. By the time spring comes around, you'll be able to best every man in that practice yard. Those who knew you before will scarce recognize you and regret they did not know you better." He smiled coldly, something in his own words clearly pleasing him in a vindictive way, but Raffé could not imagine how.

He cast his eyes over the men in the practice yard one last time then at Telmé's gentle touch to his shoulder, followed him away and to the end of the mezzanine, back into the depths of the castle to meet the men who were to be his comrades from that day forward.

TESTING

It was Prince Håkon who came for him the next morning. He was one of the most notorious of the Princes—the small, pretty, piskie-like brat prince who had been presumed dead after he had been lost at sea. He was married to the Duke of Stehlmore, part of the ruling family of the Reach of the North.

Raffé finished pulling on his tunic and belting it into place, combing fingers awkwardly through his hair, painfully aware that he must look quite plain and boring beside such a tempestuous figure. "Merry morning."

"Mornings are never merry," Håkon replied and stepped further into the room. "Telmé says you're to be tested today, and lucky us, you get me." He smiled, sharp points of his fangs gleaming. Raffé had still not grown used to his own, though his body seemed accustomed to them. It was beyond strange to have teeth that moved, though he was grateful they did because he did not know how anyone would manage with such long teeth permanently extended. "Are you ready?"

"Yes, High—" he broke off with a sigh.

Håkon laughed and offered a smile that was surprisingly friendly. "You'll get used to dropping all the formalities. It helps that everyone else is in a rush to start bestowing courtesies and such upon you. Mark my words, should you ever see your old home again, they will have rewritten history to tell everyone how much they always adored and admired you."

Raffé opened his mouth, but then closed it again before shaking his head. "So I keep being told, but I still find it all very strange."

"Strange is our way of life, to be sure," Håkon said. "Come on, get your boots on and grab your cloak and sword. We're going to test your magic first, but make no mistake, Dalibor is salivating for a chance to kick you around the yard. Half the castle is placing bets on how long you'll last."

Shaking his head, not really surprised—he sensed the castle bet on almost everything just from what little he had seen the previous night—Raffé pulled on his boots and buckled his sword into place. He settled his heavy, fur-trimmed cloak across his shoulders, marveling at the softness, the quality. His parents were not the sort to skimp on quality, but even their extravagance paled next to the luxury afforded the Princes. A new pile of clothes had been awaiting him when he'd returned to his room late in the night, along with a note that he should visit the tailor two days hence at half past the Hour of the Wind. Already it was more clothing than he was accustomed to owning.

Håkon led him along the same path that Telmé had the day before, walking along the outer edge of the second level octagon until they reached stairs that took them down a floor and then to the mezzanine that circled the practice yard. It was not hard to follow Håkon's gaze to the enormous figure in the center of what seemed to be a sort of controlled chaos—the man was as big as Håkon was small, throwing around the other Paladins as though they weighed little more than candy floss. "Is that his grace?"

"Yes," Håkon said. "He is usually the one throwing people about like a nitwit. Wait until the Titans arrive for practice. They keep him humble."

Raffé wondered if Håkon knew his attempts to sound stern and annoyed failed spectacularly. "I've never seen a Titan. At that, I've never seen most of the King's Legion. My family lives along the southern edge of Noor Hel, so mostly we see Dredknights and Paladins."

"You could not pay me to live so close to the Lost Lands, though I've heard that Alwyn is not as bad as Zyke Lorn Fall."

"No, we only get dead-walkers and the odd wraith stumbling out of Alywn. Those who live close to Zyke Lorn Fall endure much worse, at least according to all the stories I've heard."

Håkon grunted. "The reality is worse, believe me. I've had the dubious pleasure of visiting Zyke Lorn Fall numerous times." He clapped Raffé on the shoulder and urged him on. "Enough standing around. You have tests, and the Master of Magic will not be amused with me if we are late." He led Raffé to another set of stairs that led down to the practice yard floor on the western end. Leading him onward through an enormous black stone archway and down a dark hall, they spilled out into the main yard that surrounded the castle, where the auxiliary buildings were located. Looming over them was their destination: the Hall of Magic.

Raffé could feel the magic thrum in his head, like something was slowly waking from a heavy slumber. The smell of stone, leather, and old books washed over him as two guards opened the door, and Håkon ushered him inside. The Hall of Magic left him standing slack-jawed as he took in the rows upon rows of tall,

OF LAST RESORT

dark bookshelves packed to the brim with books, tools, maps, chests, and even little skeletons and pieces of creatures in jars. Scattered throughout the hall were glass globes filled with bright witchlights driving back the gloom of the place; the only other source of light were the narrow bands of glass that ran along the top of the wall all around the hall, but it was presently so gloomy and overcast that no real light poured in. From the ceiling hung enormous skeletons of various monsters, and everything hummed and pulsed with the presence of powerful magic in great quantities. "Incredible."

"Yes," Håkon agreed, mouth quirked.

The sound of boots on stone drew Raffé's attention, and he watched as a man strode down the main walkway toward them. He was dressed in heavy robes with a gold chain wrapped around his hips, the long ends of it falling almost to his ankles, clinking as he walked. The sleeves, hood, and edges of his robes were trimmed in blocks of colors: blue, yellow, purple, pink, white, and orange, all the colors of the different branches of magic. Holy blue, Summoner yellow, Shade purple, Sorcerer pink, Geomancer white, and Alchemist orange.

"Highness, Princeling," the man greeted, offering a half-bow, the long tail of his brown-gray hair spilling over one shoulder. "An honor to meet our newest Prince of the Blood."

"Raffé, this is Lord Ness Leifsson, the Master of Magic. My lord, Prince Raffé."

Smiling, the man nodded his head back the direction from which he had come. "If you'll come along, we shall begin the testing." He led them down the stone walkway to where it fanned out to a large work area, headed for the center of three enormous tables, each of them piled with books, papers, charts, slate and chalk, chests, candles, boxes, and jars of incense.

Something nagged at Raffé as he looked it all over, though he could not say what. He stared at the bookshelves against the back wall, frowning as he tried to puzzle out what bothered him.

"Is something wrong?" Leifsson asked.

Raffé shook his head, opened his mouth to apologize—and his gaze landed on the bare stone wall behind Leifsson, the puzzle pieces falling neatly into place. "The hall isn't right."

"What do you mean?" Håkon asked, though from the way his mouth tipped up at one corner, the quirked brow ... Raffé wondered if he was being tested.

He glanced up and down the hall, closed his eyes, and pictured the external wall, something thrumming, almost buzzing, flashing through his mind. "This building is seven hundred eighty-three stones long. Inside, however, I only count seven hundred fifty-one."

"I'll be damned," Leifsson said with a laugh. "There's an ability that has not manifested in quite some time. Come here, Princeling." Stepping right up to the centermost table, Leifsson gently grabbed Raffé's wrist and tugged him close. Shoving books and papers out of the way, he pulled close a small chest and a stack of metal and porcelain bowls. He opened the chest and pulled out two small sacks. One was filled with rice, the other with the small brown beans that were a staple on any table and which Raffé had always hated. Setting one of the bowls on the table,

Leifsson said, "Tell me how many beans are in this sack."

"But—" Raffé stopped as Leifsson tipped the sack and slowly poured the beans into the bowl. That buzzing, thrumming *something* flashed through Raffé's mind again, and as the beans finished falling he said, "Eight hundred forty-six."

Leifsson flashed a smile. "Now the rice." He poured the rice into a second bowl, the sound of the grains hitting porcelain echoing faintly in the open space. "How many?"

"Three thousand twenty-eight," Raffé said. "I-I don't understand what I'm doing—how I'm doing it? I've always been good with numbers, but not that good."

"You're counting faster than you can entirely follow," Håkon said, stepping up to join them, folded arms dropping to his side. "Your talent with numbers was probably a watered down, ordinary human version of this true power."

Leifsson gave a snort. "You could try not to make 'ordinary human' sound like an insult. It was only eight years ago you were such yourself, Highness."

"I don't mean it as an insult," Håkon said, making a face.

"Yes, you do," Leifsson said. "Demons can't help it. You are lucky your ordinary human husband finds it endearing."

Håkon smiled softly.

"So why can I count like this?" Raffé asked, staring at the rice and beans.

Leifsson waved a hand in the air. "It's one of your demonic abilities, and not a terribly common one. There are two hundred and three demons bound to numbers. Of those, one hundred and eleven are known to have been successfully summoned. Your demon blood comes from one of them, and their numerical affinity is manifesting by way of what we call hyper-counting. You must be magically powerful, if your latent magic is manifesting already. Have his senses heightened?"

Håkon shook his head. "No, though he has a strong sensitivity to the sun. I would imagine they'll start waking soon, and the martial testing may provoke them."

Raffé wished he had any idea what they were talking about. "Am I supposed to feel this hopelessly lost?"

They both looked briefly abashed. "If we had known that you would be the one taking the Blooding," Håkon said, "we could have taught you much of this sooner. You probably know, from rumors if nothing else, that Princes are stronger, faster, and more powerful overall than everyone else. But your sense of hearing, taste, smell—all your senses—will increase as well. It doesn't happen all at once. Usually they improve gradually so as not to overwhelm and harm you. But magic is typically one of the last to wake, not the first, unless it's especially powerful, even by our standards. My magic was the first thing to wake."

"Most intriguing, to be sure, and exciting," Leifsson said. "Håkon here is the only mage at his level at present. It will be nice to have two such talented Princes. We will have to consult the Book of Demons, see if we cannot narrow down which demon's blood flows in you." He clapped his hands together briskly, a grin teasing at his mouth, eyes bright and distant as he was lost happily in his own thoughts.

Raffé glanced at Håkon, brows lifting, and Håkon rolled his eyes. "Yes, they get like that a lot. We're their favorite specimens, I swear to the goddesses." He playfully kicked Leifsson's ankle. "Come on, we've still got the actual testing to do."

"Oh, right. Yes, of course, my apologies. If you'll stand in the measuring circle." He waved a hand at something Raffé could not see.

Stepping around the table, Raffé saw a rune circle chalked on the floor. He stepped into it, ignoring the sudden attack of nerves that ate at him, and waited while the other two joined him, standing on either side of him. "You will feel warm, a buzzing sensation. There may be some mild pain since you are powerful but nothing horrible." Raffé nodded and stood up straight, staring out at the library as Leifsson began to chant the heavy, intricate words of magic, his low, smooth voice well-suited to them.

As promised, Raffé began to feel warm and as though hundreds of buzzing insects were rubbing against his skin. He let out a soft sigh, relieved it was quite simple a matter after all. Håkon smiled briefly at him, but it was distracted, his eyes focused on the floor. Raffé looked down and saw the rune circle was glowing, and as he watched, it shifted from indigo to blue and then quickly turned green.

He began to feel hot, clammy, the buzzing turning more into sharp pinpricks. His chest felt tighter, and he could not draw a deep breath. The circle slowly moved from green to yellow, and as it turned orange, the pinpricks turned into real pain, and Raffé sucked in a sharp breath, biting his lip to avoid crying out.

The circle turned red, and Leifsson muttered something he could not quite catch—and then Raffé screamed, barely staying on his feet, holding his head as his temples began to throb as if someone had taken a hammer to it. At his feet, the circle burned brilliant scarlet and then darkened so much it nearly looked black.

Then it stopped, and he sank to his knees, hands braced on his thighs as he bent over and gasped for breath. "What— What—?" He shook his head, unable to get the question out. The room smelled like smoke, and he noted belatedly that the rune circle was scorched into the stone.

"I think of the recorded one hundred and eleven demons," Leifsson said wryly, "we can narrow it down to the seventeen princes of hell on the list." He closed the spellbook he'd been holding and set it aside on the table. Håkon offered his hands and when Raffé took them, hauled him to his feet. "Impressive, Princeling. It's been quite some time since one of you lot destroyed the circle."

Raffé winced. "Apologies."

"No reason for that. It simply means we'll have to have a care when we begin your training. But as to what the testing revealed ..." He looked to Håkon. "He is a grade three shifter and a grade three caster. I saw no indications of prophecy or mind-working, which isn't surprising if he is more of a numerical bent."

Everything they said confused him further, but Raffé was too discombobulated to voice his questions.

"I will need to speak with Telmé before we continue, see how he wants to proceed," Håkon said.

Leifsson nodded. "Of course."

"Come on," Håkon said, taking Raffé's arm briefly. "On to the second round of testing today, and I think it is going to be lively indeed."

Once they were outside, and Raffé finally felt as though he could breathe properly again, he asked, "What did all of that mean? About the ... shifter and caster and ... mind workings? Prophecy?"

Håkon clapped him on the back. "Thankfully, you do not have prophecy or mind working amongst your gifts. Prince Şehzade is a grade one prophet, but he's the only one. There hasn't been a true seer in decades, and I feel that is for the best. But a pretty common power amongst all the Princes of the Blood is a very light ... mind control, to put it bluntly. It doesn't really do anything more than subconsciously encourage people to listen to us, trust us, but it's extremely mild, and if they're truly set against us it won't stop them from showing defiance. Mostly, it just means we can keep a crowd from panicking as quickly as they might otherwise, that sort of thing. As to the shifting, a grade three shifter is as powerful as we get. It means you can shift into a non-living form—mist, specifically. It's a peculiar ability of the Princes. Premisl is a grade two shifter. He can teach you; we'll arrange the training once the ability manifests. Now, hasten your step. It's time for Dalibor to thrash you."

"Wonderful," Raffé muttered, gaining a laugh from Håkon.

Thankfully, Håkon did not lead him to the main practice yard at the south end of the castle but across the ward to the Hall of War and through the black archways to a collection of smaller practice yards. His nerves increased all over again, however, when he saw three more Princes as well as the men he'd met before: Captain Alrin of the Dragoons, Captain Boris of the Shadowmarch, and Captain Morré of the Royal Guard.

Wonderful—not only was he going to prove how hopelessly incompetent he was with a sword in front of the other princes, he was going do it in front of three of the most powerful men in the castle. Well, at least abject humiliation was familiar, if not comforting.

Dalibor grinned as he saw them, gripping Alrin's shoulder before striding to the middle of the practice ring in the middle of the yard. "There you are, Princeling. How did your magic testing go?"

"He broke the circle," Håkon said before Raffé could reply. "Grade three caster, grade three shifter, and he's a hyper-counter."

"Oh?" Dalibor said, brow shooting up, and around them, the others made noises of surprise and exchanged pensive looks. "You're full of surprises aren't you, Princeling?"

Raffé shrugged. "No one is more surprised than me."

Dalibor grunted and gestured to the other princes. The first had dark, brown-black skin, his hair in long braids ending in bright red beads. "Şehzade." The second man was short, pale-skinned, and stocky in build with a close-cropped black beard and wavy black-gray hair. "Athanasi." The last man was tall and broad, the largest man in the group, with light red-brown skin. "And this is Božidar." They nodded and lifted hands in greeting. "Come along, little brother," Dalibor said. "How well can you use that sword you wear?"

"How well do you think?" Håkon answered before Raffé could. "He was a merchant, not a swordsman, Dalibor. Not all of us teethed on steel as children."

Raffé slowly walked into the ring, painfully aware of all the eyes watching him. "So what are we testing, exactly? Because if it's whether or not I can fight, it's exactly as Håkon said—worse, likely. I was given the bare minimum of required training."

Dalibor laughed, a loud, rough-edged sound that shook his whole body, and his smile filled his entire face—he was not a man who did anything part way, Raffé suspected. "You are not the only Prince to come with no martial knowledge, Princeling, do not fret upon it. We are about to test just how much work will be needed to develop your skills—and to see if you have any more surprises for us." His grin widened. "How many stones make up the walls of this yard?"

"Two thousand twenty," Raffé said, scowling when Dalibor laughed again. He sensed his hyper-counting ability was going to be a frequent source of amusement.

He struggled to hold his ground as Dalibor prowled toward him, levity falling away as he bared his fangs and his eyes glowed brighter than ever. The air around them suddenly seemed filled with some fine tension, like sitting in a room full of angry and scared people. The closer Dalibor got, the stronger the sensation, until Raffé did not know if he wanted to scream and run, or scream and fight.

Dalibor suddenly ran, raised sword glinting in torchlight as it came down—

Steel clashed as Raffé raised his own sword, but he dropped it when Dalibor kicked him, sending him tumbling-sprawling across the yard not quite far enough to hit the wall. Raffé scrambled to his feet but stayed on one knee as Dalibor came at him again, that terror-rage feeling growing even stronger, and was he mad or had Dalibor's eyes turned red?

He jerked, flailed, and clawed futilely as Dalibor grabbed him around the throat and lifted him. "Feel it. Burn with it. *Scream* with it."

The words sank in, crawled through his blood like worms, and Raffé scrabbled even harder to get free as Dalibor squeezed, choked him, and he realized he was actually clawing at Dalibor's hand, long, black, sharp claws tearing open flesh, turning slick with blood. If Dalibor felt any pain, however, he gave no sign. "Scream!" Dalibor bellowed.

Raffé did not scream, but the worming sensation turned to fire. He felt boiled and frozen, and the world took on a red haze as he crushed the bones of Dalibor's wrist, slipped free of his broken hold and stumbled back. Dalibor growled and lunged at him—

He felt abruptly as though he had fallen apart, watched as if from afar as Dalibor went through him, saw him slam into the wall even though he had turned around. Raffé drew a startled breath and abruptly felt like himself again, though his heart was banging against his ribs, and his lungs felt full of ice and fire. "Holy Goddesses," someone muttered.

Then Håkon was beside him, hand curling around his arm. "Are you all right?"

Raffé did not answer, too caught up watching anxiously as Božidar and Athanasi helped Dalibor to his feet. "Are— I'm sorry—"

Dalibor grinned as he examined his wrist. "Well done, little brother."

"I'm glad something makes sense to someone," Raffé said, pressing one fist to his left temple. "What happened? What did I do?"

"You turned into mist. Your improved strength has manifested as well," Håkon said. "That's Dalibor's job—to wake those abilities. He has the blood of a demon of wrath, and one of his abilities is along the lines of a type of mind control. He can drive someone out of their mind with anger and to a lesser degree, fear. Once your powers awake fully it will not have any effect on you."

Raffé shook his head. "There's so much to learn."

"Yes," Håkon said. "But you'll manage it exceptionally. You seem made for the Blood."

The words were hard to believe. Raffé remembered his parents' dismissiveness. The way his fiancé loathed him so much he would not even give Raffé a farewell fuck. The whispers and laughs of the court. His glaring ignorance in ways of magic and warfare. He was used to sitting alone in his office tallying numbers in ledgers and putting together stock orders, cutting paychecks and paying bills, mailing off invoices.

It made no sense that he had gone from accountant to half-demon. He felt like a fish impersonating a bird.

He startled as someone ruffled his hair, jerking away in protest and scowling when they all laughed. "Do not look so glum, little brother," Dalibor said, his grin returning full measure. "Look on the bright side—Božidar there came to us as a whore."

"Go get buggered by a goblin," Božidar said cheerfully. "At least I did not spend most of my formative years in chains."

"Oh, I think you and I have both been in chains plenty of times, and for all the same reasons," Dalibor said, baring his teeth.

Božidar bared his own, and Raffé could not help but smile at the easy play between them. Would he ever stop being surprised at how normal they were?

Although, normal did not include his literally crushing bone and those bones healing within moments. "I'm sorry about your wrist."

Dalibor paused in the middle of another taunt at Božidar. "Eh? Oh, think nothing of it." He held out his wrist, which looked completely unharmed. "That is the least of the abuse I have taken from Princelings. Yrian broke most of my ribs, and Cemal broke three of my limbs. Those two are scrappers, make no mistake. You'll be dealing with them once your skills have sufficiently improved. In the meantime …" He pointed a thumb over his shoulder at Alrin, Morré, and Boris. "You get them."

Thankfully, the training session included no further moments of alarm, minus two more occasions of his accidentally misting. By the end of the hours of training, he had slightly improved his swordsmanship and knew the very basics for glaive and dagger.

He groaned when Dalibor finally told him to stop and dismissed everyone save Håkon. "Telmé will be extremely pleased to hear of your progress."

"There was progress?" Raffé asked, wiping damp hair from his eyes as he slumped on the ground. He wanted to fall all the way over and sleep. The ache in his jaws was growing stronger with every minute, however, and was far too distracting to let him sleep.

Dalibor and Håkon laughed. "Yes, there was progress. By spring you will be a force only a fool

OF LAST RESORT

would reckon with. The Goddesses have done us a grand turn, ensuring we Blooded you instead of your brother."

"I wish I knew where he'd gone," Raffé muttered. "Why he left."

"Men are searching for him, and they'll find him eventually," Håkon said, kneeling beside him. "He will wish desperately they had not; the king does not suffer traitors."

Raffé winced but said nothing. There was no great love lost between them, but he did not want to see his brother hanged. The only way the king might spare his life, however, was if he thought Tallas would suffice to breed more potential Princes.

He shook away thoughts of his brother, his family, because that part of his life was over. He lived to serve and protect the kingdom, and he would focus on that no matter how terrifying it got. Raffé reached up to rub at his sore jaw, swallowing against his dry, achy throat.

"Feeding time," Håkon murmured.

"I'll take him to the temple," Dalibor said. "I see your husband skulking about; I would hate to deprive you." Leering, he hauled Raffé to his feet and led him away, throwing an arm across his shoulders as they walked slowly back to the palace. "How do you like being a Prince of the Blood so far, little brother?"

"Why do you keep calling me that?"

Dalibor slowed to a stop, let his arm fall so he could turn and face Raffé. "You are my little brother. We are all brothers, the fifteen of us. We are the only ones like us in the whole world. We are half-demons permitted to walk the earth and live amongst humans, but we are not like them. You'll see as you get more comfortable.

Slowly you'll forget what it's like to be human. No matter how well we blend, we stand apart. Fifteen blood-hungry demons protecting the humans we'll never be again. A family made in blood and darkness, tempered in war and solitude. That is what we are, and it's a bond far stronger than the trivial thread of being born to the same parents. Now come, little brother, it's time to go enjoy a sweet Priest."

Nodding, Raffé relaxed as they walked, Dalibor's arm once more slung over his shoulder as he rambled on about the castle inhabitants while they walked.

MISSION

Raffé buried his cock in the Priest's body as he sank fangs into his throat, sucking and fucking in earnest as the Priest buried his head in his folded arms, leaning his weight on the wall as he begged in breathy, stilted words for more.

When his bloodlust was sated, Raffé gently removed his teeth, healed the wound, and reached around to jerk the Priest off with quick, hard movements, relishing the sweet noises he made almost as much as he'd enjoyed the Priest's blood. The Priest came moments later, and Raffé followed him soon after, burying himself deeply before finally letting the release wash over him.

He gently pulled out once the Priest had calmed, turned the man around and wiped him clean with a cloth he pulled from his belt. Smoothing his hair, Raffé sent him on his way with a smile then fixed his own clothes and sat down in one of the two chairs in the room, staring out the window at the deluge currently bloating the river and adding flooding to a long list of problems.

Håkon and two others had been sent out that morning to deal with an abnormally large pack of goblins, anticipating that something much worse was controlling them. That had been around dawn, and evening was encroaching. The rain would have slowed them some, but it should not have delayed them that long. Where were they?

Sitting around brooding would do him no favors, and sadly, his only pleasant distraction had just been used. Back to the practice yards it was, then. Sighing, he left the sitting room he'd borrowed for feeding and threaded his way through the Temple of the Sacred Three, pausing at the main doorways to pull up the hood of his water-proofed cloak.

Outside, the rain drummed down relentlessly, creating so much noise that even the crashes and booms of thunder were muffled. After four straight days of it, he had started to forget the sound of silence.

He lingered as he reached the bridge to examine the water, which was already spilling over the banks and moving swiftly up. Men worked to contain it as best they could, but the storm showed no signs of ending. Raffé had never seen a storm last so long, even out on the coast where he had grown up and storms could often feel as though they would last forever. They were so used to storms and flooding there, the houses were built high to avoid all but the most extreme of floods. Living right on the river, the royal grounds were clearly built to accommodate in their own way, but it was equally obvious they had never faced anything like the relentless downpour of the past few days.

Waving to the men diligently working along what little remained of the riverbank, he continued on over the bridge then veered right to bypass the castle entirely and make directly for the Hall of War. The barely-audible sounds of fighting drew him to the backmost yard, mostly because it was quiet, a single duel rather than dozens of sparring matches going on at once. The rest of the yards were empty, the weather having driven them all inside.

He lingered in the archway to watch the fight in progress. The combatants were so skilled, the duel was a work of art. Alrin wore only a tight pair of breeches, the bottom half of his legs transformed to a semi-dragon state, scales and claws moving easily in the mud and water, a long, wetly-gleaming tail providing unusual balance as he spun, twisted, lunged, jumped, and thrust, smoothly and playfully matching Boris blow for blow. Like Alrin, Boris wore only breeches, but he had retained his boots. Daggers gleamed occasionally as he attempted to break past Alrin's draconian arms, slipping easily about as he used the shadows that were the main magic skill of the Shadowmarch.

Blue-white light burst, filling the yard as brilliantly as day for the span of a heartbeat, followed by a boom-crash that seemed to make the stones tremble. Alrin and Boris paused, and Boris said something that Raffé could not quite catch even with his exceptional hearing. They made to resume their fighting, but then Alrin saw him and paused, lifting a hand in greeting. Boris turned around and did the same, then beckoned him close.

As a group, they walked out of the yard into the armory. The noise there was no better, the rain pounding down upon the room as it did, but at least they were not getting pounded upon themselves. Alrin clapped him on the shoulder, squeezing briefly before letting go, smiling over his shoulder as he headed for his discarded clothing, piled on a nearby bench.

"Hail, Princeling," Boris said as he stripped off his soaked breeches and pulled on dry clothes. Alrin did the same, though why they bothered Raffé did not know. "Come to spar? I take it you've not heard from your brothers?"

"No," Raffé said. "The weather must be impeding them, unless they've met with further trouble, which seems unlikely when the rain is so heavy it's near impossible for anyone to do anything. I think the river will reach the castle by morning, unless the rain tapers off, and that does not seem likely."

"The Geomancers are working to figure it out, last I heard," Alrin said, roughly drying his hair with a bathing cloth and then casting it aside to pull on a linen undertunic. Raffé let his eyes skim over Alrin's body, unable to resist a chance to admire such a beautiful, honed form. Boris was no chore to look upon either, but his bone-thin body did not appeal as strongly as Alrin's ridiculously distracting muscles-upon-muscles.

As a Prince of the Blood, Raffé would eventually be married to a pure blood human. It was not against the rules to have affairs where he chose, but it wasn't encouraged either. Better, he had been advised, not to dally save with the Priests. Not that it really mattered—even if he was permitted, or ignored advice, Raffé did not think Alrin would take up such an offer. He was ten years older and a favorite in the castle; he could have anyone. He had become a friend to Raffé in the past three months, and that was rare enough, precious enough, that Raffé would do anything to avoid risking it.

He turned away to look out a thin window at the rain and the yard that was rapidly becoming a pond. "Do they think there's magic in the storm? I'm still not terribly adept at feeling such things."

"If there is magic in it," Boris said, voice briefly muffled as he yanked his tunic over his head, "it's a very light, deft touch. That's far more troubling than a heavy, clumsy hand. At present, however, I'm more concerned that three Princes of the Blood have gone missing when something like goblins should have taken them three hours at most, and the majority of that time spent in travel."

Raffé started to reply but just barely caught the sound of feet splashing quickly, heavily, through the water. His hand went to his sword as he yanked the door open—and relaxed when he saw it was just a page. Hustling the boy inside, he closed the door again.

"What brings you out here, lad?" Alrin asked as he finished dressing, pulling on tall boots and settling his cloak around his shoulders.

"His Majesty requests Prince Raffé's immediate presence."

Raffé nodded. "I'm on my way. No, I can move faster than you. Stay here and return to the castle with the good Captains."

"See you at dinner, Princeling," Alrin said with a brief smile.

"Yes." Raffé returned the smile and bid them farewell, then slipped back into the miserable downpour and made his way quickly back to the keep. Why would Waldemar summon him? He was still training, far from ready to be sent out on a mission.

Servants greeted him as he strode into the great hall, drying him off as best they could even as they ushered him through the hall to the king's private solar at the back. Raffé had only seen the king twice since he had taken the Blooding, and he still found

Waldemar intimidating. There was something about him that set Raffé on edge, made him tense—made him feel like he was missing something. But damned if he knew what.

He knelt as he entered the solar, wincing inwardly at the water he was still dripping everywhere. The king said nothing, simply continued to eat dinner with his wives and Prince Birgir, who looked almost exactly like Telmé, save he had a beard and bright blue eyes.

Raffé waited, silent and still. A few minutes later, the doors opened again and Yrian knelt beside Raffé, the scent of amber wafting from him, firelight catching in his red-gold hair and warming his fair skin. He had been a Prince six years, and when not with Håkon, Dalibor, or Telmé, it was generally Yrian with whom Raffé spent his time.

"Princes," Waldemar finally said.

"Majesty," they acknowledged, heads still down.

"The village of Témo, half a day north and right on the southern bank, has been brutalized by this foul weather, and most of it is entirely flooded out. Survivors are being tormented by mermaids and sirens that have swum upriver from the sea. You will go to Témo, get rid of the sirens and mermaids, and bring the survivors back to Guldbrandsen."

"Yes, Majesty," Raffé and Yrian chorused. Waldemar grunted in dismissal, and they departed. Outside, servants stood waiting with weapons and bags and armor, the latter of which Raffé and Yrian both rejected, not wanting to wear the heavy mail or plate with so much rain and when they'd be heading up river.

OF LAST RESORT

Yrian gave a fleeting smile as they headed back through the great hall. "This is your first mission, isn't it?"

Raffé nodded. "I should be excited, but mostly I'm worried. They would not be sending me while I am still in the middle of training if they did not fear they would need the others for something else. I hope I do not hinder the mission."

"As much as I would love to say you are wrong, I fear you are all too right. We are the ones most easily spared, but if he did not think you capable, he would not send you. His Majesty knows this is a good training mission." Yrian's grin returned. "In this weather, there is not much point in taking horses, and there's no going by boat, either. Let's see what the Tamers have to offer us."

"That sounds ominous."

Yrian laughed but said nothing more as they plunged back out into the rain and bolted for the stables.

Inside, everything smelled like damp animal. Raffé wrinkled his nose. "I am beginning to feel like I will never be dry again. I am used to being wet, but it is getting ridiculous."

"Better than snow," Yrian said, then nodded politely as a man in the red-brown uniform of the Tamers, the chimaera crest emblazoned on his chest, approached them and bowed. "Hail, Tamer."

"Highnesses," the Tamer greeted. "What can I do for you?"

"We need to journey upriver, about half a day of travel—probably much longer in this weather. A village there is being destroyed by weather, mermaids, and sirens."

"Water is the only way you're traveling," the Tamer replied. "A horned serpent, I think. We've just three of them, but you'll only need one."

"And to get survivors home again?"

"Drag a boat behind the serpent. They can haul up to ten times their weight if they must, though have a care because it'll tire them out quickly. They eat mostly fish and can hunt for their own food, but it will probably need to feed twice a day as hard as it will be working. Come on, we'll go fetch Lucky for you."

Yrian shot a smirk at Raffé and wriggled his eyebrows. Raffé rolled his eyes, but a smile tugged at his mouth, tipping it up at one corner as they followed the Tamer out to meet Lucky. It meant going back out into the rain, but they were going to have to do that anyway, and it was nearly worth it to see Lucky.

The Tamer waded into the flooding river, almost falling over but holding steady at the last moment. Lowering his hands into the water, he began to whistle. It was a type of spell casting peculiar to Tamers, and Raffé was faintly disappointed that the weather deprived him of getting to appreciate it fully.

After a few minutes, something stirred in the rushing current, a dark, mottled blue-brown blob that turned into a winding, sinuous stream as it came out of the water and looped around the Tamer. Raffé had expected horns, but the serpent really just had long, stiff fins on each side of its head, each segment ending in a sharp point. It was not quite as wide as an average man, its scales shifting from gray-blue to muddy brown.

Turning around, the serpent still wrapped around him, the Tamer asked, "Who wants to be the controller?"

OF LAST RESORT

"You're not coming along?" Yrian asked.

"Most of the other Tamers are gone, contending with the beasts coming out because of the flooding. I'm under orders to remain on premises. Otherwise, I gladly would. So who?"

Raffé shook his head and stepped back. "Now is not the time for me to learn on the move."

Yrian squeezed his shoulder then slid down the wet, muddy bank into the water with the Tamer, who took his hands and pressed them to the serpent, whistling a tune mostly lost to the storm but which provoked a muddy, green-blue glow around Yrian and the serpent. As it faded, the serpent pushed up into his touch and wrapped around him briefly before retreating into the water to wait.

The Tamer sighed as they climbed back up the bank. "You can ride on its back, and it will heed gentle urgings, Highness. Take care of my horned serpent. We don't have a lot of them, and I know how damned beasty you lot can be."

"I learned in my first year not to piss off Tamers," Yrian said.

"Oh, you were the griffon incident."

Yrian winced and flapped a hand when Raffé looked at him, brows lifting. "A story for a quiet day. Come on. Thank you, Tamer."

"Return in peace and health," the Tamer replied.

"Be safe and strong," Yrian replied and slid back down the bank. Raffé followed him—and caught his foot on a rock, slamming into the water, flailing briefly in the current before a hand wrapped firmly around his arm and yanked him up again. "You'll be mocked for that later," Yrian said and then helped him onto the serpent before climbing on himself. Lifting a hand to the Tamer, they then slithered off up the river.

The rain continued without pause or even slowing, and the clouds grew heavier, darker, until they vanished entirely as night fell. Raffé dozed in and out, the only way to escape the arduous misery of the journey.

It was the sirens that woke him. Even through the rain their voices were clear, a perfect chorus singing a haunting melody. Raffé had encountered sirens once as a boy, when he'd been forced onto a fishing boat for what turned out to be the longest month of his life in the hopes it would 'toughen him up'. A storm had cast the boat out far to sea, where they'd come across a small, rocky island that barely deserved the name.

One man had died, though Raffé had not seen it happen. The rest had barely gotten away in time, and his father had told him later that Raffé had escaped being drawn to the island only because he was too young to be affected by the lures that tempted adults. At the time, Raffé had not understood; he'd simply been glad when they'd returned home, and no one ever made him go aboard a fishing vessel again.

He could feel what he thought was the siren's magic, trying to hook him deep and bring him in to devour, but like so much other magic he'd encountered in the past three months, his demonic nature provided a buffer. "Close," he muttered, and felt Yrian shift and nod in agreement.

The hazy shape of the village was just coming into view when the mermaids attacked them. He saw the flash of something too-pale in the water, turned toward it—and went over with a cry as the mermaid leapt from the water, grabbed him tight and dragged him off the serpent and down into the deep.

Raffé couldn't breathe. Couldn't see. Could only feel cold and wet and the hard slice of teeth cutting deeply into his shoulder—then into his throat. Rage filled him. *How dare you, beast.* The thought shot through his mind like an arrow and rage reminded him of his own strength.

He wrenched free of the mermaid, blood pouring out into the water for a moment before it was swept away in the current. Raffé grabbed it by the shoulder, sinking his claws in deep; he grabbed the arm that came at him and snapped it. The mermaid jerked, writhed, wailing loud enough it hurt his ears, but Raffé ignored the pain and kicked for the surface.

They slammed into a large cropping of rocks in the center of the river, the breath knocked back out of him for a moment. The mermaid wiggled and snarled, but he slammed its face into the rocks then threw it up onto them before climbing up and prowling toward it. Fangs bared, he hauled it up, jerked its head to the side, and buried his teeth in its throat.

The blood was foul tasting—fishy, salty, old. He pulled his fangs out and snapped its neck, cast the body back down upon the rocks, breathing heavily as he tried to see through the deluge and find his bearings.

With every breath, the rage that had overtaken him calmed, and Raffé began to tremble as he realized what he'd done. He'd never killed anything except fish his entire life, and yet he'd killed a mermaid as though it were little more than a fish itself. One less monster in the world was always a good thing, but … He lifted a hand to his shoulder. The fabric was torn clear through, but the skin beneath was already smooth again. His neck was healed as well, not even a trace of blood remaining. He half-turned to look at the corpse, blood oozing from where he had torn into its neck, the rain sluicing it away into the river. Its skin was gray-green, pale, and covered in delicate scales. The head was smooth, the deceptive 'breasts' heavy with venom it had not gotten a chance to use. Thank the goddesses the rain kept him from smelling it. Only goblins and dead-walkers smelled worse than mermaids.

Damn the earth, where was he? Where was Yrian? Raffé's only chance of finding him again was heading back up river, but should he walk or try swimming?

He saw another flick of pale fin and realized that if he did swim, he was going to have more fighting on his hands. Walking it was, then. He turned toward the west bank and gauged the distance, then backed up to the east edge of the rocks, dragging the corpse with him to get it out of the way. He threw it into the water, then turned back and ran, leaping from the rocks as he hit the edge and arching over the water to land hard, tripping to his knees on the southern bank, just barely in the water.

Dragging himself out of it, he started walking. How long it took, he did not know, but the sky had seemed to lighten ever so slightly by the time the village—or what remained of it—came into view. He could hear muffled voices, raised high in panic. Raffé slid down the sharp edge of the cove where the village was situated and dove into the water, swimming quickly toward the nearest home.

A claw-tipped hand grabbed him by the leg, and Raffé twisted, kicked, the heel of his boot slamming into something that gave way with a wet crunch. He swam on, increasing his pace, fighting the current until he finally ran into wood slimy with algae. Gripping it tightly, he pulled himself up out of the water, slowly climbing up the wooden support to the dock above, heaving up onto it, and falling to hands and knees. Water poured off him onto the dock, joining the relentless rain pouring back down and into the river.

His ankles were grabbed, and he was jerked back, almost right into the water again, but another twist-kick, and he was free, turning around and surging to his feet, drawing a dagger—

And the mermaid dove back beneath the water.

It occurred to Raffé then that he could no longer hear sirens. That made no sense. Frowning, he looked around at the village, most of it buried in water, only a few houses higher up the cove still above it. Even the dock where he stood would not be safe for much longer. It wasn't even a dock, he realized. It was a walkway, meant to wrap around where a house had been, and he could just see the remains of a set of stairs that had lead further down the cove.

Light caught the corner of his eye, and Raffé turned toward it, saw the green-blue glow of witchlights. Was there a magic user on the premises, then? Only Sorcerers, Priests, Geomancers, and Alchemists could create witchlights, and any one of those would be extremely useful.

Where the hell was Yrian?

Shoving his sopping hair from his face, Raffé trudged on, picking his way carefully along the broken walkways, checking every house as he went, not certain if he should be dismayed or relieved they were all empty. The light, it turned out, was in some sort of large building that was probably a town gathering point. He tested the door carefully, not surprised to find it barred. Pounding on it, he bellowed, "Open in the name of the king!"

The muffled voices went silent, and Raffé could just barely hear footsteps shuffling toward him—two sets, one a heavier tread than the other. After a few minutes, the doors opened to reveal an older, graying man with an eye turned completely white and a younger man who looked much like him, face mottled with bruises and his throat heavily bandaged. "Oh, thank the heavens," the older man said. "We sent for help, but we did not know if the message ever reached the castle, or if it would come in time."

"I apologize we've arrived so late," Raffé said. "My companion and I were separated; I am guessing you've not seen him?"

"No, Highness," the younger of the two men said, bowing his head.

It was strange being called Highness. Even in the castle he was still called 'Princeling.' To be treated with such deference ...

All he felt was woefully inadequate. "How many villagers remain?"

"There are a hundred and twelve in here; I do not know if there is anyone left elsewhere in the village."

Raffé nodded, looking up at the witchlights secured to the ceiling. "Where is the mage who created those?"

"Dead, I fear. We had a visiting Priest; he made them before he went to see if he could do anything about the sirens. That was yesterday."

Damn. "The sirens have fallen silent, so I am fairly certain my partner has dealt with them, and I will go contend with the mermaids now. Make certain everyone is ready to go on a moment because I cannot say precisely when we will be able to leave, only that it will be sudden and must be done quickly."

"Yes, Highness," the man said. "My name is Senth, if you've need of me. My son is Sennson."

"Noted, thank you," Raffé said with a brief smile. "Now, bar the door again behind me and get ready to move quickly. I will return when I have secured passage." He turned and left without another word, hoping it did not show on his face that he had absolutely no idea how to kill enough mermaids to get anyone out safely.

It was his problem to solve, and solve it he would. Moving to the edge of the platform in front of the community building, he let his eyes wander again over what remained of the village, picking out mermaids or the sorts of nooks and crannies where they liked to hide. Twelve definitely spotted and thirty hiding places easily marked.

There were five boats that together could transport all the survivors—if he could locate Yrian and the serpent. Otherwise, he would have to improvise something else. Did the others ever feel this lost and incompetent? Doubtful.

"Raffé!"

He spun around sharply, giving a shaky laugh as Yrian reached him. "You're alive."

"I could say the same for you." Yrian grabbed his shoulders and gave him a shake. "That mermaid—I thought it had you. I was not looking forward to returning to the castle to tell them I managed to lose you almost immediately. Well done getting away from it. How did you manage to stop the sirens?"

Raffé's smile fell away. "I thought you had."

"No …" Yrian frowned. "They must have gone into hiding because of us. I hope so, anyway. If there's something else they're scared of … but it will have to wait, as much as I hate to say it. First, I want you to come with me. I think I felt something … troubling, but I cannot be certain. Magic is not my skill."

It was not really Raffé's skill yet, either, but it was true he was getting better at feeling it. Håkon declared one day he would excel at it; Raffé could only hope that was true and keep practicing. "I haven't felt much of anything—nothing worse than usual since all this damned rain started."

"I think someone's tried to hide it, but the weather is working against them as much as it's working for them," Yrian said and led him through the fractured village back down to the river proper and then into it, where the horned serpent came up out of the water and led them across the bloated, muddy waters to the forest on the other side.

As they got closer, Raffé felt it. The presence of magic started out as little more than an itch at first, a prickling awareness similar to always knowing when he was about to get yelled at growing up. As they continued onward, however, slogging through first water and then muddy, marsh-like land that thickened as the mud-water ratio shifted, the presence of magic became sharper, almost terrifying as it reminded him of sitting alone in a boat while all the men succumbed to the lure of the sirens. He rested a hand lightly on the hilt of his sword, saw Yrian doing the same a few paces ahead of him.

Raffé saw the arm, blackened and wrong, right before it managed to grab Yrian. "No!" he drew his sword and took a lunging step forward, swinging the sword in a downward angle, cutting the arm off where it met the water.

"Behind you!" Yrian said, and Raffé turned just in time to bring his sword around and up to slice off the head of a blackened, bleeding figure lumbering toward him, water quickly sluicing away the mud that still clung to it.

After that, tens of them seemed to come at once—from the mud, the forest, even dropping down from the trees. Raffé hacked away at them, slicing and breaking and tearing his way through, but the numbers never seemed to diminish.

Dead-walkers. What in the names of the Goddesses were dead-walkers doing half a day's journey from Castle Guldbrandsen? They were nowhere near Zyke Lorn Fall or Alwyn, the two Lost Lands from which dead-walkers occasionally wandered. Raffé screamed as he cut the heads off two more, trembling with exhaustion and fear—of the dead-walkers and himself, because with every blow, every slice, it become easier and more exhilarating.

He bared his fangs and snarled as three of them came at him, swung his long sword, and took off two of their heads at once, then brought the sword down on the head of the third, cleaving it open, brain matter clinging to the metal as he yanked it free.

When the onslaught finally ceased, the realization took a moment to process. Raffé clung tightly to his sword and looked around for further attacks, but it seemed they had well and truly defeated the dead-walkers.

"Goddesses grant us mercy if there are dead-walkers about," Yrian said. "Come on. I'm glad now I did not come this far on my own." He led the way into the woods as they grew denser, darker, and for the first time in what felt like forever, Raffé was not up to at least his knees in water, merely his ankles.

They had gone perhaps thirty paces when the feel of magic grew so acute it left his temples throbbing. Another few paces and the water was discolored in swirls and patches, chunks of what was clearly flesh bobbing along in the muck. If not for the rain, Raffé sensed he would have been smelling corpses, and as they came upon the clearing, he saw he was entirely too correct.

In the center of the clearing was an old-fashioned altar, the kind not used since before the Hell Wars. Most of them had been torn down or appropriated, but a few lingered. A crescent of black stones, the largest thrice as tall as a human and the rest getting gradually smaller as they fanned out, tilted slightly back so that they turned toward the sky. Each was carved with archaic runes along the curved tops, and they had been weathered to roughness, only patches of their gleaming smoothness remaining.

Bodies had been affixed to the stones, chained at the wrists and ankles. They were all naked, but their clothes lay in sodden heaps around the base of the stones, clearly discarded in haste before the bodies were hauled up into position. The sacrifice must have taken hours to perform. There were twenty-one bodies in all, each with throat and stomach cut open, bloated and torn by the ceaseless rain, falling apart much faster than they would have otherwise.

As they drew closer, swords still drawn and senses on high alert, the unmistakable blue of their discarded robes became apparent, and the centermost figure still wore the plain circlet that marked him a senior Priest.

"Water," Yrian said behind him.

Raffé looked over his shoulder. "What?"

"This was a sacrifice to summon a demon of water. Priests do most of their work by way of the holy waters; there's no better sacrifice when attempting to call forth such a demon. Someone murdered these Priests to bring forth a demon and call this unceasing storm down upon the kingdom. Damn it! Damn them all thrice!" Though he tried to sound angry, the tremble in his voice gave Yrian away.

If Yrian was scared, Raffé was inclined to be terrified. He looked at the bodies again, shivering. He had only ever read about such sacrifices. They were a thing of the past, a magical practice outlawed centuries ago by the Great Queen who had created the Legion and ended the Hell Wars. "What do we do?"

"We destroy the bodies and then we get those people out of here and bring mages—Sorcerers, Shades, Priests, at the very least. Probably the Paladins would be a wise call. Damn!"

Raffé sheathed his sword and walked down the line to the last stone. The chains were easy to snap, and he was careful as he pulled down the fragile body, grimacing at the bloated, clammy, close-to-tearing state of it, unable to look at the horrific condition of its face. They would have to be burned, but that was a problem he would figure out once all the bodies were down.

Yrian headed for the other end as Raffé went to pull down the next body on his side. He had just started on the third one when he heard the growling followed by a scream and turned just in time to see some dark shape pull away from Yrian's prone form and collapse into mud and water.

Raffé started running toward Yrian and belatedly realized that whatever had attacked Yrian was not retreating but coming straight at him.

THE EIGHT SEALS

Mud was not supposed to have teeth, but there was no mistaking those long, jagged horrors as the mud-monster thing rose up and came at his face. Raffé belatedly drew his sword, getting it up just in time for a clumsy block that sent him tumbling to the waterlogged ground. He swore and rolled as the monster came at him again, getting to his knees just in time to bring his sword up again, catching the monster in the hinges of its enormous mouth, slicing down into them.

It snarled and fell back, collapsing into the mud and water—immediately camouflaged save in the way it moved, and even then it was damned hard to track. Raffé's skin prickled with magic as it hovered close, making wet, garbled, spitting sounds as it tried to get at him even as its jaw still healed.

Raffé followed it, sword at the ready, but it remained just too fast for him to get a fix on it and attack. Something fast enough for a prince, and given the location …

Not a demon, or it would already have him dead. It was probably a minion, a sliver of a demon's shadow set, in this instance, to play guard dog. He didn't have time to work out why it wanted to guard the sacrifices, too busy hoping it wouldn't remove his face with those nasty looking teeth. He could not even gain enough time to check on Yrian, damn.

The minion lunged up, and Raffé screamed as he brought his sword slamming down, grunting as the jolt of impact vibrated up his arms. For something that seemed composed mostly of mud and teeth, the damned thing was hard.

It lunged again, then dropped and went for his feet. Raffé jerked back, tripped, dropped his sword to protect his face, and felt the cold, tingling rush as instinct overtook and misted him out. He thought of rolling, standing, and rippled through the rain. The monster made a sound heavy with mucus, a growl or something, and the way it twitched and shifted, Raffé had the sense it was trying to sniff him out.

Clinging fiercely to thoughts of mist, ignoring the fear that remained whenever he did it—and he still could only do it by accident, much to his instructors' frustrations—he drifted over to Yrian, who lay far too still in a pool of blood that was rapidly being washed away by the rain. Grief tore through Raffé. If he had been stronger, better, relied less on Yrian to know what to do, perhaps they would have made a better team, and Yrian would not be dead.

He turned away—and froze when he heard a whimper, whipped back around, barely noticing that he had returned to his normal state, and examined Yrian more closely. His throat had been torn open, but the wound had partially healed. He needed blood and rest, but he was not quite dead yet.

Raffé laughed-sobbed in relief—then yelped and threw his arms up as the mud monster came at him again, sinking its teeth deeply into his left arm. Raffé screamed as he fell over, but it quickly turned to choking and sputtering as water and mud filled his mouth.

OF LAST RESORT

Desperate, he grabbed the minion with his free arm and rolled over, getting his knees about it and holding fast despite its bucking and writhing, the wet, slippery nature of it. Those damnable teeth were still slicing apart his arm, but he managed to draw a dagger, take rough aim, and drive it down into the top of his closest approximation of the minion's skull.

It clamped down even harder on his shredded arm then abruptly let go and flopped back, dissolving into the water and mud, a pool of black-red blood, mucus, and teeth that was soon lost in the steadily deepening water.

Raffé looked at his arm and bit back hysterical laughter, closing his eyes as his arm began slowly, painfully, to repair itself. When the pain eased to a dull ache, he slowly opened his eyes and stared at the fading bruises that remained. He crawled over to Yrian and reached for his dagger—then remembered it was gone, and damn it all, so was his sword.

Snarling in frustration, he tore his wrist open with his teeth and pressed it to Yrian's mouth. "Drink, damn it."

Yrian made a soft noise, lips moving whisper-gentle against Raffé's skin, and then his lips clamped down, mouth working as he drank. It was not the best choice for blood, but it was better than nothing.

After several long, terrible minutes, Yrian pushed his wrist away and sat up, throat nearly black with heavy bruising but whole. "Thanks," he mouthed. Raffé nodded and stood up then helped Yrian to his feet. Yrian pointed to the bodies that still needed to be dragged down.

Raffé nodded and trudged back to the far side of the crescent to resume where he had left off. It took them far longer than it would have before the minion to finish the job, and when they finally had all the bodies stacked, he still could not think of a way to burn them. "Do we have to burn them here?" he asked, hating his knowledge was so pathetic. Yrian shook his head. "We'll have to take them back to the village, then," Raffé said. "Use an empty house to burn them."

Though Yrian wrinkled his nose, he did not argue. Raffé felt tired just thinking about it, but there was no helping the matter. If they were going to stop the rains, the bodies needed to be burned, and if he recalled correctly, they would next need to locate a Priest to purify the place.

One challenge at a time.

They carried the bodies back through the woods four at a time, two apiece, trudging back through water, thick mud, the increasing debris from trees and the ruins of the village. By the time they were half done, it hurt to move, hurt to breathe, and if he dared to think of how much they still had to do—get the rest of the bodies out of the woods and then all twenty-one across the river to the village—he would collapse.

He pushed on, swearing when he stumbled but immediately dragging himself back up. He had mud in places it had no business being and had given up hope of ever being dry again, but if they managed to survive the long night ahead of them—a night too quickly descending—he would declare it a victory.

They had just dragged the last of the bodies from the woods, piled with the others on top of a cropping of rocks not quite yet flooded out, when he heard the roar. It was faint, so faint he thought he had imagined it until it came a second time, and Yrian's head snapped to the sky. "Oh, my Goddesses." Yrian still could not speak, but Raffé had no trouble reading his lips.

"What is that?"

Yrian grinned and just pointed up as another faint roar, louder than the previous, cut through the din of the rain. As Raffé stared, brilliant green light punched through the clouds. Not light—fire. That was dragon fire. It appeared again, brilliant against the dark, and was followed by the ponderous dragon itself, dark green scales gleaming before the fire went out and all returned to dark.

But he could still see the shape of it as it headed toward them, an ominous mass of muscle and scales. Though it landed carefully, water still splashed up high enough to wash over Raffé's head and nearly knock him off his feet. He shoved his hair back out of his face as witchlights flared to life, until at least thirty of them filled the clearing around them.

Raffé nearly sank to his knees in relief when he saw Håkon heading toward them flanked by four Priests, with more men moving behind them. "You're both alive. Good." The hard set of Håkon's shoulders eased slightly. "I'm going to throttle that fool for sending them out so recklessly!"

"That fool is your king," drawled Captain Boris as he crept from the shadows to stand with them.

Håkon made a face. "Let's get on with it. We have to find—" he broke off and stared at the bodies, still just barely secure on rocks that would vanish in a few more minutes. "What are those?"

"Bodies," Raffé said, and then shook his head. "I mean, we found an old altar and these unfortunates had been recently sacrificed. Yrian said it must be connected to the water, so we were going to haul them back to the village and burn them."

"Well done," Boris said. "But we can burn them right here. Clear the area!" The others who had clambered up onto the rocks hopped back down into the chest-deep water, moving up closer to the woods. Raffé took Yrian's arm and helped him down, and they held fast to each other as they slogged to join the group. They had only just reached them when Håkon turned to the dragon. "Burn them to dust, Captain."

Captain? Raffé's eyes widened as he stared at the dragon. Captain Alrin? Raffé hadn't known he could shift into a full dragon. He gawked as Alrin growled and reared his enormous head back then leaned in and let loose with the green fire. Even from a distance, despite the ceaseless rain, Raffé could feel the heat of it, but they said very little could stop dragon fire. He had always thought the tales exaggerated.

It took only minutes for Alrin to destroy the bodies. He lowered his snout to the blackened rocks, sniffing and grunting, then finally drew back and snorted softly at Håkon.

"Good," Håkon said. "Priests, your turn. Raffé, Yrian, can one of you lead them to the altar?"

Raffé nodded, removing his arm from around Yrian's shoulder. "I'll do it. He needs to be tended, the minion we encountered nearly took his head off, and I had to feed him before he would entirely heal."

Håkon swore softly and swam toward them, hauling Yrian up against his side. "Will you be all right?" he asked.

"Yes." Raffé turned away and pressed to the front of the group waiting for him and then trudged on back to the woods, stumbling more often than he managed to walk properly, vision blurring in and out, doing him no favors when it was already hindered by rain and dark.

Finally, finally, the woods opened up into the clearing. Hands squeezed his arms, clasped his shoulders, and then the Priests were surging past him, five of them, dressed in leather armor and blue tunics. Raffé's skin buzzed, stomach churning, as they began to chant and holy magic filled the clearing, spreading out from the pentacle formation they'd made.

He stumbled back into the relative safety of the trees, not wanting to get burned by holy magic, or worse, corrupt it and cause the purification to fail. His foot caught on something in the water, sending him tumbling back to slam into a tree. Raffé would have happily remained sitting if it had not meant the water came up to his eyeballs, and he whimpered as he dragged himself back to his feet.

Looking up, he realized there was a branch just barely reachable if ... Mustering his remaining energy, he jumped up and grabbed the branch, hauled himself onto it, and then climbed up one more branch so that he was settled on a wide, relatively firm limb. Settling as comfortably as he could manage straddling a waterlogged limb, he rested his head against the trunk and passed out.

A lack of water jerked him awake, though it took several moments of staring blankly about to figure out what had changed. Raffé laughed softly when he realized what it was. Looking down, he saw the Priests in the clearing. His body screamed in protest as he dropped from the tree, but the pain of overtaxing himself was worth it to be free of the deluge. "Well met, Priests," he said as they reached him. "How are you?"

"About as exhausted as you look, Highness," one of them replied, mustering a tired but genuine smile. "Shall we go see if they've been good enough to prepare hot meals for us?"

The other Priests chuckled, and Raffé managed a laugh as he turned to lead the way through the woods back to where their companions waited. By the time they reached them, the dire clouds had dissipated, and Raffé was able to see the stars. He let out a soft sigh as Håkon approached him and slung an arm across his shoulder. "If this is his Majesty's idea of a training mission, I would like to rescind my status as a Prince of the Blood and go back to accounting."

Håkon laughed. "Too late, I'm afraid." His laughter faded into an approving smile. "You did well, though I strongly advise that you not lose your weapons next time. I can tell you from experience that it always turns out poorly."

"A lesson I have already well-learned," Raffé replied with an answering smile. "I will have more care."

"We also need to work harder at your magic. If you had been comfortable with it, the matter would not have been nearly as difficult for you."

Raffé grunted as Håkon began to move him through the water, slowly leading him to one of the various boats that had appeared in Raffé's absence. "The mist thing certainly saved my life. I would like to be able to do that on purpose."

"Good, we'll work harder to ensure you can," Håkon said and helped him climb into one of the boats, sitting down across from him and motioning for the Dragoon at the oars to go.

Raffé belatedly noticed he was leaning against someone and saw Alrin slumped over awkwardly, dead asleep, skin pale and almost bruised looking. The boat rocked, and he slumped to the side, head lolling against Raffé's shoulder. Raffé reached out to steady him, surprised at how cool he was to the touch. He had thought Dragoons ran warmer than most. "Was he really that Dragon? Is he all right?"

Håkon laughed. "Look at your face. Yes, he was the Dragon. Impressive sight, isn't it? He doesn't do that full shift often because the pain is excruciating and it leaves him too exhausted to do anything else for at least a day, but he was the only one who could get off the ground in this weather, and dragon fire will burn in almost anything. He will be fine with food and a great deal of rest. He was worried about you—we all were. You are proving your mettle as a Prince, no mistake."

Raffé ducked his head against the praise. "So do we know who was responsible for bringing the storm?"

"No," Håkon said, mouth tightening. "We also fear the problem is much bigger than a single, albeit horrendous, storm. But you need to feed and rest; I can update you once those matters are addressed." He gripped Raffé's arm for several seconds. "You did well and deserve praise. Without you, we would not still have Yrian, and I don't know that we would have gotten here in time to save any of the villagers."

Raffé wanted to ask what that meant because he and Yrian hadn't accomplished anything in particular—they hadn't even yet managed to burn the bodies—and it was clear Håkon and the others better understood what was happening. Before he could get the words out, however, he was being helped out of the boat and down a hastily-repaired walkway to a small house while Alrin was hauled away by the Dragoons and taken down another path.

Inside the house sat Méo, drinking a cup of tea as he sat beside a sleeping Yrian. "Greetings, Highness."

The form of address drew Raffé up short. Méo always called him Princeling, not Highness. But the thought slid away as Méo approached him and wrapped arms around him, tilting his head to offer his throat. Raffé was too tired and hungry to do anything other than bite down, moaning as hot, sweet blood filled his mouth and slid down his throat, beginning almost immediately to fill the cracks and holes the mission had left in him, soothing the aches and healing the lingering traces of his wounds.

As he withdrew and healed the wound, exhaustion washed over him so sharply he tipped backward, barely hauled in by Méo in time to avoid cracking his head against the floor. Chuckling softly, Méo dragged him to an empty bedroll and lay him down on it. Raffé grunted as his head hit the pillow, groaning in complaint when Méo made him shift and move about while he got rid of Raffé's clothes.

When he was finally naked, Méo pulled blankets up over him, murmuring something that made Raffé's skin prickle as he drifted off to sleep.

It smelled like night when he woke, and a glance out a nearby window confirmed it. Raffé looked around the room, could see clearly despite the dark that Yrian still slept, Méo beside him. Next to Raffé's bedroll was a pile of fresh clothing, and he quickly pulled them on, tying hose into place then pulling on a black undertunic followed by the red tunic of the Princes. Pulling on boots and retrieving the sword someone had left him, grateful to have his weapon back, he stood and quietly padded across the room to the door.

The soft murmur of voices drew him down a narrow walkway to a large, round platform where Håkon, Boris, Alrin, and a man who Raffé belatedly realized was Kristof, Håkon's husband, sat around a small fire in a stone pit, talking and drinking. They paused when they saw him. "Merry evening, Highness," Boris greeted, motioning to the empty seat beside him. "Join us, please. You look well-rested." His eyes glowed pale lavender in the dark, the mark of his hellish magic. After the Princes of the Blood there were few legally permitted to use black magic: Summoners, Shadowmarch, Shades, and Dredknights. They all paid a heavy price for their abilities. Bone-thin and almost sickly, the Shadowmarch sacrificed much of their bodily strength in exchange for the manipulation of light and dark and the extrasensory abilities that made them ideal spies and assassins. "We found the remains of the minion you mentioned and the remains of your dagger. How in the world did you kill a minion of that power with just a dagger?"

"I stabbed and hoped," Raffé replied, reflexively rubbing his arm, trying not to recall how it had looked shredded into gory strips and pieces. "He'd already destroyed my left arm, and I was bleeding out rapidly. It was all I had left."

Håkon grunted. "We are most definitely working on your magic when we get home."

"If we get home," Alrin said quietly. He still looked wan and bruised, hair even messier than usual, and his hands were barely holding onto the mug of tea in his lap. "We still have six seals to locate, not to mention the demons that have already come through."

"Seals?" Raffé asked. A tense silence fell around him, as though he had said something displeasing. "What is going on?"

Håkon raked a hand through his hair, scowling at the fire. "Have you ever heard of the Eight Seals of the Entrance?"

"No." Where would he have ever heard of such thing?

It was Kristof who replied, "There are three main ways to summon a demon. The first, and safest, is to prepare a vessel. Almost any object will work, from necklace to person. Once the object is properly prepared, the summoner cages the demon in it, to be used according to the whims of either the Summoner or the person to whom the Summoner grants control. This is how the majority of demons are summoned. The second method is to open a Door to Hell, which permits only the demon or demons explicitly summoned to pass through. Dangerous, because the demons have a better chance of slipping their bindings. Most often when there is a demon on the loose, it's because it was summoned in this way. The third method is called a Hell Gate, and once it's opened, whatever wants to get through can. The size and strength of the gate can limit that but not by much."

Tension coiled through Raffé, pulled taut. "I suspect none of those methods was used here."

"Yes and no," Kristof replied. "Someone is using Doors to Hell to call forth eight very specific demons. We know at least two of them have already been brought forth successfully, and the others will be brought out soon. Those eight demons ..." He stopped and rubbed a hand over his face, letting out a frustrated sigh.

Håkon reached out to brush the back of his hand against Kristof's cheek, a smile flitting over his lips as Kristof took his hand and kissed the back of it, sharing a look that made Raffé ache with unexpected longing. He was pretty certain he would never have someone with whom he could exchange such a look.

Not that it mattered right then. There were far more important matters to attend. "What makes these eight demons so special?"

Turning back to him, Kristof said, "Back during the early days of the Hell Wars, a group of mages managed to open the main entrance to hell. Demons of all shapes and sizes poured out, and it cost hundreds of lives to close it again—not counting the thousands who died in the chaos. Twenty-four mages, the first to be called 'Summoners,' managed to close the gate again. They died in the process, but they made certain the sacrifice was worth it. They closed the gate and locked it, and then bound the keys inside eight demons that were subsequently returned to hell. The only way to open that gate is from the outside, but all of the keys are locked inside. Those are the Eight Seals of the Entrance. And two of them have been brought back out of hell."

"Merciful Goddesses," Raffé said faintly.

"Yes," Alrin agreed and drained his tea. He glanced around the group, sharing a look with the others that made Raffé anxious—even afraid.

"What is it?" he asked.

Håkon made a rough noise. "The first seal we found, the one that made us realize what might actually be happening, was in the great plains of Noor Hel, at the site of an altar that was torn down decades ago. Like the one here, twenty-one bodies were sacrificed. All possessed a great deal of demon blood, though for various reasons they were never chosen to become Princes. But the main one …"

There was only one reason they would all be so damned hesitant. Raffé felt numb. "Tallas."

"Yes," Alrin said quietly. "I'm sorry."

Raffé shook his head, stared at his hands. "There was—there was no love lost between me and my brother. I don't— don't— why him?" They all shared a look. "Just tell me!"

"Because he was a potential Prince. Because he had sufficient amounts of demon blood—and the blood of a powerful demon at that. The Priests killed here were used to summon Raab, a demon prince with dominion over the seas. Tallas and the other potential Princes were used to summon Belza, a prince with command over countless legions of hell. That is one seal from the Mortal Seals, the Seal of Water, and one seal from the Divine Seals, the Seal of Hell."

"Thank you for telling me," Raffé said. "Excuse me." He stood up and walked off aimlessly, stopping only when he'd found a broken, empty house, a cool, dark quiet in which to mourn Tallas. Goddesses, Tallas hadn't deserved that—no one did. Pinned to a rock and sliced open to bleed out a slow death knowing it would lead to terrible things. He leaned against an open window, arms braced on the sill, and rested his forehead on his arms. Poor Tallas. Goddesses, his poor parents. Bad enough they thought their eldest had run away—to find out he had been murdered, sacrificed ...

Raffé wanted to hit something. Instead, he lifted his head and looked out at the village, the small slice of stars he could see from his angle. After the thunderous deluge, the stark quiet was strange, almost alarming. He would still rather not hear the sound of rain for as long as possible.

A bitter, pungent scent caught his nose and made his eyes sting and water, ruining his ability to smell anything else. Raffé went for his sword and realized he was a goddess-damned idiot because he'd left it back at the fire pit. Damn. Well, he was freshly fed and rested; he could take whatever came at him.

He started to turn—and froze as a calloused hand curled around the back of his neck, heavy and warm and even more than three months later, so achingly familiar. His eyes stung anew, unrelated to the smell that was throwing off his senses. "You can't be." It was pitch black, and his eyes were too swollen, too sore and his vision too blurry, for him to see clearly. How was it possible for a damned smell to befoul his senses so? But the thought flew away as he was turned and his face taken in hands he would never forget. "Cambord?"

"Not such a little prince anymore," Cambord said softly. "But still so sad. I was sorry to hear of your loss and pray the Goddesses carried your brother away to sweet eternity."

"Thank you," Raffé whispered, reaching up to curls his hands around Cambord's. "How are you here? Why are you mucking with my senses? What is that smell?"

Cambord laughed softly. "If I told you all of that, they would not be secrets. I only wanted to make certain my prince was well, no matter how unwise my actions." He tilted Raffé's head up and brushed a feather-soft kiss across his mouth. Raffé gave a soft whine when he pulled away, feeling suddenly cold and lonelier than ever when he realized he was alone again. He scrubbed at his eyes as he stumbled out of the house, hoping to catch some sign—

And huffed when he saw absolutely nothing past the distant campfire, only a single figure still sitting at it. Swearing, he moved to the edge of the walkway and sat down, letting his legs dangle over the edge and bending down to scoop up a handful of water to flush out his eyes.

He was patting his face dry with his sleeve when he heard footsteps again, recognizing Håkon's familiar tread. Raffé looked, lifting a hand in greeting, letting it fall to his lap as Håkon sat down beside him. "You need to stop leaving your weapons behind."

"Yes," Raffé replied. "I was mad at myself the moment I realized what I'd done. I'm sorry."

"Forget it," Håkon said. "I am sorry about your brother."

Raffé nodded. "Do you think he ran away, then, or was he taken?"

Håkon did not immediately reply, save to sigh. After a few minutes he said, "I don't know. I wish we had a definitive answer because if it is 'no' then someone was able to sneak him out of the castle, and that should be impossible. If the answer is yes, then how did they find him, know what he was? There is no reassuring answer."

It was what Raffé had expected. "Are my parents being informed?"

"Yes," Håkon said. "I wish I could spare you to go see them—"

"Seeing me won't help," Raffé said. "Seeing me would make them angrier, more depressed. They would want to know why the bastards could not have taken me instead." Though it was probably for the same reason the king had chosen Tallas—no one thought Raffé worth anything. For once he was grateful.

Håkon gestured crudely. "Fuck them all. Tallas was a good man, I have no doubt, but you are proving to be an excellent Prince. It is not often that we choose poorly, and on the surface, Tallas seemed the better fit, but the Goddesses clearly knew better than us and chose to step in."

"What?" Raffé asked, almost dropping his sword in his surprise. He hastily set it aside before it did wind up in the water. "Tallas was much more fit—"

"Bigger and stronger and better trained, perhaps, but it is not strength of body that makes a Prince. You should know that by now." Håkon glared at him, eyes blazing like torchlight. "It's strength of spirit, strength of heart, and a taste for darkness."

Raffé flinched. "Well, I don't know about the first two, but I definitely have the last."

Håkon's anger went out like a doused fire. "I intended to speak to you at length about what happened. Yrian was not able to tell me much; he is still recovering. Tell me what happened to you."

So Raffé did, starting with when he was dragged into the river by the mermaid all the way through to their arrival. By the time he was finished, he felt drained, ready to crawl right back into his bed roll.

"All in all, well done. Your only mistakes can be attributed to lack of experience, and we can work on all of it when we return to the castle. Impressive work killing the minion; my first encounter with one did not go even half as well," Håkon added wryly. "Do not worry too much upon the fact you killed so easily and enjoyed it to a degree. You are becoming more truly settled in your demonic nature. As long as you never let it get the best of you it will make you the nigh-unstoppable weapon you're meant to be."

Raffé shook his head. "How do I keep it from getting the better of me?"

"Don't forget how to be human. Keep something in mind that reminds you of what it was like to be human."

"Cambord," Raffé said softly, before he thought to catch himself.

Håkon frowned at him. "What?"

"Nothing," Raffé replied, shaking his head. "It was a memory, that's all, from the night before I undertook the Blooding."

"I see." Håkon clapped him on the shoulder before standing and giving Raffé a hand up. "Come on, the Priests and the Summoners have been working to figure out where we must go next, and we must be ready to move on a moment—unless you prefer to return to the castle? You are not required or expected to go on this mission."

Raffé shook his head. "If I am meant to be a weapon then I should be a weapon. A Princeling tucked away in a castle is of no use to anyone."

Smiling, Håkon clapped him on the back as they walked back to the others, rattling off tips for fighting minions, fiends, and several other types of hell creatures, and Raffé was grateful for the flurry of information that kept him too busy to be afraid.

Part Two
Obsession

PAIN

"Fall back!" Alrin bellowed.

Beside him, the horn-bearer blew the retreat, and the men closest to him immediately broke free of their opponents as quickly as they could and fell back.

Alrin waited until his men were clear before hastily stripping off his clothes and giving himself over fully to his dragon. Transforming always hurt; it was like no other pain he'd ever experienced. Being kicked repeatedly in the balls with spiked boots for a year straight would hurt less.

He screamed until the transformation took that ability away, then fell to the ground, writhing, jerking, and twisting as bone, muscle, guts, and all the rest altered—and then grew. The growing hurt worse than the shifting, everything pulling, stretching, tearing, and then starting over again at pulling. He couldn't breathe, couldn't see, couldn't hear anything except the horrid noises of his own body.

When he could breathe properly again, he stood there panting, dug his claws into the earth, flexed and stretched to ease the worst of the bone-deep ache. Expanded his wings, then slowly brought them in again. He roared at the dead-walkers, lowered his head and summoned fire.

The fire sacs deep inside him churned and gurgled, sending fiery liquid up his throat, smoke pouring out of his mouth and nostrils as he held the fire ready.

He waited until the rotted, rancid bastards were close, waited and let them think he was still recovering from the transformation—then opened his jaws and spewed bright green dragon fire, scorching, melting, obliterating the vile dead-walkers.

His flames only destroyed the first wave, unfortunately, and until they could reach the necromancer, the damn things would just keep coming. But he wasn't Captain of the Dragoons because he was a thrice-damned pushover. Alrin roared, enormous claws raking the earth.

Another wave of dead-walkers came at them, eyes glowing sickly red with the power of the twisted, hellish necromancy that was giving them a twisted imitation of life. He knocked several over, then rounded sharply and took out dozens more with his long, spike-tipped tail.

He preferred to use his fire sparingly since it would not last forever before he needed time to produce more of the liquid that made it, and he had no idea how long the fight would last. They needed the Princes, but there was no telling when—or even if— they would arrive. The field was supposed to have been secure, damn it.

The dead-walkers built in numbers, and far across the rotted, barren field Alrin could see the glow of necromancy. Bastard. Alrin roared again, the sound shaking the earth and sky. Behind him he could hear his men and the remaining Paladins readying for the command to mount a second assault.

So many dead-walkers. The numbers were horrifying. How had the necromancer amassed so many without being noticed? There were thousands of them. If Alrin and his men did not break their numbers, the dead-walkers would overrun them and move on to the villages on the other side of the canyon. They would also convert his men to do it. Alrin bellowed again as fury overtook him. He would not falter. He would not let more people die.

Spewing fire, he cut down the latest wave of dead-walkers, then heaved himself into the mess to attack more of them with teeth, claws, and tail again. His scales were too thick, too heavy, for them to cause him real harm, but he suspected the necromancer was simply using his pawns to clear the field a bit.

He could feel the tension in his men as they continued to await his order, but that was an order Alrin would not give. It was a hopeless fight, and he was not going to throw their lives away. The best he could do was try to hold the dead-walkers back until help arrived—hopefully the Princes, but he would take whatever came. Any help was better than none.

The feel of magic in the air abruptly increased, like a burst of cold air through a warm room, and he turned his ponderous head to see that the necromancer had deployed new menaces to fight: wraiths and revenants.

Damn. Dead-walkers he could handle, but those nightmares required holy or hellish magic.

Alrin had always known he would die in battle, but finally meeting that day was still horribly depressing—and he had really hoped it would not be at the hand of wraiths or revenants. Both were a miserable, agonizing way to die. Wraiths were violent, eager to destroy as they had once been destroyed in life. Revenants were a more powerful type of dead-walker, born from mages, that sucked the life out of those they encountered.

He went after another wave of dead-walkers, clawed at the earth and dug in to settle himself firmly. Behind him came the sound of men running; Alrin turned to snarl at them, order them back, huffing out smoke when his men ignored him.

The wraiths drew closer, the masses of dead-walkers separating to let them pass though it was unnecessary. Alrin had always hated the wraiths enslaved to Castle Guldbrandsen, guarding the ward between the second and third curtains. Anyone set upon by wraiths was guaranteed to die screaming for mercy.

Alrin lowered his head and braced to breathe fire. It would not do much, but it was all he had.

He froze in shock as he heard the cry of griffons, and Telmé's deadly red lightning cut through the sky to strike at the masses of dead-walkers. A scarlet figure dropped to the ground in front of the wraiths. He threw his hands out, and dark red flames burst out to wash over the wraiths. They screamed, a high, glass-shattering sort of sound, and then were gone, leaving behind the scent of belladonna, sulfur, and hot metal.

Alrin's heart gave a lurch as the Prince looked over his shoulder to grin, then drew his sword and threw himself into the battle with a challenging bellow. It had not quite been six months since that day—that night—but his little prince had become a truly breathtaking sight.

The griffons landed behind him and his men; Alrin roared in gratitude and relief as Paladins and three more Princes rushed into battle, far more suited to it than Dragoons. A battle that had only moments before seemed a lost cause became an almost laughingly-easy fight. The Princes cut down the dead-walkers and the wraiths as though they were little more than foot soldiers too new to their swords to be of use, laughing and calling to each other between violent bursts, filling the air with their demon-like glee.

Alrin set his flames upon another group of dead-walkers, leaving behind only ashes, then made to press on.

"Stay," said a sharp voice, and Alrin growled as he turned to face Prince Dalibor. "See to your men. We'll tend this mess. You've done more than enough, Captain. Take your well-earned rest." He did not wait for a reply, simply charged on.

The Princes, assisted by the Paladins, rapidly cut a swath through the dead-walkers, pummeling them with sword and spear and levels of hellish and holy magic that reduced the wraiths and revenants to minor threats. Alrin turned to face his men, growling at them. The Dragoons nodded, dragging out all the injured they could carry before retreating over the hill to their makeshift camp.

When they were gone, Alrin stood at the top of the hill to guard their retreat. He was not going anywhere until victory was assured.

It did not take the Princes and Paladins long—an hour, at most, to fight their way through the hordes of dead-walkers. Prince Telmé himself took the head of the necromancer and stood watching while a Paladin destroyed the body with holy blue fire.

Alrin waited until the Paladins and Princes returned and once he was assured it was safe, began the slow and painful transformation back to his human form. He was the only Dragoon who could make the full transformation. Most Dragoons could alter only pieces of their bodies. The two most favored tricks were covering the entire body with impenetrable scales and transforming arms or legs. Dragoons were most useful because they were tough, enduring, immune to fire, and nearly impervious to cold.

He curled up in agony as the transformation completed, struggling just to draw breath, tears pouring from his eyes and every part of him feeling as though it had been stabbed with broken glass.

"Captain," Telmé said soothingly and helped him to sit up, wrapping his own cloak around Alrin's body. "Dalibor, fetch his flask; those look like his clothes there."

A couple of minutes later, mercifully cool liquid poured down his throat. Alrin slumped against Telmé, waiting for the tonic to begin its work, not quite unconscious as he listened to the voices around him.

"Raffé, take about twenty men with you and see if you can find where the necromancer was holed up. I sense we will find another seal broken. Nothing else would explain such an alarming number of dead walkers."

"Yes, Telmé," Raffé said, his voice quiet but steady—impressively so for a man who had only been a prince a little more than five months. It was pleasure and pain all at once, that voice. Alrin would always remember how scared he had sounded that day in the throne room when he had offered to take his brother's place, the gut-tearing sadness in his voice when his fiancé had so cruelly rejected his last wish. His occasional doubts about himself even as he showed the same breathtaking acumen for the Blood that Telmé showed.

And Raffé was probably the only one not aware that Telmé was slowly and quietly grooming Raffé to inherit his role someday. That Telmé had never chosen an heir had been a source of growing concern, especially given the way Telmé himself had come to power. Raffé would not take the role for years yet—and Telmé could decide he was not suited for it after all, though Alrin doubted that would happen. It made him burst with pride even as his heart hurt. But he had known since the maze that it was never going to be more than a single night. Alrin had not thought that would be a problem; it was why he had done it.

He could only imagine how hard the Goddesses laughed at him. Despite the months that had passed since that night, Alrin remembered it so clearly that it may as well have been yesterday. He still wanted to kill the heartless Almor who had fled like a coward because he had known he could not measure up to the man Raffé had proven to be that night. Alrin was also reasonably certain the poxed oaf didn't know how to use his dick.

So far as Alrin was concerned, it was Almor's eternal loss and his eternal gain—even if it was a sweet, twisted pain. He would never be able to touch Raffé again, but no one else would ever be able to give Raffé his first kiss, his first release. No, Alrin had been the first to give Raffé the pleasure he'd so shyly and sadly asked for, and with that he would be content.

He dragged his eyes open and watched Raffé walked away, then pushed away from Telmé to stand on his own feet. "Thank you for the help."

"I'm sorry we arrived so late," Telmé said, yellow eyes far too pensive for Alrin's liking as they regarded him. "How are you, Captain?"

"I'm fine, Highness, merely exhausted and in pain, same as most every man here."

"Every other man here does not turn into a creature the size of a house," Dalibor said with a snort.

Alrin shuddered, not needing to be reminded about the growing part. Magic added the mass, a complicated shifter-magic that no one completely understood though they never stopped trying, but it was not a painless process. Alrin just knew he could happily go the rest of his life without ever having to do it again—and that he would probably be doing it again tomorrow or the day after that because he was an asset not to be wasted.

"Help him back to camp," Telmé ordered, motioning one of the Paladins forward. "If he keeps trying to work, don't hesitate to tie him down." He cuffed Alrin lightly when he tried to protest. "How many times must we have this argument? Do as I say."

Making a face, Alrin let the Paladin lead him away, determined to ignore the order if he must. The Princes of the Blood held rank on the battlefield, but that did not mean they could run roughshod all the time, and Alrin's men came first.

It was still a relief to reach his tent; he groaned as he fell face first onto his cot, never happier to have a scratchy camp pillow beneath his cheek. He grunted out a thanks when the Paladin stripped off the cloak and covered him with a blanket. No doubt it should have been a concern that he was completely naked otherwise, but Alrin had lost all sense of modesty a long time ago. There was no time to worry about everyone seeing his dick when he was consumed by pain and enemies were closing in.

He fell asleep thinking of Raffé's smile and the memory of how those lips had felt, shy and sweet and earnest, against his own.

OF LAST RESORT

The sound of laughter greeted him as he woke, along with the smell of smoke and roasting meat. Rolling out of his cot, Alrin stumbled groggily over to his trunk and pulled out clothes: undergarments, hose, a quilted black undertunic, hauberk, and then the dark green and steel gray tunic of the Dragoons emblazoned with their dragon crest. His was in gold, marking him Captain. He buckled his sword belt into place, strapped daggers on, then pulled on heavy, knee-high boots.

Food. He definitely required food. Leaving the tent, he headed for the circle of campfires where men were clustered around eating, cleaning weapons, playing chips, or otherwise relaxing while they could. The conversation lulled as they saw him, the Dragoons cheerfully hailing and the Paladins calling a more subdued greeting.

"Merry evening, Captain," a familiar voice said behind him, and Alrin swallowed.

Bracing himself, he turned and smiled brightly. Friends. Only friends. No matter how badly every piece of him screamed that Raffé was his. It was an element of his draconic nature that he had to work constantly to keep in check—something that would get him in trouble, thrown out even, if he could not control it. But he was far more dragon than his fellow Dragoons, as tenuously close to being a beast as the Princes were to being demons. Fighting the bone-deep drive to claim and keep the man his dragon had decided to hoard was harder than going solo against an entire pack of hungry, berserked goblins. "Greetings, Highness. Did you have luck with the necromancer's lair?"

"That is why I'm here," Raffé replied, and he nodded back toward the red-black tent that belonged to Telmé, erected while Alrin slept. "I found a campsite and another successful sacrifice. Come, there's much to discuss. I ordered food be brought for you, though."

"You're my favorite, Highness," Alrin said, dropping an arm across his shoulders as they walked to Telmé's tent. Normally he would not be so informal with a Prince, but Raffé was a good friend. He would never be the lover Alrin so desperately wanted, but he would not deny himself an abiding friendship.

He dropped his arm again as they slipped into the tent and moved to stand with Boris and Kristof on one side of the table. Telmé, Dalibor, and Raffé stood on the other side. Alrin glanced at Kristof and lifted his brows. Kristof gave an irritated shrug. "His Majesty recalled Håkon to the palace to help the Master of Magic try to better determine where the rest of the sacrifices will happen. We've been one step behind this entire time and his Majesty is about to string all of us up for it." His face twisted for a moment as he battled his grief. The broken Seal of Heaven had entailed the sacrifice of twenty-one Paladins, and most of them had been Kristof's men.

Alrin reached out and gripped his arm tightly, leaning in to rest his head briefly against Kristof's shoulder in comfort. "I thought the necromancer three years ago was more than enough to handle."

Kristof's mouth tightened at the mention of the unpleasant memory. Alrin had been the only one to listen to him, to believe him, and they had both come very close to imprisonment for their defiance.

"We won't lose anyone else," Alrin said, reaching out to grip his wrist and squeeze firmly. Kristof grunted in agreement, and Alrin let him go. "Now, Prince Raffé promised me food. Where is it? I will make like a dead-walker and eat the lot of you if someone does not feed me soon."

"Dragoons," Dalibor said, rolling his eyes, and jabbed a finger at something behind Alrin.

Turning, Alrin brightened at the wide, shallow wooden bowl heaped with meat, bread, cheese, and dried fruit sitting on a table a few paces away. Grabbing the bowl, he kept it with him as he rejoined the group, asking, "So we are four seals down and four to go, correct? What is our plan?" He bit into a hunk of sharp, bitter cheese and followed it with dried peach, thinking wistfully of fresh peaches and sweet cream.

Telmé raked a hand through his hair, a rare show of agitation—well, rare in the past decade or so. Alrin well-remembered the days when Prince Telmé had been far from the stoic, capable leader everyone knew. "We need to get ahead of whoever is behind this, whatever the cost. Håkon is working on it now. I fear if we do not manage it this time we will not get another chance. Raffé, how many dead-walkers did we kill today?"

"Four thousand, two hundred and seventy-three," Raffé replied promptly. "I cannot count the number that Captain Alrin and his men obliterated before our arrival, but I would put the total number at approximately five thousand."

"Many of them were far gone," Dalibor said, folding his arms across his chest. "There were some fresh ones in there, but most of those dead-walkers had been dead for some time."

Raffé grimaced. "They also smelled of belladonna. That's a trait common to the dead-walkers that come out of Alwyn. How did so many Alwyn dead-walkers get this far north? We're in Taakar, for Goddesses' sake. Zyke Lorn Fall is much closer."

"I'm sure whatever the answer to that question, we won't like it," Telmé said. "So far they have broken the seals of water, earth, heaven and hell. They'll go for fire and death next, but we don't know where they'll perform the sacrifices."

"None of this is recorded?" Raffé asked.

Telmé shook his head. "No. Records weren't kept back when this happened, and the accounts that do exist are third or fourth hand at best, grossly exaggerated, and incomplete. We know the seals, the demons attached to those seals, and that the keystone seals—air and birth—cannot be summoned until the other six have been. We can make educated guesses as to the sacrifices, but the locations are impossible to determine. Too many places they can be done and no way to search them all in time."

"So what do we do?" Alrin asked, finishing the last of his food. He set the bowl back where it had been, then leaned on the table covered with a map and dozens of markers. "I realize Håkon and Leifsson are working on the matter, but I still think they'll be too little, too late.

"We're going to keep them from gaining access to the necessary sacrifices," Telmé said. "The next mortal seal they need is fire. Want to hazard a guess, Captain, what they'll need to sacrifice to summon a demon of fire?"

Alrin went still, eyes snapping to Telmé's face. "If my men and I are a liability why are we still out here?"

"You're leaving momentarily," Telmé said. "All Dragoons, Shades, Shadowmarch, and Dredknights are being recalled to Guldbrandsen immediately.

Under no circumstances are you to leave it again. Understood?"

"Yes, Highness." Alrin fought the nigh-overwhelming urge to go find his men, gather them up, and count them over and over until he was certain they were all accounted for and safe. Until he had touched every last one of them and was absolutely certain they were there and in no danger of being sacrificed.

"Prince Kristof and his men will escort you."

Kristof nodded. "What are you three going to do, Highness?"

"Korin and the wolves are on their way to us," Telmé replied. "Ideally with Håkon and new information, but if not then we will improvise."

Alrin glanced at Telmé, surprised and not—it was not often that High Priest Korin left the grounds of the castle or temple, especially since Korin had produced an heir four years ago. If the king was ordering Korin into the field, matters were far worse than they had already surmised. "I'll go see to the preparations to leave. We should be ready to depart within the hour."

Telmé nodded, dismissing him, and Alrin stole a last glance at Raffé, who was half-turned away speaking to the Paladins, before he slipped from the tent. Looking around, he did not immediately see Åge, his second in command; Alrin bellowed for him. Åge came bolting around the side of a distant and ran across the camp, clearing two campfires in the process, stumbled to a halt, and drew to attention in front of Alrin. "Captain?"

"We leave before the next bell. Get the camp broken down immediately. Also—no Dragoon is to leave camp without permission and Paladin escort. No exceptions, and anyone who decides to make himself an exception will be locked in a cell for three full moons. Am I clear?"

"Yes, Captain," Åge said with a sharp salute. He cast Alrin a confused look but did not ask questions, merely turned sharply on one heel and began snapping orders out across the camp.

"Look out!"

The words registered just as something heavy slammed into Alrin's side and tackled him to the ground. He landed on his back with a grunt, Raffé sprawled atop him. Alrin gaped at him a moment and then saw the black shape flying at them again, long, sharp claws out and a spiked tale whipping—

He flipped them over, covering Raffé with his body, mild pain flaring as he shifted his back into scales. The spikes slammed down on him, jarring him to the bones, but they were unable to get through dragon scale. Rolling off Raffé, Alrin climbed to his feet, restored his back to normal, and shifted his face, torso, and arms, growling as the damned bone wyvern came at him.

It attacked claws first, wrapping them around Alrin's arm to try and lift him. Alrin grabbed the wyvern's ankle with his free arm and held it just long enough for two more Dragoons to come up and help him drag it down to the ground. A Paladin came up, long sword flashing in firelight as he hacked at its neck.

"Captain!"

Alrin turned and caught the glaive one of his men tossed him. "Form a star!" he bellowed as he saw more shapes in the sky rapidly descending. His men moved to obey, hissing and growling as they fell into a formation that helped them control where the bone wyverns would have to attack, allowing for stronger retaliation.

He counted ten before the fighting began, but he knew the number exceeded that, and if there was an entire gathering of wyverns then something still out of sight was controlling them. Alrin snarled as one of the wyverns came crashing down, felled by a Paladin's lance. He swung his glaive, slicing open its throat. He shifted and swung again to catch the edge of the blade where the wyvern's scales were soft, and from there tore open its gut.

"Behind!"

Alrin whipped around, dropping to a defensive crouch as a figure in a mix of leather and plate armor came charging at him with sword drawn and shield up. He tensed to lunge—and relaxed when a Paladin got the bastard in the back with a well-placed dagger before bolting off to the next assailant.

And there were plenty of them coming over the rise, reeking of black magic. Alrin yanked off his boots, brought up his scales, retrieved his glaive, and threw himself into the fight. Swords were all well and good, but Dragoons favored their pole arms for a reason.

He snarled when something grabbed him by the shoulders, reaching up to grip the hard, leathery ankles of the wyvern that had managed to snatch him. Holding fast, Alrin swung his body up, landing a solid kick on the underside of the wyvern's squat, fat head. It snarled but did not let him go.

Then they were high in the air. Damn, damn, and triple damn. Alrin braced himself for pain and went for a shift he had tried only a few times in the past. He screamed as his back tore apart, bones snapping and cracking, blood soaking his shirt as bone extended from where it had not been before, unfurling into leathery wings. Tears streamed down his cheeks, but Alrin focused on the next step, shifting his nails into long, thick talons that he hooked into the wyvern's body right where legs met underbelly and the skin was still soft. He closed his eyes as thick, blue-red wyvern blood fell on his face.

The wyvern let him go with a scream and Alrin plummeted. His wings snapped out, catching the air, stealing his breath as he jerked to a near-halt. Alrin drew a shuddering breath, bracing himself, then folded his wings in and dove, opening them toward the end to slow his speed and land with relative ease on the ground.

He folded his wings in out of the way, picked up a discarded sword, and charged the nearest cluster of soldiers.

A familiar cry drew him, and he saw more bone wyverns trying to carry off two of his men. Alrin crouched, braced himself, then jumped forward and up, wings spanning as he rushed the escaping wyverns, catching one in the wings and sending it tumbling back to the earth. Alrin snatched his Dragoon free and threw him toward an empty patch of field, then whipped back, looped around, and surged upward to save the second captive.

He met it at an angle, using speed to drive his sword in the patch of skin between belly and throat where the scales were soft. It screamed and released its captive. Alrin caught the Dragoon and flew him back down, letting him go a few stones from the earth before landing several paces away.

Turning back to the battle, which was still rife with chaos and no clear winner apparent, he tried to figure

OF LAST RESORT

out what he should do next. With the wyverns and the hundreds of hellish soldiers that kept pouring over the hill, only the presence of Three Princes of the Blood gave them a bare advantage.

Then the smell came: wild roses, hawthorn, and garlic flower. Demonsbane. It wafted across the battlefield in noxious clouds of smoke, annoying to most but potentially deadly to the Princes of the Blood because it crippled most of their senses, leaving them vulnerable.

But the secret of demonsbane was not commonly known. It was not even written down anywhere, merely passed along between those who needed to know. "Protect the Princes!" Alrin bellowed. "Somebody find the source of the demonsbane now."

He bolted across the field to where Telmé was collapsed on the ground, covering his face but obviously already struck. Grabbing his arm, Alrin hauled him up and dragged him out of harm's way. Three men came at them, and Alrin dropped Telmé back on the ground, snatched up Telmé's sword, and fought off the assailants, slamming the sword across the face of one and buying himself time to break the defenses of the second. Alrin slashed upward and tore open his face, then shifted his free hand into dragon form and slammed it into the face of the third man, claws shredding it open, blood pouring hot and sticky over his scale-covered hand.

After that, killing them was easy. He hauled Telmé up again and made for his tent, throwing him at two Paladins who came rushing up.

A familiar voice screamed in agony, and Alrin's world went still and quiet and white. He turned in time to see Raffé fall, his throat torn open by one of the wyverns, Raffé's blood dripping from its claws.

Alrin did not remember moving after that, remembered nothing but blood and pain and fury. No one would take his treasure from him.

Eventually it all came to a stop, though it took Alrin a moment to process that the fight had finally ceased. He stood staring at the battlefield littered with bodies, rank with death, trying to recall all that had transpired, but he remembered little past the emotions, sensations of flying, falling, fighting. He was wet and sticky with blood and gore. What had happened?

Raffé. Something had happened with Raffé. Where was he? Alrin looked anxiously around, letting go of the glaive he had acquired at some point. There. His heart, already beating furiously with fear and the residue of combat, began to thud even faster as relief flooded his body. Stumbling over to Raffé's prone form, Alrin made a low, ragged noise as he realized that Raffé was alive and already recovering from his wounds. Alrin knelt down beside Raffé, reached out to touch his cheek—and passed out.

Consequences

Alrin dragged his eyes open slowly, wishing quite fervently that he were dead. He had not even attempted to move yet, but his body burned with pain. Goddesses, he wanted to go one day without pain, without feeling as though he had been torn apart and sloppily put back together. Tears stung his eyes as he burrowed his face into his pillow.

He remained still, breathing slow and steady, until the sharpest edges of pain dulled. He still felt raw and ill-used, as if he were being held together by cheap thread and dumb luck, but he would be able to manage. Swallowing, he shifted to brace his hands and slowly levered himself up. Sweat slicked his skin, and he felt fever-hot, but he kept going until he was off the cot and standing on relatively-stable feet.

That accomplished, he looked around his tent for clothes because he knew what he was going to face the very moment Telmé knew he was awake, and he did not want to face it with his dick hanging out. Pulling on clothes was almost too much for him, but Alrin grit his teeth and muscled through it, though he had to sit down again when he was finished.

If he was still in a tent, they were still afield. Strange. Telmé should have ordered everyone home immediately. That attack had to have been meant to obtain Dragoons for sacrifice. Hopefully none had been carried off. He had hazy memories of flying and breaking two of his men free—but he also remembered going berserk, sort of, and anything could have happened in the seconds or minutes that had passed.

He tensed at the sound of approaching footsteps, relaxing only slightly when the tread and jangle of spurs marked Kristof. He wrapped one arm across his stomach, cramped with misery and anxiety, balled his other fist in the blankets, and half-curled over himself as the tent opened and Kristof slipped in. There was a beat of silence before Kristof quietly spoke. "You're awake. For a while, we weren't sure you would wake." Kristof crossed over to the cot and gently rested a hand against Alrin's face, knowing better than to touch him too much. "I'm glad you made it this far, you crazy bastard."

Alrin gave a shaky laugh. "I think I might have been better off dying." He squeezed the bridge of his nose between his thumb and the knuckle of his first finger.

Kristof sat down next to him and gently rested a hand on his thigh. They had been more or less strangers to each other three years ago when Kristof had returned from a mission with the news that Håkon had been lost but insistent he was alive and they needed to find him. Alrin had been the only one to believe him, and the only one willing to join him in defiance, and they had become fast friends. Alrin leaned into his shoulder, grateful for Kristof's steadying presence, the warmth that always leaked from Paladins that was almost on a par with Dragoons. "How long was I out? What has happened?"

"We are about three days travel from the castle. Too many men died, and the rest are in no shape to travel quickly. You've been out about five days. We stopped here to rest because the Priests insisted that continuing to press on would do more harm than good for everyone—especially you. As much as Telmé is ready to kill you, he does not actually want you dead."

Alrin winced and slowly sat up. "I didn't mean to do it. I know I can't—I've been careful—" He broke off, hung his head. "I had it under control."

"If Telmé thought you'd acted so foolishly on purpose, he would have killed you himself, you know that. He's worried about you, more than almost anyone else in camp. But he's still going to have to tear you apart."

"I know," Alrin replied and briefly gripped the hand still resting on his thigh for comfort and in gratitude. "Thanks."

"You know if there's anything I can do, you've only to say," Kristof said. "Not just because I still owe you a debt."

Alrin rolled his eyes, shaking his head. "There is no debt, you idiot Paladin."

Kristof tugged at a strand of his hair. "We'll rehash the argument later. You have a far more brutal one to face first."

"Stop reminding me," Alrin muttered. "You still haven't told me what happened."

"You happened," Kristof replied wryly. "The Princes were holding back the worst of it despite the damned wyverns when the demonsbane came wafting over the hill. They must have burned piles of it to get so much smoke flowing. It should have crippled the hell knights, too, but something protected them. We started to lose, and then you berserked. Most everyone is attributing it to general casualties, that you gave in to panic when the Princes fell. Only a few of us know it was Raffé specifically who tipped you. He hasn't been told yet. Telmé is waiting until you are gone before he has that discussion."

Alrin sighed, heart hurting at what he knew was coming. Castle Guldbrandsen had been his home for as long as he could remember, and he enjoyed being Captain of the Dragoons. But he was also as near to being a full-blooded dragon as it was possible to be and still shift between forms, and he had just tipped over from acceptable risk to liability. "Best to get it over with," he said and with Kristof's help, stood up and pulled on a cloak.

Kristof hugged him carefully, then helped him walk out of his tent and across camp to Telmé's. "Goddesses be with you," Kristof said quietly and with a last, gentle squeeze to his shoulder, left Alrin to his fate.

When he was gone, Alrin motioned to the guards standing duty. One of them slipped inside but reappeared almost immediately and waved for Alrin to pass. Stepping through the flap, Alrin bowed low. "Highness."

Telmé sighed. "Sit down before you fall down, Captain." He waited until Alrin had done so, then shoved a cup of tea across the table. The bittersweet smell of melbark tea with honey wafted over him. Alrin curled his hands around the rough clay cup and lifted it, drinking the scalding tea down in one swallow.

"Thank you, Highness."

"Captain, for all that I want to throttle you right now, I do not want to see you dead. Between all your shifting and the berserking, I am impressed you are on your feet already—but you have the tenacity of a Prince, I swear. Unfortunately for all of us, you are too much a dragon."

OF LAST RESORT

Alrin flinched, but there was nothing to say because it was true. His father had been half dragon and his mother a full dragon. His father had brought Alrin to Guldbrandsen to be raised human, then returned to his mother—at least that had always been the best supposition since his father had remained at the castle only three days to ensure his son would be well. Alrin had been raised alongside a handful of other orphans in the care of a man and woman who were both heavily dragon themselves. But even with their knowledgeable care, Alrin had always been a high risk, dragon enough to get fiercely, murderously attached to someone or something. The possessive, protective tendency—hoarding—was mitigated somewhat by pouring it into his Dragoons. Across a large group it wasn't as severe and mostly manifested as being extremely loyal and devoted.

So far as relationships went, he never spent time with someone with whom he might get attached. Lovers were people he could let come and go with ease. The few times he thought he might get too attached he had walked away.

If only he had been that smart with Raffé.

"Why, Alrin?" Telmé asked with a sigh. "You are so smart, have always been so careful. The king has said that if you found someone to be a suitable spouse that he would grant permission. Why in the name of heaven, hell, and earth did you decide to fixate on the impossible! You know that a Prince of the Blood cannot marry a Dragoon! He needs a human. And I cannot have you in the way, on the edge of losing it, while he is training and unattached and constantly in danger! You know all this!"

"I didn't know I had," Alrin said, hanging his head. "I only meant—he was so fucking sad—" He broke off, unable to get the words to come out the way he wanted, balling his hands into his fists.

Silence stretched on for a long, arduous moment before Telmé broke it, his voice stern but soft. "Tell me."

Alrin drew a deep breath and let it out on a long sigh, fighting the exhaustion that washed over him, a combination of his still recovering, the stress of the conversation, and the pain-dulling tea. "I noticed him straight away, as did most of us." Telmé nodded in agreement. Raffé had stood out—quiet demeanor, soft-spoken, and plain-looking, but he also endured well, was smart, and without hesitation, had been willing to risk his life to do the right thing.

Since becoming a Prince of the Blood, all that buried potential had been steadily coming out, augmented by all the special abilities that being a Prince gave him. When he was completely comfortable and had a few seasons of experience behind him, he would become a strong leader in his own right and a suitable heir to Telmé. "I admired him, but it was distant—he does not live here, he was engaged, and even if he were not, he was the only child his parents would have left after his brother became a Prince. I was sorry he was not given better opportunities, but there my interest ended. But the night before his Blooding …"

He sighed again then described to Telmé the encounter he had overheard between Raffé and his odious fiancé. "I only meant to give him what he wanted. I didn't know—I thought I had walked away unscathed. When you introduced us that day he woke up, I realized I was wrong, but I have kept it buried ever since. I know the dangers of trying to hoard him, and I would not endanger anyone that way."

"If I thought breaking your face would accomplish anything I would," Telmé said, raking a hand through the long, loose strands of his hair. He was dressed with unusual casualness in only his hose and a long-sleeved undertunic, a long, beautiful stretch of pale skin and dark clothes, the yellow eyes adding an eerie touch. Alrin knew his own eyes were probably such a deep blue they'd look black to most—a sign of pain. Most people thought the phrase 'a green dragon is a healthy dragon' came from the condition of their scales. Really it came from their eyes. A dragon with green eyes was healthy and whole. Blue was pain. Red illness. Notoriously self-contained about such matters, the only way to tell how a dragon felt was by eye color.

"I didn't mean to fixate on him, I swear," Alrin said, though it little mattered in the end whether he did or not. The problem was that he had fixated. It wouldn't be a problem if he had focused on another dragon, or a civilian who would be happy to marry him, did not mind a dragon's possessive inclinations, and could build a relationship that would help it settle over time.

But to fixate on Raffé, who was out of reach and would never be in a position to settle with him even if he wanted—and Alrin was painfully aware Raffé saw him only as a friend—only meant that he risked going mad with it, so many times worse than his brief fit on the battlefield.

Only distance and time would fix the problem before it reached a point it could not be fixed. But that meant removing him indefinitely from the Dragoons, from the Legion, and that was as heart-breaking as severing all ties to a man he had known he'd never be able to claim. "What's to be done with me?"

"I don't know," Telmé said, settling back in his seat, looking twice his age and three times as exhausted as Alrin felt. "His Majesty said he would address the matter himself upon our return, and he has altered our orders to have everyone return there as quickly as possible. I wish we were making better time, but nearly everyone is too badly injured. Until we are home, you are to stay confined to your tent unless absolutely necessary. Am I understood?"

"Yes, Highness."

Telmé jerked his head toward the door, and Alrin obediently rose and left, keeping his head down as he walked in slow, halting steps back to his tent. Nearly there, the last twenty or so paces seemed like a hundred. He stood where he was, body feeling as though it had been filled with glass, tears streaming down his face from exhaustion, agony, heart-break, and fear.

"Alrin—"

He jerked, looked up, and reared back when he saw Raffé. Swallowed. No one would ever describe Raffé as beautiful; he did not possess the stunning features that seemed to come so easily to men like Håkon and Telmé. But he was appealing, like falling into his own bed at the end of the day, or gathering in the hall with friends for a meal, hearing the minstrels play his favorite ballad after a long day. His hair was long, loosely braided back, strands falling in his face. He hadn't shaved in a couple of days, giving him a rough edge that Alrin wanted to feel. And he would give away everything he possessed to taste Raffé's lips one last time. "H-Highness."

"Do you need—"

"Raffé!" Telmé called sharply from across the camp. "To me now."

"I just want—"

"Now!"

Raffé huffed in irritation, glaring in Telmé's direction as only another Prince would ever dare, and with an apologetic look at Alrin, stormed off.

A familiar weight wrapped around his waist, hauled him close, and Alrin was more than happy to let Kristof more or less carry him back to his tent and set him on his cot. "It's entirely annoying how easy it is for you to carry me around when I know you do not weigh that much more than me. Thank you."

Kristof snorted and went over to the table in the corner where someone had left a fresh pot of tea. Pouring some and adding honey, he brought it over and pressed it into Alrin's hands. "So what is Telmé going to do with you?"

"Nothing," Alrin said and downed the tea. Kristof scowled at him, making him smile briefly. "Apparently King Waldemar wants to deal with me personally."

"Oh." Kristof winced. "I can speak from personal experience as to the unpleasantness of that."

Alrin cast him a withering look.

"Well, you're too valuable to execute, right?"

"Maybe," Alrin muttered, not even half-convinced, not when this was his second major foul up.

Kristof squeezed his shoulder. "I don't know if it's better or worse for me to say it, but I think you would have been a good match for him."

Alrin gave a dry, sour laugh, scrubbing at his face, longing for a hot bath to soak in or a roaring fire and a pile of warm blankets. "He is a young, new Prince of the Blood and fitting well into the role. All he has to do is look at someone, and they are his for the taking. I sincerely doubt an old Dragoon is anywhere on his list of desires."

"You're not old, and you're what—ten? Twelve years apart? That is not so great a distance, and it is not like you to be so hard on yourself. I also think you've been wallowing a bit too hard if you have not noticed he is always looking at you. It is circumstances that deny the two of you a chance, not a lack of interest."

"Telling me there is a chance, but that it's denied me anyway, does not help."

Kristof winced. "Sorry."

Shaking his head, Alrin reached out and gripped his forearm. "Your support is all that is keeping me from losing my mind. But I think, for now, I am going to escape back into sleep. If you have the time, come and visit me again sometime. I am confined to my tent unless ordered otherwise, and it will not take me long to go cage crazy."

"I'm sure I can find you something to do," Kristof said with a grin.

Alrin rolled his eyes. "If you even try to give me your paperwork, I will tell your husband about this conversation and make it sound filthy."

Gesturing crudely, Kristof returned the empty cup to the table and snatched up a spare blanket from a chest behind it. "He wouldn't believe you. Get in bed." He set the blanket aside and pulled off Alrin's boots, then helped him strip down to his hose before getting him under his blankets. Settling the spare in place, he flicked Alrin's cheek. "Sleep well, dragon." Extinguishing the lantern hanging above, he murmured a farewell and left Alrin in peace. Despite his tumultuous thoughts and the knot of dread over what awaited him at the castle, Alrin fell immediately asleep.

When he woke, it was dark, though the noise outside indicated it could not be terribly late. Alrin turned over so he lay on his back, loath to leave the warm nest of blankets—it was not as though he had anywhere to go. Åge would have the men well in hand, and Alrin was not needed for anything else.

A painful reminder he did not need right then because it only reinforced his fear that his punishment was going to be a swift execution. One could only defy the king and jeopardize the Legion—and therefore the kingdom—so many times and expect to live. Last time he and Kristof had received the beating of their lives.

Brooding would not help him. Alrin rolled out of bed, relieved the pain had mellowed to bearable levels, and went to the entrance of his tent. "Merry evening."

"Evening, Captain," the Dragoon and Paladin on duty chorused, saluting smartly. The Dragoon added, "Good to see you awake, sir."

"Thank you." Alrin smiled and lightly gripped the Dragoon's arm for a moment. "I do not suppose one of you would have a bath called for me? If I do not clean up I am afraid my stench will convince the camp I'm actually a goblin."

Laughing, the Paladin raised a hand in acknowledgement and strode off to see it done.

"Are you well, Captain? Begging your pardon." The Dragoon ducked his head, hand white-knuckled where he held his glaive, the other balled into a fist at his side.

"Dénes, isn't it?" The Dragoon looked up, clearly startled his captain would know his name—evidence he was more human than dragon and did not possess their dangerously obsessive behavior. Alrin knew all their names, knew where they were from, their strengths and weaknesses—all that he needed to keep them alive and as safe as it was possible to be in the King's Legion. "I will be fine. I am sorry to distress you and the others. All will be well when we reach the castle. All that matters right now is protecting each other. Do not worry about me."

"Yes, Captain."

"Good. When the Paladin returns, seek me out food."

Dénes nodded and again said, "Yes, Captain. Prince Telmé said we would be heading out in the morning. He will be glad we don't have to put you in a cart again."

"Me too," Alrin said, making a face. "Notify me of anything important, and if you see that reprobate royal Paladin, bid him attend me."

Poorly smothering a laugh, Dénes nodded. Alrin retreated to his tent and tidied up his cot while he waited for the bath. After the bed was made he wandered over to his work table and sorted through the pile of papers that had accumulated haphazardly while he slept. Why did the paperwork remain when all the rest of his duties had been taken away? He picked up his letter opener—

And dropped it when he heard a horn calling out an emergency. Turning on his heel, Alrin bolted from the tent, leapt over the bathing tub being carried by two Paladins, and ran for the center of the campsite in time to see a message hawk alight on Telmé's arm.

The look on Telmé's face was explanation enough, but Alrin clung to hope until he said, "Another seal has been broken."

Dread dropped into Alrin's stomach like chunks of jagged ice. "Which seal?" He tensed further as Telmé signaled to someone behind him, knowing what was coming—

"The Seal of Fire," Telmé said quietly. "I'm sorry."

Alrin screamed, fury and pain and shame cutting through him like a serrated blade. Hands grabbed his arms and shoulders firmly, holding him in place as he thrashed and wailed. Which of his men? Which twenty-one of his men had been strung up and sliced open to bleed out slowly for the sake of a demon?

He couldn't take it—not with the pain, the pending loss of his position, the knowledge he'd never be allowed near Raffé again. If he hadn't lost control and let his damned draconic nature get the better of him his men might be alive.

A Priest strode up to him and gently cupped his head, and Alrin was grateful when the dark closed in on him once more.

DEMON OF NIGHT

They were met by a castle that was far too quiet, a collection of solemn faces that felt too much like staring into a mirror and seeing his own pain reflected a thousand fold. Alrin kept his eyes firmly in front of him as they walked on through the crowd that parted for them and into the great hall. Only half the torches were lit and the fireplace was banked, the colorful tapestries that minimized drafts and helped hold heat draped in pale mourning gray.

The tables had been cleared away and the bodies laid out for viewing—all the Geomancers, Paladins, Dragoons, and potential Princes who had been sacrificed but not yet burned. The ashes of those already burned were arranged on the tables pushed against the walls. Some of the bodies were uncovered; others were far too decayed and so had been draped in burial linens. Priests formed a loose wall around them, quietly singing prayers. Alrin pushed through them to go to his men, crying as he said goodbye to each one and leaving a dragon blossom on their chests. Most of those laid out would be burned, but Dragoons *couldn't* burn and so must be destroyed and set free by other means, usually a grisly chemical developed by Alchemists that reduced a body to nothing in less than a bell.

A hand fell heavy on his shoulder, and Alrin looked up to see Telmé standing over him. He gave a nod of gratitude and slowly stood, looking across at the others who were paying respects to their fallen. "We have to stop the other seals."

"I am hoping that if his Majesty has recalled all of us then he must have a plan," Telmé said. "Come, he is waiting."

Alrin fell into step behind him, silent as the others joined them, reaching out a hand to briefly grip Kristof's arm in comfort. He felt Raffé's presence somewhere behind him and swallowed against the raw pain that cut through him. Too much, too much. He needed space, a chance to breathe and mourn in peace. Soon, hopefully—if he survived the audience with the king.

Guards pulled open the heavy doors to the king's solar as they approached and closed them again once everyone was inside. Alrin knelt and bowed his head, Kristof on one side, Boris on his other, with Telmé, Håkon, and Raffé in front of them. Around the room, all the other heads of the Legion were gathered. The king's solar was not by any definition a small room, but it felt like a wardrobe right then.

"I'm glad you're all finally here," Waldemar grunted and motioned for them to rise and join the others. His wives were curiously absent—normally Waldemar did not do anything without them, having no taste for his father's practice of keeping women tucked away. It was troubling they were not present. The crown prince, Birgir, was present, however, on his father's right and looking decidedly unhappy. Strangest of all, Korin sat on Waldemar's left, and the Master of Magic sat beside Korin.

Alrin sincerely doubted that the most powerful people in Castle Guldbrandsen had been assembled to see the king flay him, so what was wrong that it required all the captains and masters of the Legion? They never gathered together so closely all at once, not unless the risk was worth taking.

The king looked them all over, expression pinched, shadows heavy around his eyes. Finally he leaned forward, hands folded on the table, and said, "You are all aware of the situation with the seals. At this time, only three demons have yet to be summoned. The next seal will be the Divine Seal of Death, and to do that he will require twenty-one Shades." The Master Shade swore softly, and Boris and the Captain of the Dredknights looked no happier. "Protect them at all costs. No one leaves the walls of the castle without my express say so, not until this matter is resolved. If the Legion must be sent out, Shades, Shadowmarch, and Dredknights are absolutely forbidden. Unfortunately there is little we can do to prevent the collection of candidates for the final two Seals. The Seal of Air requires a sacrifice of twenty-one women, and the Seal of Birth twenty-one children."

Alrin bellowed in outrage along with everyone else in the room at that until there was so much noise it was impossible to hear anything except the anger. Why in the name of heaven, hell, and earth would anyone stipulate women and children be slaughtered to summon demons? Who would be that reckless, that fucking cruel? Women were the core of everything—to slaughter twenty-one of them was—and *children.* What sort of bastard son of a demon murdered children?

He startled when someone grabbed him, and only as he stared at Kristof did Alrin realize he had been growling and on the verge of completely losing it. Waldemar bellowed for silence, and around Alrin, everyone subsided, though they all shifted about restlessly, anger palpable. "We cannot guard every woman and child on this continent, though efforts are being made anyway, and those of you we can send out will be to further contribute. But have a care that what we are doing is kept quiet because people will riot—and for good reason, but it will do more harm than good. Now I want everyone out. Orders await you in your quarters. Telmé, Raffé, Håkon, you will stay, along with Captain Alrin and Prince Kristof. Everyone else, go."

Alrin shared a looked with Kristof but said nothing, only waited while the others departed. He felt the prickle of a stare and looked up, frowning when he caught High Priest Korin staring pensively at him. Why? He knew the High Priest, but they had very little to do with each other. Alrin looked away, anxiety burning higher than ever. No one ever drew the attention of the High Priest for a good reason, except Prince Telmé.

When the doors finally closed again, it felt too much like the clanging of prison gates.

"High Priest, Lord Leifsson, if you please," Waldemar said quietly.

Standing, Korin walked with Leifsson to the middle of the room and faced the doors, Leifsson turned toward the king's table so that they stood pressed together back to back. Alrin's skin prickled, heart spiking with alarm because such a stance was only used when holy and hell magic were used in concert—something that was rarely done, not least of all because it was dangerous.

"Nobody move or speak," Telmé said softly right before Korin and Leifsson began to chant, their separate parts of the spell coming together in a strange duet that sounded as though there should be a disharmony that was never quite reached. Bright, lightning-blue light and heavy, blood-red light cascaded from where they had lightly tangled their fingers together, spreading across the floor to climb up the walls, melting away save for those places where the runes had been created—or woken, Alrin realized belatedly. They were waking a spell that had been put in place a long time ago.

When the chanting finally ceased, the silence that remained was thunderous, pulsing with magic. Korin and Leifsson stepped slowly, stiffly apart. Telmé surged forward and caught Korin up close, clearly displeased if the tone of his words was anything by which to judge. Alrin stepped forward to help Leifsson back to his seat and pushed Korin's abandoned glass of wine into his hands. "Are you well, my lord?"

"Yes, thank you," Leifsson said.

"What was that?" Alrin asked.

Prince Birgir raised a hand and gestured for all of them to sit at the table. Alrin did not like any situation where a simple captain was not just permitted but ordered to sit with the king.

When everyone was seated, Waldemar spread his hands on the table. "What is said in this room—what occurs in this room—does not leave it. On pain of however many deaths it takes to ensure it remains a secret. Am I understood?"

"Yes, Majesty," they all chorused. Alrin's fingers curled and uncurled in his lap. He wanted to be out, wanted to be *moving*, not locked away in a magic-drenched room learning secrets of state he was happier without.

When they had all fallen silent again, Waldemar sat back in his seat, reached out, and took his son's hand. Korin stepped up behind Waldemar as he closed his eyes and removed the heavy gold chain that was always around Waldemar's neck. Alrin recoiled, damn near lunging from his seat, as the presence of *demon* rolled out from the king, and when he opened his eyes again, they were blood red from corner to corner, a black and yellow ring in the center.

Almost as one, Alrin and the others stood, pulling whatever weapons were to hand. Magic filled the air, sharp and hot. Alrin shifted his torso, his arms, scales coming up to cover even his face, feeling the fire and smoke building—

"Enough!" Korin shouted. "Sit down, all of you—now."

Alrin shook his head; he was doing no such thing. That was a fucking *demon.*

"Sit," Korin ordered, eyes flashing holy blue. "No one here will do any of you harm. Sit down." His stern expression eased to something softer but far more somber as he looked at his husband and said gently, "Telmé."

Telmé gave Korin a look of such rage and hurt—of betrayal—that Alrin was achingly grateful he was neither of those men. Trembling, Alrin slowly resumed his seat, unable to tear his eyes away from the demonic king. He could hear the others grumbling and moving restlessly beside him, no one relaxing, the air still heavy with magic not quite banked. Beneath the table, Alrin kept his arms shifted, claws ready to strike in a moment and his fire easy enough to recall.

Though he remained standing, Telmé sheathed his sword, finally tearing his eyes away from Korin to glare at the king instead. "What is the meaning of this? How long has this been going on, and why are we only now being told of it?"

"I have always been this way," Waldemar replied, but the cadence of his words had changed. "Since the first Queen, though when I stole her body she was nothing but a broken girl. I have been passed down from heir to heir ever since." He squeezed Birgir's hand, eliciting a faint smile.

"Why?" Telmé demanded. "Why in the name of the heavens are we following the dictates of a demon?"

"Sit down, Commander," Waldemar said firmly, and it was strange to hear anyone call Telmé that. He was always Telmé, or Highness. "You and your men will not come to harm; you may all rest easy."

Alrin kept his claws out anyway, and around him the others made no move to relax either. Telmé remained where he was, kept one hand resting lightly on the hilt of his sword. "Who are you, demon?"

Sighing, Waldemar replied, "I am Satrina."

Alrin did not know what that meant, but from the way Telmé, Håkon, and Kristof hissed and recoiled and nearly drew their swords again, that was not a good answer. He growled, rested his claws on the table.

"Demon Queen," Håkon said. "Why in heaven, hell, and earth is our royal family possessed by the Demon Queen of Night?"

"Because I like it here," Satrina said quietly. "Because I was summoned and escaped and meant to destroy all that was here and make it my own, for hell is no place I want to be for eternity. But I came to love the mortal plane, damn everyone, and I want to take care of it."

Alrin stared at her, then shared a look with all the others.

Telmé heaved a sigh and finally sat down, motioned for the others to finally relax. Reluctantly, Alrin shifted fully back to human and tried to rest easier in his seat, though he still was ready to attack the moment things went wrong. Telmé suddenly seemed every bit of his long, hard, forty-two years, so much so that looking at him hurt. "Why do you tell us this now? I can only assume it must pertain to the seals."

"Yes," Satrina replied. "The eight seals will be broken; that can no longer be prevented. They will find a way to obtain the twenty-one Shades, if they have not already, and as much as we all hate it—hate ourselves for it—we know it is far too easy to make off with twenty-one children and twenty-one women to break the seals of birth and air. Now we must concentrate on making certain the Entrance is not opened. Luckily, there are restrictions enough that we stand some chance, but it will not be easy or without cost." Her gaze shifted to Alrin and rested there.

Alrin wished that he could have said he was surprised, but everything the Legion did was difficult and came with a high cost. He only wondered how exactly he was going to die. "What must we do?"

Satrina replied, "There are three requirements that must be met for whoever is behind this to open the Entrance: location, the Master Key, and the Ninth Seal."

"Master ..." Kristof shook his head. "None of our records say anything about a Ninth Seal, Majesty."

"It was not recorded," Satrina replied. "None of the Second Opening was recorded. Six hundred years ago the Hell Wars began when a small feud between two noble houses spun out of control. Twenty-five years after the pivotal battle that was the start of it all, a group of amateur mages, some of the earliest to bear impure blood and therefore the gift of magic, managed to open the Entrance. What is not known is that a little over two hundred years later, twenty-four rogue Summoners tried again. That was not long after I had decided to try and end the wars and build a new kingdom. A group of Summoners fighting for the same goal managed to prevent the opening of the Entrance and built in new protections. They did not survive, but they had anticipated that, and I kept my promise.

"I destroyed their bodies, destroyed all sign that anything had even occurred. I hid the location, hid the secrets of the Master Key and the Ninth Seal, and went on to end the Hell Wars. I had hoped the matter of the seals would never come up again, but someone or something has dredged up enough knowledge of them to make of it a problem—but I do not think they know of the additional precautions. That is why it is vitally important none of what we say leaves the people in this room."

Silence fell for several minutes before Raffé asked in his soft, endearingly polite way, "So what do we do now, Majesty?"

"Telmé, you and the rest of the Princes are going on the offensive. You are going to find the person or persons behind this affair and drag them out into the light. Take back the seals, we're going to need them to return the demons to hell. At all costs you will do this, am I clear? Everything we've tried so far has failed, so I am leaving it to you to figure out something new. Whatever it takes."

"Yes, Majesty," Telmé said quietly.

"Good." Satrina shifted her attention to Kristof. "I am going to tell you the location where the Breaking of the Seals must be done. You are to take the full weight of our holy forces and protect that place at all costs. Never has it been more important that we have holy might to counter hellish force."

"Yes, Majesty."

"Then you and the Princes are dismissed."

They all stood and bowed, the Princes heading for the door as Kristof rounded the table and bent for Satrina to whisper the location in his ear. Rising, Kristof departed.

Alrin had never hated the sound of a closing door so much. "You've yet to mention the Ninth Seal or the Master Key, Majesty. Which one of those am I to die for?"

"The Master Key," Satrina replied. "Despite the precautions I have taken, I still fear our mysterious foe will discover our secrets and send one of his own to claim the Master Key. You will ensure that does not happen by being the one to claim it."

He supposed it was better than being executed and dissolved by alchemical concoctions. "So where do I go and what am I to do?"

"High Priest Korin knows the location. He will escort you to it."

"And the Ninth Seal?"

Satrina shook her head. "That is not for you to know, little dragon. You leave in the morning. I suggest you make the most of your night."

Alrin nodded, wanting to scream and cry and rage and run. He wanted to find Raffé and hold him tightly, pretend that all would be well. But duty came first, came last, came always. So he only bowed his head and replied, "Yes, Majesty." He started to stand but paused when the king spoke again.

"Captain, you have always been the most fiercely loyal man in my castle. People say that Dragoons feel things like loyalty and love only as a twisted byproduct of their obsessive nature, but I have never known that to be true. Draconic obsession, in my experience, is born from strong emotion; it does not give birth to it. Sometimes that obsession comes out a warped, evil thing, and this makes dragons dangerous. But I never knew you to be anything but a gift to the Legion, Captain. This is not the way I would treat you, Captain. Whatever mistakes you've made, you've been an honor to the Legion. It is for all these reasons, and more, that I trust this mission to you. I am sorry you must leave us this way."

Those were not the words Alrin expected to hear. He blinked back tears, ducked his head. "Thank you, Majesty." There was more he should say, things he should express, but the words stuck in his throat, jumbled on his tongue. Alrin stood and backed away from the table enough to bow properly. "I will be ready at dawn, High Priest, unless there is a different time you want to leave."

"Dawn is fine," Korin said quietly. "I will walk with you, if you'll wait for me outside."

Alrin nodded, too adrift to argue or refuse, and left the king's solar. He leaned against the wall opposite the doors, scrubbing at his face with both hands, raking them through his hair, clenching and unclenching his fists, and was just about to start pacing up and down the hall when the doors opened. Korin bid a quiet farewell to Leifsson and watched him

OF LAST RESORT

vanish down the hall before turning to Alrin. "Shall we?"

Falling into step alongside him, Alrin walked in silence as Korin led the way through the halls and down stairs to the main floor of the castle, though he stopped before they reached the grand hall, already as loud and raucous as it had been silent before.

"Captain," Korin finally said. "His Majesty spoke true. Whatever your mistakes, you are one of the best things to ever happen to the Legion. The Dragoons were never as strong as they are now, and they are not the only ones who look up to you. Nature is nature, and we have always been aware that expecting a dragon not to act like a dragon was unfair. You managed to meet, and even exceed, that expectation anyway. That is why you are being given this task— you, above anyone, can be trusted to see it through to the end, no matter what. Please know it leaves us all despairing and wishing there was any other way. That we were not driven to these means of last resort."

Alrin gave a wobbly laugh, some of his despondence and self-pity bleeding away because he might have distrusted those words from many, but Korin would not speak so if the words were a lie. "Thank you, High Priest. Do you know more of … what we will be about?"

"Yes, and I will tell you all when it is safe to do so," Korin said. "Meet me in the stables at the Hour of the Rose."

Nodding, Alrin bowed respectfully then turned and walked off.

"Captain," Korin called after him, and Alrin half-turned toward him. "His Majesty said to make the most of your night, and he meant it."

Alrin stared at him, the words scraping him raw, leaving him feeling beaten and bled out. "I can't—"

"I believe it was king's orders, Captain. Goodnight." Korin turned and walked off, the smell of incense lingering on the air.

Elation coursed through Alrin before he realized there was one major flaw: just because he wanted to spend his last night at Castle Guldbrandsen, his last night before he headed off to die, with Raffé did not mean ...

He laughed as the irony of the situation struck him, feeling stupid he had not seen it sooner.

Then it turned his stomach because if he confessed, if he asked, Raffé would say yes, would repay that night all those months ago without hesitation. Alrin did not want that night to be repaid. He hadn't done it out of pity, hadn't done it as a *favor*.

He wanted Raffé to want to spend time with *him*, not a memory of an amorous stranger in the dark.

Leaving the keep, he strode along a stone path that took him around the Hall of War to the training grounds of the Shadowmarch, the maze and gardens that looked harmless enough but could become dangerous when certain spells were activated.

The Shadowmarch had been amused, if slightly offended, that a little stripling of a human had so quickly picked out three of the nine routes to the center of the maze. In the months he had been training Raffé had not yet been subjected to the full abilities of the maze, but Alrin had no doubt that he would master it beautifully.

Alrin had never particularly excelled at it. He was much more of the 'barrel through the walls' method, but he had been dragged through the damned thing often enough he knew a couple of the paths. A need for solitude, near-impossible to come by in Castle Guldbrandsen, had driven him into the maze that long-ago night, and since then he had not been able to return to it.

Right then, it felt like the only place he could go—the place he needed to go, if only to be as close to those precious memories as was possible. When he reached the spot, however, Alrin found it was too much to take. It had been far too dark for an ordinary human to see, but Alrin ... he remembered everything. Raffé's wide eyes, how very young and scared he'd looked, how he had called himself a coward even as he seemed amused rather than frightened that he was being shoved about in the dark by an unseen figure. Perhaps it had only been because Raffé did not give himself any worth, but there was courage there too, peeking through cracks and yearning for a chance.

Alrin moved on, not wanting to relive the evening more than he already had. There was only so much torture a man could inflict on himself. He walked slowly through the rest of the maze, wrinkling his nose at the lingering scents of smoke and chemicals, residue of the traps designed by Alchemists to keep the training Shadowmarch from getting complacent.

The center of the maze was a training ground of an entirely different nature. To most it was just an empty pavilion of black marble, the center covered by a canopy of wrought iron overtaken by bitter ivy. But to the Shadowmarch, Dredknights, and Shades, the compass rose in the very center was a door only they could easily slip through, though protections ensured the High Priest and the Master of Magic could bypass it if necessary. Down in the safety of the rooms beneath the castle, they could practice their hellish magic without risk of interfering with or being affected by the holy magic that was most prevalent because of the Temple.

Moving under the iron canopy, Alrin stretched out on one of the long benches framing it and tried to decide what to do with his evening. What he wanted was to approach Raffé, but he had no reason to think Raffé would want anything to do with Alrin, and he refused to cheat his way in by admitting he was Cambord.

He should go say goodbye to his men, but it would not take them more than a moment to realize that something was wrong, and they'd already endured enough grief. Alrin was not certain he would be able to let go if he went to see them right then. Åge would look after them.

"You know—"

Alrin jerked at the sound of Raffé's voice, nearly falling off the bench before he regained his balance and sat up instead, twisting around to straddle it and watching as Raffé walked toward him with slow, not-quite-predatory steps, like some dark, shadowy version of his former self, a demon twin of the Raffé he had first met. Strange, but oh what a sweet rush, to see the darkness that had once been Raffé's enemy become more like a lover.

Raffé's mouth ticked up at one corner as he continued prowling toward Alrin. "All this time I thought Cambord must have been Shadowmarch. It makes the most sense—this is their maze, and the Cambord line does run through a handful of the Shadowmarch. They would be able to see in the dark with perfect clarity. They have the improved senses to hear a conversation that should not have been so easily overheard. It made sense ... but it never stuck."

Alrin swallowed, throat suddenly dry, and stared at the stone bench when Raffé's gaze proved too intense to match.

"Mostly I tried not to think about it because it was just one night, someone bidding me farewell. There was never any reason to think Cambord would want to be known, want to see me again."

That elicited a faint laugh because only Raffé would think himself so disinteresting when Alrin had overheard more than a few lewd comments that required cuffing insolent soldiers upside the head.

"Then one of my closest friends—the kind of person I never thought I would be allowed to call friend—nearly dies going berserk, and my commander tells me that I am the reason he snapped. That he has become unstable, a danger, because he became obsessed with me."

Alrin scowled. "It's not your fault. The blame lies with no one but me. I'm the idiot who knew better, knew to be on guard, knew what would happen if I dared to become obsessed with someone I cannot have. You had nothing to do with it."

"Oh, he made that clear enough," Raffé said, sitting down on the bench and half-turning to face him. "I just wish I better understood what was going on and why I am suddenly forbidden to go anywhere near one of my best friends. I don't understand what everyone means by 'obsession', and Telmé did not explain it well, only that it was part of a dragon's nature. I don't understand why you— why it's a bad thing you—" Alrin almost smiled to see Raffé's awkwardness return, but the expression wouldn't hold, too weighed down by a heavy heart. "Why it's so wrong that you want me. You haven't *done* anything, and I— it's not as if I'd refuse any offer you made me."

Jerking his gaze up, Alrin stared, elated and depressed all at once. "I— it's more complicated than that, but it's hard for a non-dragon to understand, let alone explain."

"My impression is that this is … something unique to you," Raffé said and made Alrin jump when he shifted to swing around and straddle the bench as well, hands covering Alrin's. "What makes you different from your men?"

"I'm more dragon than human," Alrin replied. "Most of my men fall in the forty-fifty percent range, and only three of them push anywhere close to sixty percent, which is the limit. Any further than that and too many draconic tendencies come out in a force that's hard to contain. Generally, we come off as nothing more than jealous and possessive—a little worse than ordinary people but not much. Dragons are possessive, Princes are arrogant, and Shadowmarch are smug. We all of us have our quirks and extremes, aspects of personality that are both element and result of what we are.

"Dragons … well, dragons are wild animals, to be perfectly blunt. We aren't demons or granted holy power or born with magic or anything. We are part-monster, humans who can turn bits of ourselves into dragon. In my case it is more accurate to say that I am a dragon who can turn into a human—I just barely have enough human in me to retain this shape as my dominant form. My mother was a dragon. My father was half dragon."

"Goddesses," Raffé said.

"Dragons are territorial by nature, aggressively so; that is where their reputation for possessive, obsessive, behavior originates. It's called hoarding. We always knew the tendency was in me, but I've kept it in check, taken precautions when I could feel it crawling out."

And then Raffé happened.

"You don't seem ... different, though," Raffé said, confusion and hurt in his voice. "That's what I'm not getting."

Alrin laughed—just laughed and laughed until it hurt and his eyes were wet and stinging. "Because I'm trying to resist it, trying to keep it smothered, but the longer you're around me, the harder that is going to be."

"I—"

Pulling his hands free, Alrin pinned Raffé's down, leaned into his space and let out the growl in his voice that he normally kept down because it made him sound even less human than he already was. "Whatever I feel for you as a human—and believe me I do feel strongly—I am almost completely dragon. I want to *keep* you. I want to lock you up and hide you away and not let anyone else near you. I don't want others touching you, I don't want them able to smell you. I want you hidden and safe. I want to *hoard* you and never share you with anyone again. I would shape my entire life around your every want and desire, around pleasing you and satisfying you, keeping you where I am not just the center of your world but all of it. That's not *right*. Not here, not in humans. Do you understand now?"

Raffé stared at him, eyes wide, then dropped his gaze to where Alrin still had his hands pinned. Alrin almost moved them, abruptly aware he might be hurting—but no, as strong as he was, Raffé was far stronger still, and if he had wanted his hands free he could have managed it easily. "I think," Raffé finally said, voice soft, slightly sad, "that whatever I feel about being hoarded doesn't matter because it was clear to all of us that you are not meant to survive. It is, of course, dubious that any of us will, but you were specifically chosen to die."

Alrin's hopes withered. "Is that why you're here? Returning—" he looked away, words ending in a rough-edged noise, gazing hard at the far wall.

"I came because I'm selfish," Raffé said. "I always yearned to know Cambord's identify, and I was devastated to know that one way or another, I was losing a friend. I've never had those before, you know. I never thought I would. I thought I was going to *die* and that nobody would miss me or mourn my passing. That I would have been nothing in life and less than nothing in death." His mouth twisted. "Cambord was the first person to do something for me, for no reason at all, with no expectation of something in return. And the Captain of the Dragoons spends hours of time he probably cannot spare just to give me extra training and sparring practice. You let me sit with you while you eat and ask you a thousand questions. You don't mind that I'm always flustered and awkward and don't know what I'm doing. You're my friend. I didn't want you to die before I got a chance to say goodbye, orders to avoid you or not."

Silence fell between them, pressing so heavily on Alrin's chest it felt like something was about to break. He stared at their hands, his still pinning Raffé's the bench. He froze when Raffé pulled them free, shuddered when they cupped his face, and it was as easy as falling over to lean in as Raffé tugged slightly and meet his kiss. Raffé's lips were slightly chapped but warm and so achingly familiar, though the bold confidence behind them was delightfully new.

He whimpered softly and gave up, gave in, surging forward to break free of Raffé's careful hold and shove him down on the bench, doing his best to climb on top of him, pin him down, and devour him. Raffé was almost cool to the touch, so different from the warm human he had once been, so opposite the heat that Alrin put off.

Claws scraped along the back of his neck and Alrin moaned, drawing back to stare into the gold eyes watching him so intently. "As fond as I am of this maze, what say we take this to my quarters?" Raffé asked.

Alrin nodded and drew back, climbed off the bench, and followed Raffé back to the keep.

Farewell

Getting out of all the cumbersome layers of his clothes had never been so damned difficult. Alrin threw it all in an untidy heap then went over to the bathtub in front of the fire, grateful for the chance to get clean. There was probably a similar bathtub in his quarters in the barracks; he hoped someone else made use of it when it became clear he would not be returning.

It felt marvelous to be clean again, to strip away dirt and blood and sweat, the reek of battle and hard travel—the sour memories of all they'd lost and everything he'd done wrong.

Climbing from the bath water, he glanced to where Raffé was sprawled on the bed, watching him with eyes that glowed from within and flickered with the reflected firelight. "You already bathed."

"Earlier, while you were still with the king," Raffé replied. "I ordered another in case I managed to convince you to join me."

Alrin finished drying off and threw the cloth to the floor before prowling to the bed and climbing in, sliding up to brace on hands and knees over Raffé. "You've come far from the little prince in the maze." Too much of him snarled and snapped in jealous fury at the knowledge, ached and cried that his treasure had been with others, learned from others, found pleasure with others when it should have been his duty to give such things. But the human part of him was simply happy that Raffé had thrived in his new life, was getting to live.

And nobody else would ever have the maze.

Raffé reached up and traced the lines of his face with light, barely-there touches. Alrin felt fragile. He dropped his head as the fingers reached his throat and curled around to cup the back of his neck, going eagerly when Raffé drew him into a kiss that was soft, easy, lingering. Raffé's free hand trailed along Alrin's arm, moved to his side, thumb running over the edge of an old scar that cut just beneath his ribcage and wrapped around his side.

Drawing back, Raffé licked Alrin's lips playfully, mouth ticking up as he said, "It's probably sad that I did not notice until this moment that your skin is so different. Thicker, firmer."

"For the scales," Alrin replied, matching Raffé's grin. He levered up and back so he was straddling Raffé's hips, swallowing against the distracting press of Raffé's rapidly firming cock. He spread his arms as he called up scales to cover them and his torso. They were a rich, dark forest green, gleaming as firelight bathed them.

Raffé braced himself on one arm while he reached out with the other to splay it across the scales. "What can you feel through them?"

"Pressure, if it's firm enough," Alrin said. He had done it on impulse, proud as any Dragoon about what he was and could do—but it was not normally something other people were amused to see in bed. Raffé was far too comfortable to be around for his peace of mind. "Extreme cold. Not much else unless it manages to cut through the scales, which rarely happens—" He squawked in protest when Raffé gave an abrupt shove and sent him toppling back, sucking in a startled breath as he found himself covered in eager prince, hands splaying across his chest and a mouth licking and sucking at his lips, urging him to surrender.

Alrin did so happily, letting his scales vanish as he wrapped his arms around Raffé, holding him close and rolling his hips, grinding their bodies together in the best way. He spread his legs and let Raffé settle between them, raking hands down his body to grab hold of his firm, highly-distracting ass. Raffé pulled back, and Alrin chased after him, desperate to get at that mouth again, to taste every crevice of it, not letting Raffé go until he trembled and moaned.

Holding him tightly, Alrin rolled them over, putting himself back on top and lightly pinning Raffé's arms to the bed on either side of his head. "I want to taste every piece of you," he rumbled, dragging his tongue along one wrist, liking the way it tensed. He scored his teeth along the so-soft skin. "You had more color before you were Blooded. You've become a little night crawler. Sunlight too strong for you, Prince?"

"Y-yes," Raffé said as Alrin's teeth marked the soft underside of his arm before he lapped his way steadily to Raffé's shoulder, dipping down to bite and suck at his collarbone.

"I want to taste you, mark you," Alrin said. "Want everyone to know you were devoured by a dragon." He nosed his way up Raffé's throat, bit at the soft lobe of his ear, and then nuzzled over to eat at Raffé's mouth again, licking and sucking and biting until his own mouth ached.

Then he started working his way back down, biting into the meat of Raffé's right shoulder, tongue dragging down across the smooth, beautifully muscled chest. There was not a single mark upon it despite all the time Alrin and the others had cut him open, left holes with claw and sword and glaive.

Alrin let go of Raffé's hands to span his chest, dragging scaled thumbs over Raffé's nipples while he sucked at the spot dead center between them. Raffé gasped, jerked, and writhed in his hold, sinking his hands into Alrin's hair, holding his head down. Alrin smiled against his skin, left off his nipples with one last teasing scrape, then scored his claws down Raffé's sides until he reached those heavy, trembling thighs. Teasing his way around Raffé's cock, hard and wet at the tip, Alrin lapped away sweat and drips of pre-come, then rubbed a stubble-rough cheek against the smooth skin of one inner thigh, tongue flicking out to taste Raffé's heavy sack. He spread Raffé's legs wider, shifted him up so that he could get deeper, farther, tongue flicking out to taste and torment. Raffé jerked and writhed, words coming out a garbled mess, and at one point, Alrin thought he was going to tear away completely, so overcome by what Alrin's tongue was doing he nearly forgot to check his strength.

Laughing, Alrin pulled away entirely and sat back to admire his work so far: the pale skin flushed shell-pink, hair disheveled, the pupils of his yellow eyes huge, body glistening with sweat, and his fangs descended. Alrin felt a brief pang that he could not provide blood the way Raffé wanted, be a source of sustenance as well as sex. That he could not let him bite anyway because he could not afford to be left weak.

"Are you going to fuck me or not?" Raffé demanded, reaching down to grip his own cock, strokes confident and easy, the best contrast yet to the uncertain figure who had not even been able to baldly ask for a farewell fuck from his fiancé. "No one has since you. The Priests aren't really—" He broke off swearing when Alrin knocked his hand away and replaced it with his mouth.

Alrin took him as deep as he knew how, sucking hard, tongue and throat working, growling deep in his chest, knowing what the vibrations did. He flushed with satisfaction at the breathy, jerky noises that got him, nothing else able to escape an overcome Raffé's throat. Alrin worked his cock until his jaw ached and Raffé was a broken mess of cussing and twisting and hair-pulling, Alrin's name spilling out on a jagged cry as he finally came.

Swallowing as much of Raffé's release as he could, Alrin pulled off and licked the rest away before kissing his way back up Raffé's body to take his mouth. Raffé draped heavy arms around him, held him fast, and ate at Alrin's mouth with sloppy, hungry need. Alrin trembled against him, so desperate to find his own pleasure his body ached with it. Raffé unwound one arm and dragged it clumsily down his body. Alrin trapped it with one of his own, drew back, panting heavily, and said, "If you want me to fuck you, then let me fuck you. I'm not going to last much longer."

Raffé laughed and gave him a playful shove, sending Alrin falling onto his back. He leaned up on his elbows and watched as Raffé rolled sinuously forward to the head of the bed, groaning at the sight of that perfect ass exactly where he wanted it. Reaching beneath a pillow, Raffé twisted and tossed a small porcelain jar at him before lying on his back, limbs sprawling. "I would have loved to see your face when you asked for this," Alrin said, grinning at the way Raffé flushed.

"One of the Priests gave it to me. I didn't have to ask. Now get to it."

"Yes, Highness," Alrin murmured, removing the lid and scooping a generous amount of the slippery cream inside. He slicked his cock before pressing teasing fingers against Raffé's hole, pressing one inside only after Raffé started in with the colorful threats. Alrin pressed in close, rubbing against Raffé, reaching around to grab hold of his cock, amused that he was slowly hardening again. He pushed in a second finger, scissoring them, twisted and reaching until he found that spot and Raffé bucked against him.

"Damn it, dragon. Stop torturing us both and—" he broke off on a groan.

Deciding he had really had enough of torturing himself, if not Raffé—never Raffé, he could spend eternity keeping Raffé wild and hungry and desperate—Alrin withdrew his fingers, lined up his cock, and slowly pushed inside, withdrawing slightly and pushing in deeper, steadily working into Raffé's tight body until he was fully seated and plastered to Raffé's back, holding him tight and drawing steadying breaths. He nipped lazily at the back of Raffé's neck, drunk on the way he smelled—the way *they* smelled.

Stealing one last lick and bite, Alrin drew back and grasped Raffé's hips, pulled nearly all the way out, and drove back in, managing to keep his movement smooth and steady at first but quickly going mad from the trembling, desperate pleas, the tight heat of Raffé's body, and the consuming need to come. He muffled his shout in the hollow of Raffé's neck, sinking in deep and holding fast as he spilled.

Finally collapsing from sated exhaustion as he finished, groaning as Raffé made him roll to his side, Alrin wrapped his arms around Raffé. He was desperate to keep Raffé close, to stay inside him as long as possible. He started to say something, but the words came out a yawn, eyes slipping shut as he nuzzled into Raffé's damp hair.

Alrin woke to the feel of hands trailing lazily along his body and opened his eyes to see Raffé studying him, sleepy and intense all at once. Alrin, still more asleep than awake, leaned in to kiss his brow. Raffé's eyes snapped up to him, glowing faintly in the dark. "You're absurdly hot," Raffé said. "The fire went out at some point, but I can't tell lying next to you."

"Heart of fire," Alrin mumbled.

Raffé snorted but did not argue. "Hungry?"

"Starving," Alrin said. "I could eat every scrap of food in the kitchen."

"I've heard that you often attempt to do precisely that—you and every other Dragoon."

"Not our fault that what we do burns energy at ridiculous speeds. I bet if you were made to turn into mist for twelve hours straight you could go through a few Priests without trying."

Raffé laughed as he rolled out of the bed and went over to a table in the corner where platters of food had been arranged. "Come eat."

Dragging himself out of bed, Alrin joined him at the table, sitting down and making quick, greedy work of the roasted meat and vegetables, fresh bread, and soft, crumbly cheese that had been piled in large enough quantities for a Dragoon. There was even a sweet pie, sticky with fruit and honey, for him to finish off with, and two pitchers of hot cider.

OF LAST RESORT

Alrin set his empty cup aside and used a damp, warm cloth to clean his face and hands—then found himself with a lapful of eager, squirming Prince, claws scraping along the back of his neck as Raffé feasted on his mouth as though he were the meal awaiting a diner. Alrin spread his legs slightly to better accommodate him, grabbing his ass and returning the ravenous kiss until his lips were bruised, chin wet, and they were both panting for breath.

"I want to fuck you," Raffé murmured against his mouth, rubbing against him, cock hard and wet between them. Alrin leaned in to suck and bite at his throat, feeling as much as hearing the way that made Raffé moan. He had yet to meet a Prince who did not have or develop an obsession with necks. It was vastly more hilarious to most of the castle than the Princes realized—and no one was in a hurry to tell them.

Raffé shoved at him, slid off his lap and pulled him to his feet—then nearly climbed Alrin to wrap around him and resume the bruising kisses. Alrin tried to walk them toward the bed but was far too determined not to stop kissing to manage it without nearly killing them in the process.

He struck the bed with a grunt, landing on his side, twisted to push himself up, and instead found himself held quite firmly down, legs kicked wide so Raffé could stand between them and bend to press sucking kisses down the knobs of Alrin's spine.

Alrin tried to rub against the bed, the unexpected manhandling having done absolutely nothing to calm him down. He whined low in his throat when the press of Raffé's cool body vanished. He returned a few moments later, however, mouth warm at the base of

Alrin's spin, fingers slick where they began to press into him.

"Don't need them," Alrin gasped out. "I can take it as I am."

Raffé did not reply, but his fingers slid away and then his cock was pushing in. Alrin fisted his hands in the bedclothes and lifted one leg higher to open himself up more, moaning into the heavy blankets as Raffé pushed all the way inside, fingers digging into his skin. Alrin hoped they left bruises he would be able to feel until he died.

He groaned and grunted as Raffé began to fuck him in earnest, pounding into him so hard the wooden bed trembled and creaked. Alrin had never been fucked so hard in his life, could only cling desperately as Raffé took him as ruthlessly as a Prince of the Blood could take a battlefield.

His throat was too raw for him to scream when he finally came, all the strength stolen from his limbs, leaving him limp and used when Raffé finally pulled out. He climbed slowly up onto the bed and flopped down, grunting when Raffé sprawled on top of him, slick with sweat but still almost cold against Alrin's heat. "Fire probably feels cool to you, doesn't it?" Raffé mumbled into his neck. "How can one person be so hot?"

Alrin laughed, cheeks flushing pink. "Um. Fire feels nice. The servants love us because they just have to bring cold water to the barracks and we can heat it ourselves just fine. The rest of the barracks love us because it's the only way they get hot water, and we can get it way hotter than the servants could anyway."

"I'm supposed to be the all-powerful demon, but fire still hurts me," Raffé replied.

"Yes, but you would also heal. Someone shreds my arm to pieces I'll probably die, or at the very least lose my arm."

Raffé did not voice a reply, but he seemed to nod against Alrin's chest. A short time later, he settled more heavily, breaths evening out in sleep. Alrin smiled faintly, wondering if Raffé had slept at all earlier. He suspected not.

The good and bad thing about Princes was that when the slept, they slept. If he did not know better Alrin would swear they were corpses. Certainly their already peculiarly low body temperatures dropped even further. Raffé did not even twitch as Alrin slipped away. Padding across the room, he knelt before the fire and quickly got it burning again, then transformed his arm and waited a short time for it to heat up. When the scales were glowing like green embers, he moved to the bucket of water left over from his bath and plunged it in. The water hissed, steam curling up as it began to boil. Alrin withdrew his arm and fetched a clean cloth and bit of soap and scrubbed himself clean.

Going to the door, he pulled it open and was not surprised to see two guards stationed outside. "Would one of you be kind enough to bid a servant fetch my belongings from the barracks? Any of the Dragoons will know what I require."

"Yes, Captain."

"Thank you." Closing the door again, he wandered over to the corner of the room that held a writing desk. There was a long shelf attached to the wall over it that was half-filled with books. Most seemed to be on history and war, a bestiary, a book on the basics of demonology ... and one palm-sized, slender volume of poetry. Alrin pulled it down and flipped it open. The back cover did not bear the king's mark, so it was a personal acquisition or a gift, not something Raffé had borrowed from the library.

Alrin put it back, loathe to so much as wrinkle a page. Books were expensive, and if Raffé had somehow found time to pause long enough in a town to obtain a book of poetry it must mean a great deal to him. Instead he pulled down the largest book, a volume on warfare that he had seen many times about the castle and read more than once himself. He thumbed through it again, smiling faintly at the different sections Raffé had marked with scraps of paper.

It was fortunate he was studying so earnestly because he was probably going to need all the knowledge he could muster in the very near future. But thinking of futures just woke fear and despair, so Alrin ruthlessly shoved all such thoughts aside and turned instead to admire the view: Raffé sprawled on the bed, breathing so lightly Alrin could only see his chest move if he looked for it, dark hair spilling in every direction, pale skin soaking up the fire light.

He could just barely hear the bells as they began to toll, marking the Hour of the Angels. One more bell until dawn. One more bell until he never saw home or family again. Alrin closed his eyes and took several deep, slow breaths—

And jumped as a soft rapping came at the door. Rolling his eyes, he went to open it, not entirely surprised to see Åge standing on the other side of it holding his clothes and equipment. "Thank you."

"You'll come and see us, won't you? Before you leave?" Åge asked. Alrin wondered how they knew— or maybe they just sensed that something was wrong when even the High Priest was being called out along with every last single Prince of the Blood, and all those who practiced hellish magic were being ordered to stay within the castle walls.

"Of course," Alrin replied. "Let me get dressed and I'll head that way. I'll go ahead and say now, however, that you're Captain until I return."

"Yes, sir," Åge replied, mouth tight, eyes downcast.

Alrin stepped forward and embraced him tightly. They'd been through much together, him and Åge. Letting go, he nodded and slipped into the room, carrying his clothes to the fireplace and slowly pulling them on. Unlike most of the soldiers in the Legion, Dragoons did not bother with heavy plate armor, their scales being far more effective.

He pulled his clothes on quickly, feeling almost ready to face his last hours. Casting a glance at the bed, Alrin deliberated between waking Raffé then or going to see his men and returning, and finally decided to leave because he wasn't quite ready to say goodbye.

Leaving Raffé's room, he headed quickly through the keep and across the inner bailey to the barracks behind the Hall of War and the wing that belonged to the Dragoons. His men were already assembled in the hall there and hailed him when he walked in. Alrin raised a hand in greeting and fell into the crowd, accepting embraces, pats on the back, clasps of shoulders and arms, assuring all he would be fine and return to them, that he was not going to let his mission get the better of him.

No one admitted he was lying, for which he was grateful. He stayed there talking and advising until he heard the bells toll the Hour of the Rose. "I must go," he said and hugged Åge one last time. Climbing the stairs back up the hallway, he turned to face the hall, raised his hands in the air, and bellowed with his men as they gave their war cry. He then turned sharply on his heel and strode off before he lost all decorum, hastening back to the keep to make his last farewell.

Raffé came tumbling down the next to last set of stairs that led to the floor where the Princes lived, eyes wide, motions frantic—all of it turning to anger when he saw Alrin. "You snuck out! You son of—" he snarled and jerked away as Alrin reached for him. "To the depths of—don't touch—" He bared his fangs in a hiss when Alrin grabbed his wrists, eyes burning a yellow as brilliant as summer sunshine.

"I went to bid my men farewell," Alrin said. "I was returning to you this very moment. I promise. You're my final goodbye." He couldn't bear to see anyone else. He would lose his mind completely. Why, he couldn't say. He faced death every time he left on a mission. A mission explicitly meant to kill him should not have been so different. At least the death was a certainty, not a surprise.

It still seemed far more awful anyway.

"You were gone," Raffé said quietly. "All I could hear were the bells. That you were leaving soon and you hadn't even said goodbye."

Alrin tugged him in close, held fast to his wrists, and bent to kiss him with everything he would never be able to say, every thought and emotion they would never get to share. Raffé jerked his arms free and wrapped them tightly around his neck, holding so tightly Alrin worried briefly for his ability to breathe before he simply stopped caring. He memorized the salty-sweet taste of Raffé's mouth, the slightly rough feel of his lips, the press of his body, the pleasantly warm feel of his skin, and softness of his hair.

When they finally broke apart, it was the most difficult thing Alrin had ever done. "Be safe and strong, Highness."

Raffé nodded but did not otherwise reply. Alrin leaned in one last time and kissed his brow, then turned and walked away. Leaving the castle again, he headed for the stables, unsurprised to see Korin was already there, waiting with two griffons. "Not horses?"

Korin shook his head. "Not where we're going."

Mountains, then, mostly likely, or an island somewhere. Griffons were stubborn beasts but also hearty, so they were good for arduous journeys. Alrin extended a hand to the one closest, letting it nuzzle its sharp beak, clicking and growling as it examined him. When it gave a low squawk of approval, Alrin rubbed his hand over the soft, warm feathers of its head and down its neck to where tawny feathers met golden pelt. A saddle had already been placed on its back, just in front of the wings, with bags of supplies strapped to its stomach.

The sound of footsteps drew Alrin's attention, and he turned to see Telmé walk toward them. "Highness."

Telmé clasped his shoulder then pulled him in tightly. "You've always been there for us, Captain. Even when Korin and I were out-of-control brats in need of thrashing."

Alrin nodded and returned the tight embrace, then stepped back. "Find and stop whoever is behind this, Highness."

"We will."

Mounting up, Alrin waited while Korin and Telmé said their farewells. When Korin mounted up beside him, he called out for clearance, mostly from habit because the stable yard was empty save for them, and then gave the signal to the griffon. With a screech, the griffon obeyed, and within minutes they had vanished into the sky.

Sacrifice

The griffons dropped them off at the base of the Harth Mountains, a mountain range that spread between the northern province of Stehl and the eastern province of Mykne. In olden days the mountains had been host to various temples, towers, shrines, and altars that had eventually given rise to the Temple of the Sacred Heart. But the history of the Reach of the North was an especially bloody one, rife with the sorts of sacrifices that had compelled the crown to outlaw the practice once and for all. The Harth Mountains still held shadows of those dark days, and people avoided them as much as possible. Those who desired to travel to a different reach usually went by sea. Every few years the High Priest sent Priests and Paladins into the mountains to ensure all remained well.

Though they could have gone almost anywhere on the continent, Alrin was not surprised they had wound up at the Harth Mountains.

He waited, silently staring up the path they would be walking, while Korin sent the griffons off back home. "So where are we headed? What exactly is waiting for me?"

"Us," Korin said quietly, pulling up the hood of his dark blue cloak, the white fur that trimmed and lined it blending with the snow falling lazily around them. "There is an old temple near the central peak. It's nothing more than a pile of ruins now, but once it was an early incarnation of what eventually became the

Temple of the Sacred Heart. I've been there thrice in my life in the course of my training, and though it's been out of use for centuries, it still holds a great deal of power. That is where the Master Key is sealed, and it is up to us to break the seal."

Alrin had more questions, but the daylight was not to be wasted. He settled his pack more firmly on his shoulders and began to walk, leading the way up the snowy, icy-slicked trails. It was tempting to shift into his dragon form and simply fly them up, but if something went wrong and he had to shift back, or was forced to shift back, he would not have adequate time or supplies to recover. Better to save transforming in case they had to get off the mountain should something go wrong and the sacrifice had to be aborted.

They made good time at the bottom of the mountain, where the path was slippery but otherwise an easy hike. By the time they began to climb upwards in earnest, Alrin had to remove his boots and shift his arms and legs to get decent traction, hauling himself up the path more than climbing. Behind him, Korin followed carefully, using the path Alrin cleared combined with special boots and gloves.

When Alrin cleared a scrub of trees and stumbled across an open stretch of rocky white field, he raised a hand, fingers fanned out. Korin replied with the same gesture, and Alrin trudged a few steps more until he found a small patch of ground, partially free of snow due to the rocks that leaned out over it, and called up sparking green fire to clear a bit more of it.

He kept the flame glowing, extending his palm as Korin came up to him. Spreading his fingers, Korin cupped them over and around the green flames and began to softly chant a spell, hands glowing with bright white light that spread out to form an orb around the green flames. Alrin jerked his hands away, and with a last, sharp word to close the spell, Korin captured the flames within—and the light solidified into witch glass, creating a witchlight.

Shrugging off his pack, Alrin sat down on the cleared ground and pulled out small packs of food and a skin of water. A few minutes of fumbling and he managed to find a cup and packet of tea as well. He hated when he didn't get a chance to pack his own bag. "T—" He broke off and cleared his throat, but Korin nodded and handed over his own cup. Alrin simply called up a small flame in one hand and heated the two cups of water in his palm, adding the tea leaves once it had started to steam.

Handing Korin's cup back, he traded sips of his own with bites of jerky and bread. "How far of a trek do we have?"

"Four days, more if the weather works against us, which it is very likely to do once we pass the royal markers. The temple is difficult to reach even when you know exactly where to go and how to get there. Without that knowledge, it's impossible save by way of fortune—or misfortune, depending on your perspective."

"What—what am I meant to do when we arrive?"

Korin sighed, scowling into his tea. "I know only this: Access to the Master Key spell is two-fold. I must break the first barrier, being a pure human with penultimate holy powers. The second rests entirely upon you, and about that I know nothing. I wish I could tell you more, but details were purposely lost. That is part of the security measures that were taken to prevent this entire debacle. They're utterly brilliant until the whole damned thing fails anyway." He finished his tea. "Would you mind?"

"Of course not." Alrin took his cup, refilled it, and fixed him a fresh cup of tea.

Korin took the cup as Alrin held it out. "Thank you. Whenever I must leave the castle, I always hope I will at least go in the company of Dragoons." He took a sip of tea. "I wish there was another way to end this."

Alrin nodded, fingers tightening around his own cup, memories and the rush of emotion they provoked scraping his throat and stinging his eyes.

"I truly am sorry. You do not deserve to die this way."

"People rarely get the death they deserve," Alrin said. "I was going to be executed anyway—better to die doing my duty than as a criminal."

"Executed ... I do not think his Majesty was going to be that harsh. Banished, perhaps, but not executed."

"Then he would have been a fool." Alrin drained his tea. He brewed a second cup, scowling at it throughout. "I was always a liability. We all knew that."

Korin's mouth tightened. "No one should be punished for what they *are*. You have as much right to be you as any of us. And you can't say you're too dangerous because there are fifteen men a thousand times more dangerous than you out there right now. You might be obsessive, but they are *demons*. You will kill to protect. If they lose control, they will kill for the pleasure of killing. You don't see the king executing them."

"Håkon would say otherwise," Alrin said quietly. "They're always killed if they come out of the Blooding too much a demon."

Flinching, Korin conceded with a nod. "That doesn't mean you should be killed for one mistake."

Alrin did not bother pursuing the argument. They were climbing to his death; the matter was decided. He fixed and drank a third cup of tea, then cleaned the cup with snow and tucked it away again, shoving a last bite of jerky in his mouth before packing everything else away. He climbed to his feet, held out a hand to help Korin up. "Do you want more witchlights to travel with us? I feel it will grow dark long before night even begins to fall, and we want to go as far as we can."

"I'm leery of drawing attention. I'm not entirely certain what lurks in these mountains. We've never been attacked, but that just makes me more nervous." Korin settled his own pack, pulling up his hood and fastening it securely in place before pulling up the strip of heavy cloth to cover his mouth and nose. "We'll keep the one for now and see what it provokes. If the answer is 'nothing' then we'll add more."

"Yes, High Priest," Alrin replied and gave a deep bow before turning neatly around and plunging back into the snow.

As they had expected, with the combination of the dense forest, the increasingly tumultuous weather, and rapid fall of evening, it grew dark quickly. A prickle along the back of his neck was the first sign Alrin had that something was amiss. He stopped, raising his right fist. Behind him Korin silently halted. A moment later, the witch light lowered and dimmed, leaving them in a dull circle of light mostly obscured by falling snow and thick trees.

The prickle ran across his neck again, then down his spine. A moment later, Alrin heard a soft, heavy snort, followed by the crackle-snap of icy branches beneath ponderous footsteps. Lifting his right hand again, Alrin spread his fingers then pulled in the thumb and middle two fingers, flicking the remaining two fingers.

A soft touch to his back acknowledged the order, and a few seconds later he felt the warm tingle of magic spread over them as Korin wrapped them inside a protective barrier. "Secure," Korin said quietly. "Do you know what is coming? I cannot get a clear read on it, but I do not like what I am feeling. It's powerful."

Alrin shook his head as he knelt to pull off his boots. Thrusting them at Korin, he stood up again, shifting his legs from the knee down to gleaming scale and long, sharp talons. "No, but I agree it's powerful—alarmingly so. I wish I could smell it, but the snow and wind are making that impossible right now." He had not brought his glaive because it would have just been in his way with the hard traveling they were doing, and he hardly needed it to fight.

"It may wander off. With only two of us to protect, I was able to get more elaborate with the barrier; it should block scent and sound. Unfortunately, I've not had enough practice with blocking sight to trust it now, though I can take the risk if you feel it necessary, Captain."

"I'm not Captain anymore. I don't think it's necessary. Sight is usually the least important sense to most beasts."

Korin smiled. "You'll always be Captain. You—" He broke off, eyes widening, and until that moment Alrin would not have thought it possible for Korin's dusky skin to lose color. He whipped around, shifting his arms to heavy scales and long talons—and froze.

He had thought until that moment he knew every beast, monster, creature, and terror that roamed the earth, but he had no name for the *thing* that strode toward them. It ... it seemed vaguely human in shape but only barely. It had six arm-like appendages extruding from a wide, squat chest and two leg-like things that did not touch the ground because there were twelve fleshy wings extending from its back. The legs and arms all ended in narrow points, like the tentacles of a squid. It was a sickly gray in color, and nearly all of it was covered in eyes, each one a vibrant flame blue. The largest of them took up most of what vaguely resembled a head, set in the center and surrounded by thirteen smaller eyes in a perfect circle. "What in the name of the Three is that?"

"An angel," Korin replied, the words only barely audible. "At least, it's *part* of an angel. Like the minions that demons leave behind. An angel's shadow, either left here or ..."

"Sent after us." Alrin braced himself, facing it head on even as he began to tremble and encroaching fear made him cold. "I heard it stomping. I heard it breathing. It's *not even touching the ground.*"

"You hear the force of its presence, not the reality."

"I ..." Alrin swallowed as it drew closer, not even twenty paces away and closing fast, and the barrier Korin had cast began to crackle and spark. "I cannot beat an angel."

"I can. It must be here for us—to stop us or use us. But what do *angels* have to do with any of this? Angels just don't—get down!" Korin shoved, and Alrin was surprised enough he dropped as told, feeling the numbing-tingling rush of holy magic as Korin countered whatever the angel had just done.

He caught nothing but brilliant blue light.

Hands grabbed him by the back, tugging hard, and Alrin climbed to his feet. He saw a smattering of what looked like starlight scattered across the field. "It won't stay that way long," Korin replied. "I can contend with the sliver of angel, but I need you out of my way. You have to get to the summit. Head for the central peak, look for a path of black stones. There won't be many at first, but the closer you get, the more solid the path. Follow it until you see the temple ruins. I will follow after you once I've taken care of the angel's shadow."

"High Priest, I can't leave—"

"You're a liability to me! Go. In the name of the Three, Captain, *go*." Korin's hands slammed against the sides of his face, and Alrin jerked at the feel of too much magic flooding his system.

He was still tingling from it, hot and cold and numb all at once, when Korin shoved him from the barrier. Fighting an urge to look back, to *go* back, Alrin started running. The sparkling shards of starlight began to slowly gather together, so brilliant that the clearing seemed flooded with daylight. He heard a whining, keening sound, felt the prickle of the angel's growing strength—and then he was out of the field, back into the woods, chased by white-hot light and Korin's screams.

Alrin's eyes stung. He stopped, half-turned, but at the last, swung back and continued up the mountain. He had his duty, and Korin was ensuring he'd get the chance to do it. He would not throw that chance away.

OF LAST RESORT

Ducking his head against the wind, shifting scales over all of his body, he pressed on.

The going grew rapidly steeper, made even more difficult when night fell, and the cloud cover remained so heavy that even when the sun rose again Alrin could only just barely tell. He abandoned his pack on the second night. Shifting as far as he could while still retaining a human shape, he breathed out fire where the ice was too thick for him to hold, digging his talons into the rock as he slowly climbed. The cliff was almost sheer, handholds few and far between. When he found a reasonably stable ledge, he rested until night once more gave over to day, too exhausted to continue.

His body screamed with agony when he finally resumed his climb. Alrin's heart seemed permanently lodged in his throat, beating an alarming rhythm every time he slipped or fumbled. He cried out when a rock broke to pieces beneath his hand, talons scraping ice as he fumbled futilely—

And at the last, caught hold just long enough to dig in the talons on his feet and get a fresh grip with his second hand. Shuddering, shivering, he clung to the rocks until he'd calmed enough to try climbing again.

The temptation to shift to dragon grew stronger with every breath, but he wanted to save that for getting off the mountain, and if he needed to be human for whatever was necessary to get the key, he would not be able to manage the transformation twice.

When he finally reached the top of the cliff, Alrin clung to the ground for a moment, drawing the deepest breaths he could manage. The cold fought to get hold of him but stood no chance, melting as it struck his scales, turning into steam and mingling with his billowing breath. Heaving to his feet, Alrin pressed on, fighting the snow, the dark, and the increasing cold as he trudged, climbed, stumbled, fell, and struggled back to his feet to do it all over again.

He looked frantically for any sign of the black stones but saw only white, gray, or brown. Increasingly he saw only white, nothing but a world of snow and treacherous hidden slicks of ice. Two more cliffs nearly sapped what was left of his strength, and he had to crawl several lengths before he managed to climb to his feet. He had to be headed toward the center peak, he *had* to be ...

Alrin's foot snagged, and he went down hard, slamming into rock and ice, felt the scrape of rough stone against his scaled cheek, grateful he could still maintain his scales because otherwise his cheek would be a bloody mess.

Heaving himself to his hands and knees, he drew breath and braced to stand—and stopped when he spied what was beneath him. Black stone. He wiped the snow and ice away to better see it, half-afraid he was starting to hallucinate.

No, it was definitely black stone, strangely warm to the touch and gleaming wetly. He scraped and pushed snow away another couple of paces on, slowly digging out the bits and pieces that remained of a long-forgotten path.

It was extremely slow going from then on, a few paces at a time as he sought out the remaining bits of black stone and carefully followed them along a winding course ever deeper into the mountains. Eventually the path led him back into woods, the trees so dense that they blocked a good deal of the snow, and he was able to move at a faster pace. Lighting his hands afire enabled him to see even when it grew dark, green dragon fire gleaming on the black stone, drawing out opalescent color like someone had trapped magic deep within the stones.

Exhaustion had begun to blur his vision when the frequency of the stones increased, and shortly thereafter he walked along a black path that was virtually unharmed, slipping from the woods and back out into open field. The solid path seemed to repel the weather, a perfect curving strip of black against the snow like some strange reversal of the sky, a strip of night set in a sea made of stars.

It led him into a small canyon, barely wide enough for two people to walk shoulder to shoulder. He felt the prickle of powerful magic along his skin—

And stopped as he turned the corner, spilling out of the canyon into a pavilion made of black stone save for the center where dark red stone formed a mosaic of the Sacred Heart broken into three pieces, the symbol of the Great Goddess torn apart by a jealous brother. Instead of dying, she had become the Sacred Three: Heaven, Earth, and Hell.

There was very little left of the temple. The pavilion was shattered in many places, entire stones missing. Two of the five columns in the front of the temple had collapsed completely, and of the remaining three, one looked set to collapse at any moment. The roof itself was long gone, broken and scattered.

But still the presence of magic was strong enough that Alrin hesitated to approach without a Priest to convey the Goddesses' permission. Korin was not there, however, and he had orders. Leaving the artificial safety of the canyon, he forged on across the broken, snowy pavilion, scales scraping, claws clicking, the fire still burning on his hands turning snow to steam for fleeting moments. More snow melted on his scales and into his clothes before it too was turned into steam by the heat of his body.

The temple seemed to hum softly, the sound growing louder as he drew closer—but it ceased as he crossed the threshold. Rubble littered the ground, and it was slow going again as he picked his way over and around the enormous chunks of collapsed roof.

Alrin paused in front of the large doorway surmounted by three archways that still had hints of the gold-paint prayers written along their edges. Only a smattering of letters were still legible, the old language that only Priests and scholars still could read. "Goddesses guide me," he murmured and passed through the archways into the room beyond.

Most services were conducted in the main sanctuary of the Temple of the Sacred Three, though there were other rooms where smaller services and private ceremonies were conducted. The true work of the Priests, the magic they cast and used in the name of the Three, was conducted in private prayer rooms. Alrin had seen the prayer room of the High Priest, the Chamber of the Beating Heart, only once, and only for a few seconds.

The room in which he currently stood reminded him strongly of the Chamber. The floor was a rose pattern of black and white stones, the very center of it a blood red stone that seemed to faintly glow. All around him the high walls were intact, and though from the outside the snow had seemed to be flying in,

OF LAST RESORT

there was no sign that even time had passed through there.

Extinguishing his hands and retracting his scales, Alrin ventured further into the room, headed for the blood red stone at the heart of the rose. The wall burst into brilliance in front of him, glowing as red as the stone on which he stood, then raced along the wall, shifting to orange, yellow, and on through a rainbow spectrum until it crashed into red again, and the whole room burst into multi-colored light.

Magic wrapped around Alrin like a warm blanket, temples flaring briefly with pain before he heard a voice softly resonating through his mind. *No Priest.*

"No." Alrin fisted his hands, but they continued to tremble anyway as Korin's words at the start of their journey came back to him. *Access to the Master Key spell is two-fold. I must break the first barrier, being a pure human with penultimate holy powers.* "High Priest Korin fell behind to stop the angel trying to kill us."

Angel ... the voice whispered. The glowing runes flared sun-bright; Alrin lifted a hand to shield his eyes. A moment later the light died, and he slowly lowered his hand. Before him stood a shadow that rippled and ran with softly-glowing runes, like some sort of crude puppet given life.

"Who are you?"

Shadow of Satrina.

"I've come for the Master Key."

There must be a Priest. What was sealed by penultimate holy magic must be unsealed by the same.

Damn them all thrice. "Then I guess I had better go back and fetch the High Priest." He spun around sharply—and yelped as he was slammed from all sides by a force he could not see.

Once in, no out.

"Fuck you and the bloody Queen for creating such a needlessly—" He broke off, jaw clenching, thinking of all who had died, would die, and the mess they were still cleaning up centuries later. If anything, he wondered if the steps taken had been enough, if there would ever be enough precaution to stop power-hungry fools from getting what they sought.

But precautions hindered the good as well as the bad, and right then he needed a thrice-damned fucking High Priest.

Dizziness washed over him like a tide, and Alrin let it take him down, sore, half-frozen ass barely feeling it when he landed hard on the surprisingly warm ground. He folded his legs in front of him and rested his elbows on his knees, planting his chin atop his hand as he tried to think of something—anything—he could do while he was trapped in that damned room.

The answer seemed obvious, however: Nothing.

He ... Alrin wanted to be angry, afraid. And he was both those things, but they were dulled by a numbing exhaustion and the despair slowly creeping over him like ivy. What more could he fucking do? "What happens to me if the High Priest does not come along to break the barrier? And what do you mean this place was sealed by holy magic? Satrina hid the key, not a Priest."

Demon Queen of the Night. Priest of the Broken Heart.

Priest of the Broken Heart ... that was the formal, old-fashioned title of the High Priest. Alrin had never heard it used outside the types of religious ceremonies done once or twice a decade. So a High Priest had helped Satrina seal away the Master Key. Why had she not mentioned that?

Precaution, no doubt. Fucking secrets. "So I sit here until I die or a High Priest happens by?" The shadow did not offer a reply, but one was hardly necessary. Alrin sighed. Unfolding his legs, he fell back to stretch out on the warm stones, scales coming out again, scraping against them. He stared up at the sky, marveling at the way the snow seemed to melt away or simply vanish before it fell inside the prayer chamber.

His eyes grew heavy, and despite everything pressing down upon him and the time he did not have to spare, Alrin fell asleep.

He jerked awake to sunlight searing his eyes—then heard the pained cry, which must have woken him. It sounded ...

Clambering to his feet, he tried to move. "Let me go! It's Korin, damn you. It's the High Priest."

He must come.

"He's hurt!" Alrin snapped around, hands fisting at his sides, and he almost wept when he saw a hand come around the edge of the archway, followed by Korin, who looked gaunt and ready to fall over, his clothes stained with red and sticking to him but still alive. "High Priest ..."

Korin paused and slowly lifted his head, staring at Alrin through wet, blood-matted clumps of hair. Alrin sucked in air through his nostrils, words lost. Korin's eyes had gone blue—solid blue, with the pupil and everything lost.

He stumbled into the prayer chamber, and the rainbow shimmer wrapped around the wall again, the shadow glowing with a blue aura. *Priest of the Broken Heart.*

Korin said something, but the words were too garbled for Alrin to make them out. He slowly moved closer, tripping at the last, and Alrin shot his arms out to catch him, haul him close. Korin twisted and shifted until he was pressed back to chest with Alrin. He touched Alrin's arms lightly and rested against him then brought his hands up to clasp them together in prayer and began to chant.

Alrin shivered as the pulse of magic washed over him again and again in rhythm with the cadence of Korin's words. The runes carved into the wall began to glow again, starting at red along the top and falling like rain to the bottom, shifting through the spectrum of the rainbow as it went, and then drifted toward them along the floor, coalescing in brilliant, silver-blue light.

Too much. Alrin closed his eyes and focused on holding tightly to Korin as the light grew ever brighter and the chanting louder—

Then it all stopped and Korin went slack in his arms. Alrin opened his eyes and barely caught him up in time to keep Korin from landing hard on the floor. Shifting his hold, he scooped Korin up and then knelt to lay him down more gently.

Snow began to fall down upon them, cold air sweeping in. Alrin summoned flames to one hand, holding it close enough to help keep Korin warm without hurting him.

Movement caught the edge of his vision, and he looked up to see the shadow. It had a more definitive shape, something reminiscent of a woman in full armor with a diadem upon her head. *Seal is broken.*

"What do I do?" Alrin asked, quenching the flame and rising to his feet. "Will he be all right?"

I do not know. The Priest's aura is nearly gone. He will sleep for a long time; it is up to him if he ever wakes.

Alrin's stomach churned, depression washing over him and leaving him exhausted in its wake. All he could hear was Telmé's anguished screams. The devastation of the Priests, many of whom would all too well remember the last time they had abruptly lost a High Priest. And Korin's heir was not yet old enough to take his place.

The anguish of the castle, to lose someone they held so dear, a young boy who had once spent his days picking fights with Prince Telmé or being punished for those fights. A young boy who had been burdened with too much responsibility but had taken it and thrived. They had changed so much—had come so far.

And Korin was more or less dead. Telmé would break.

But there was no time to mourn. He had a mission to complete. "What do I do?" Alrin asked again.

The Master Key requires a two-fold sacrifice. Half of you now. Half of you later.

Alrin swallowed, tried to lick his suddenly-dry lips, but his tongue was just as parched. "I know the cost. I am here to claim the Master Key."

Not to claim. To become.

"What—" The words choked off as the shadow touched him, cold slicing through him so sharply it was, for a moment, even hotter than his own flames. Was this how other people felt the cold? He stared at the long, dark fingers curled over his shoulders then slowly dragged his gaze up to the shadowy face that only barely held the hint of shape where eyes and nose and mouth should have been.

His eyes widened, body shaking, as the shadow leaned in—

He screamed as that bare, black hint of mouth covered his and fed him all new levels of hot and cold. It felt like his body was being licked with flames of flickering ice. A smell like brimstone and hot metal filled his nostrils, the odd, clammy, faintly sweet taste of blood filling his mouth.

Only when he felt a much more familiar, bearable pain against the palms of his hand did he realized he was free, and he'd scraped his hands on stone. His eyes blurred with warm tears, and he reached up to wipe them away, only managing to mingle blood with tears and leave sticky smears across his face.

Alrin stared at his hands. Something was wrong. What? He almost had it, but then cold and lingering aches swept his thoughts away again. Cold. He hated the cold. Why could he still feel it so acutely? He snorted and summoned—

Nothing. His flames wouldn't come. Alrin tried to summon his scales, but they were not there either.

Fresh tears stung his eyes as he dragged them up to the shadow. It was gray rather than black and growing ever lighter as he watched. "What did you do to me?"

Two fold. Half now. All your power and strength sacrificed to make you the key. It will take your light to use the key.

He was *human*. An ordinary human. "How am I supposed ..." he trailed off as the shadow vanished and was gone as though it had never been and then finished sourly, "to get off a fucking mountain when I cannot fly or stay warm—" As though on cue, a sharp wind howled through the prayer chamber. Shuddering, Alrin pulled his cloak more tightly around him and wished he had not abandoned the bag that had carried all his supplies, including his boots.

Alrin turned to Korin, still fast asleep and nearly as pale as the snow slowly falling down upon them. He reached out to touch—

Pain cut through his gut, radiated up his chest as if he were being sliced open for butchering. He wrapped his arms around his body and collapsed to the ground, head landing on Korin's stomach. The pain radiated out, wrapping around his arms and legs like vines, spiking out as though sprouting thorns until he felt hot.

Heat. So strange to feel it as something problematic. To feel it at all, maybe. Had he felt it as a dragon? He'd always thought so, but comparing it to how a human body reacted ...

Thoughts of hot and cold chased him into unconsciousness, but when he woke again to sunlight, all he felt was a sad ache. Something warm rose and fell beneath him, and Alrin finally dragged open sore, sleep-crusted eyes to stare at Korin's bruised, sickly face.

Everything came back to him, and Alrin groaned, turning to his side and getting an arm beneath him to leverage himself up—and nearly fell back over when he saw what had become of him. Memories of all the twisting, spiking, slicing pain flooded him as he gaped at his skin: it was covered in tangling vines and hooked thorns that seemed to be made out of bruises. The ... marks or tattoos or whatever they were seemed to glisten like wet ink, but when he reached out to slowly run his fingers over his forearm, they were warm and dry and smooth to the touch.

He pulled back his shirt and saw the damned thing covered nearly every last stitch of him, all radiating out from a lurid-looking heart on his chest. It seemed to pulse in time with his own heart, broken in two places precisely like the mosaic on which he and Korin lay. The Sacred Heart.

A soft voice whispered in the back of his mind. It sounded a bit like the shadow and a bit like himself. *Master Key …*

Alrin pushed himself to his feet, groaning as stiff muscles protested, brushing off snow. He frowned, flexed and unflexed his fingers. Something felt … he willed his fingers to shift into talons—and yelped, jerking in place as his nails turned black and extended into long, thin, needle-sharp claws. What? He looked down at his feet to see shorter, thicker, but still finely-pointed claws in place of his toenails.

At least he had a rough idea about how to control them. His mind and body had not forgotten shifting. What else could he do? Cold, he realized. He did not feel it as he had before passing out. What had taking the Master Key done to him?

All of this changing was giving him a fucking headache. Dying was supposed to be a simple matter. Why was it turning out so bloody complicated? Alrin closed his eyes and tried to make it simple. *All your strength and power to make you the key.* That was what the shadow had said. So he was the Master Key.

And its protector. He had been stripped of his own power and strength to make him something suitable to protect the key—himself—against the types of beings that would come after him. Had Satrina known that when she had sent him? What would have happened if she'd sent someone else?

Not that 'if' really mattered.

At present, the only thing that mattered was getting off the mountain. Where he had to be from there ... *the Ninth Seal.* There was a tugging sensation in his chest, a twisting, aching need. Alrin closed his eyes as images flooded his mind.

A castle made of dark brown stone shot through with red veins. Fields of red flowers, a banner of a stone tower with a scarlet roof on which rested a giant gold raptor. The tower was the crest of the Reach of the West. That gold raptor ... that was the crest of Zyke Lorn Fall.

Is that where the others had gone? How had he known that?

Alrin increasingly hated being the Master Key with every passing moment.

How was he going to get them down the mountain? He no longer seemed in danger of freezing, but Korin ... Alrin knelt and ran his hands gently over Korin's body, searching for damage and signs of internal injuries. Thankfully, he seemed only faintly too warm and heavily bruised, all of which could be tended to easily enough. Alrin was more concerned by the way touching Korin left his hands tingling, as though they had gone numb and the blood was rushing back into them.

Damn everything. If he were a dragon he could fly—

Alrin yelped again as heat flared through his shoulders and down his back, clear to his ass, and the sounds of tearing fabric momentarily filled the room. The weight and strain of wings was familiar, as was the way they tried to pull and jerk, battling with the wind, before he got control and settled them down. But he was not accustomed to *bird* wings, the dark purple-black feathers, the softness of them, or the faint hint of something smoky in the air. They were heavy and light all at once, pulling at muscles …

That had not hurt when his body changed. Being a shifter meant there was always pain. The terrible combination of magic and monster was what allowed shifters to alternate between forms, but neither human nor dragon was meant to undergo such a change, and so it always hurt.

His new … form or abilities … caused him no pain at all. Hot tears blurred his vision before they spilled down his cheeks as the realization sank in and took hold. He was no longer a dragon, but he was no longer going to be in pain damn near every single day of his life.

He did not care that that life was only going to last a few more days. They wouldn't be spent in *pain.*

Alrin knelt and gently lifted Korin up into his arms, cradling him close and tightly. He crouched, staring up at the sky, felt and smelled the air—then launched himself up, wings snapping out to catch the wind. Double checking that Korin was secured, he slowly banked around toward the west and headed for Zyke Lorn Fall.

Part Three
Defiants

WORRY

Raffé watched Alrin until he was out of sight, then turned and stiffly walked back to his room. He breathed in deeply and out slowly, silently counting stones, threads, scuff marks—whatever he saw that he could count.

Anything that kept his thoughts away from Alrin. If he thought about Alrin he would scream and do something stupid. He gripped the edges of his tunic to keep from putting a fist through the wall, from tearing the room apart before starting on the rest of the castle. The agony tore through him like blessed steel through his flesh. It was a thousand times worse than having his arm mauled to pieces by a minion.

Until the moment when he knew that Alrin was Cambord and was going to die and there was nothing he could do about it, Raffé had thought he understood that duty meant sacrifice. That he could handle it. What could possibly be harder than sacrificing himself for his family?

He should never have asked that question. He didn't even *like* his family, and as much as he had hated to die it had also been a relief to escape them. Dying for them did not compare to having to watch the man he loved go off to his death. He would rather kill himself a thousand times than live with the knowledge that Alrin was headed off to die alone on a mountain. Being left behind was far worse a hell than dying.

The room still smelled of them, so much it drove him mad. It brought the taste of Alrin back to him, made his mouth ache to have that taste back. Recalled the feel of his skin, smooth and hot, slick and rough when his scales appeared. Alrin smelled like smoke and fire, a hint of earth.

Raffé stripped off the clothes he'd hastily pulled on when he'd thought Alrin had snuck away without saying goodbye. Walking over to the bowl of cold water, he quickly washed up then pulled clothes from the wardrobe and armor from his trunk. He dressed with jerky moments, unable to focus with the smell of them lodged in his nostrils. He bared his teeth at the bed before turning sharply away, deftly finishing the buckle on his sword belt as he strode to the door and headed out.

He found the others assembled in the great hall. Some of the tables had been dragged back out, all signs of the bodies that had been lined up long gone, but most of the hall was still eerily empty. Raffé had never seen it so, except perhaps in the earliest hours of the morning.

But he could hear the clamor in the bailey as the Paladins departed, headed … wherever they were headed to help stop the opening of the Entrance.

"Raffé."

He obediently strode over to the table where Telmé and the other princes were waiting. They formed a loose ring, some sitting at the table, others gathered around it. Rare to see all of them together—the last time had been his Blooding.

Axel beckoned to him, and he and Şehzade made space for Raffé to sit between them. Şehzade smiled, welcoming and sympathetic, gripping Raffé's arm briefly in comfort. Raffé smiled gratefully back, gave another smile to Axel in thanks for the cup of dark red wine he pushed toward him.

Telmé clapped his hands for silence. "Our orders are to find the bastard orchestrating this mess and stop him. We will not prevent him from gaining the Eight Seals. In that endeavor, the Legion has regretfully failed. But we still have a chance to stop him from doing anything with them."

"How do we do that when we don't even know where to find the remaining seals, which are probably the only places we'd ever hope to catch the bastard," Yrian asked. "Why not just go with the Paladins and make a last stand?"

"Because hopefully we can still do better than that," Telmé replied. He picked up a map lying in front of him on the table, a fine one made of cloth rather than the usual parchment ones they used for day-to-day matters. Unrolling it, he then opened a battered wooden box that had been set alongside the map. He grabbed a handful of scuffed, faded markers and plopped them down on various parts of the map. "These are where six of the seals were summoned: Water in Guldbrandsen, Fire in Whitt, Earth in Krimkoryn, Heaven in Taakar, and Hell in Noor Hel. It cannot be coincidence that each seal is broken in a different province. That leaves Ecklemore, Stehl, Mykne, Boorst, and Lass. We are splitting into five groups, decided by me, and will each go to a different province accompanied by Priests and Shades. Whatever it takes, stop any threat—blatant, perceived, or otherwise. Use caution, be smart, but be ruthless. This is our last chance."

Şehzade frowned. "Those are not small territories; we need more information just to know where to start."

"We can provide that," said a familiar voice.

Raffé turned to see Méo standing a couple of paces behind him, a Shade beside him, ominous looking in his dark purple robes and firelight making the silvery threads of his crest shine. Like the Shadowmarch and Dredknights, the Shades' crest was a mask, but theirs was decorated with a crescent moon rather than stars or slashes.

Méo shoved his hair from his handsome, open face as he stepped closer to better show the heavy book he carried. Runes were etched into the blue leather binding it. The Shade held what looked like a map sketched in charcoal with several red blots that resembled blood covering it. His voice was soft but clear when he said, "We've been examining records and can at least provide some starting points."

Gesturing to the Shade, Telmé said, "This is Shade Edvin, the third most powerful Shade in the castle. He is an expert at demonology and ancient sacrificial practices, which makes him ideally suited to assist us. Thanks to him and the Priests, we still have a chance."

Raffé could have guessed Edvin's abilities by his frailness. His dark, brown-black skin seemed dull, leeched of healthy color and paper thin, and the bones of his fingers and wrists were painfully prominent. If not for the fact they were essentially half-demons and so naturally bestowed hellish magics, the Princes would fare no better for using them. But the Shadowmarch, Shades, and Dredknights, like the rest of the Legion, could do things the Princes would never be able to.

OF LAST RESORT

Edvin gave them a brief bow then moved in closer and leaned over Raffé's shoulder. The way he kept shifting made it clear he still could not see well. Nudging him back, Raffé stood and slipped by, then urged Edvin down into his seat while he stood next to Méo.

"Sadly, it is not my magic that makes me especially useful in this case," Edvin said. "I was a cartographer before I learned I had an affinity for hellish magic. I've extensive knowledge of the lands, and combining that with what I and the Priests know of old rituals and where they were performed, we've been able to pick out several places for each group to explore and marked the ones that we think most promising." He smoothed his map out and, taking markers from the box, began to plot them out on Telmé's larger map. "Four locations in Mykne, three in Ecklemore, five here in Stehl, and seven apiece in Boorst and Lass."

"Why so many in those last two?" Raffé asked.

Méo replied, "Because Lass shares a border with Zyke Lorn Fall, and Boorst may as well share a border, given the way it borders Krimkoryn and so practically wraps right around Zyke Lorn Fall. Guldbrandsen and Stehl are the seats of holy power now, but that has not always been the case. Zyke Lorn Fall was not where holy magic was born, but it was where holy magic first flourished. Lass and Boorst were part of a sprawling empire backed by the weight of the goddesses. It was only much later that Zyke Lorn Fall began its slow decay. Lass and Boorst broke away from it—and then began to fight each other. Eventually holy power moved to other places. One Priest fled to eventually settle in Stehl and form the Temple of the Sacred Heart. Guldbrandsen later became the heart of the newly unified kingdom by the authority of the Great Queen and formed the Temple of the Sacred Three. Although the majority of that power is long gone from those places, the ruins of it remain in the broken altars and collapsed temples."

"Interestingly," Edvin added, "Lass now boasts the finest Alchemists, and I am one of many Shades who come from Boorst."

"We don't need historical tidbits, no matter how interesting—we need information we can use," Raffé said. "Why did we not know of these locations sooner? Were there some we could have reached in time to prevent earlier sacrifices?"

"There were too many at the start," Edvin said, ducking his head. "We tried, but our guesses were too many, and every time we wound up being wrong or figured it out too late. I swear we have done our best, Highness. I'm sorry that was not good enough."

"Yes," Méo agreed, dipping his head slightly but keeping his eyes up to meet Raffé's gaze. "All of us are sorry."

Raffé shook his head, dismayed by his own words, and looked to Telmé for guidance. These men owed him no apologies, and he'd had no right to be so terse with them. It was not even like him … except that increasingly it was. He had been told innumerable times over the past months that he would change, that the demon elements that had woken in him would come more to the fore. But that did not make it easier or less disconcerting. It had always been his habit to keep his mouth shut and walk away.

But those memories felt more and more as though they belonged to another person, a man he had once known and would never see again. A man who hid in his office or his bedroom, who sighed and stewed in bitterness at every dismissal and reprimand. He could not reconcile that man with fresher memories of having his arm shredded, of throwing demon fire at hordes of dead-walkers. He could not see that sad, timid man fucking a dragon.

Telmé seemed to smile at him, ever so faintly, and tip him the barest nod before he dropped his folded arms and spoke to Méo and Edvin. "We know our brothers in the Legion always do the best they can. We have something now; that is all that matters. Now we divide into teams and get to work. Méo, Edvin, are your Priests and Shades sorted out?"

"Already waiting at the stables, Highness," Méo replied.

"Good." Telmé gestured to the Princes. "Athanasi, you're with Lassē and Božidar. Head for Mykne. Dalibor, you've got Magnus and Premisl. You're headed for Ecklemore. Tollak, Cemal, and Şehzade, you three are covering Stehl." The indicated men divided up, and Telmé sorted the remaining. "Håkon, take Yrian and Göker and take care of Boorst. Raffé and Axel, you're with me."

Raffé frowned but did not voice his confusion. He bid farewell to the others, tightly embracing Håkon and Yrian, bidding them be as careful as they could. When they had all gone, and his group was alone in the hall, he finally turned to Telmé. "You do not want one of the others with you?"

"No, they are best sent elsewhere," Telmé replied, then smiled faintly. "We have an excellent Priest and one of the best Shades in the Legion with us, and you and Axel are certainly nothing to be scoffed at. We will be more than fine."

"So we get Lass?" Axel asked, pulling on the armor and sword belt that had been on the table. He then buckled his arrow holster across his chest, shrugging and twisting until it settled just so across his back. When that was done, he picked up his bow and strung it.

Normally archery work was left to others in the Legion. Princes of the Blood were most useful right in the thick of the fight. But Axel had been an archer before he was marked as a little prince. He had been discovered late and undertaken the Blooding at age twenty-seven, but he had taken well to it and with his new power he was a marksman of unmatchable skill. His arrows were specially made for the increased power Axel wielded, though Raffé had never heard the details of how.

"Yes. It's the most dangerous, given how close it is to Zyke Lorn Fall. Our job is to make certain our enemy does not make it that far."

"Even with every single Prince on hand we could not hold that border," Raffé said. "There is no way we can do it with three princes, a Shade, and a Priest."

Telmé shook his head. "We don't need to hold the border, we only need to guard a part of it. An arduous task, to be certain, but I have every confidence we will do it."

"How are we getting there?" Axel asked, testing his bow before relaxing and focusing his full attention on Telmé. "We are moving large amounts of the Legion all at once and in countless directions. The castle has not been this empty in a long time."

"We are taking the griffons," Telmé replied. "We should head out—not you, Raffé. I want another word with you before we depart."

Raffé froze, startled, but then realized that after everything that had transpired with Alrin he should have anticipated Telmé wanting to speak with him privately. He fought an urge to fold his arms across his chest and forced himself to keep his head up as Telmé drew close.

"How are you?" Telmé asked quietly.

Raffé almost said he was fine, but the stern look Telmé leveled at him stopped the words short. He sighed. "Managing. I do not know what else to do. If I hold still too long or do not keep my thoughts otherwise occupied ... But I am not the only one saying goodbye today. I am not the only one who will have to live with the fact that someone I love will not be coming back. If I have learned anything since coming to Guldbrandsen, it is that everyone here is old friends with death and grief."

"That does not mean your pain is less, and you better than anyone know what it is like to be where Alrin is right now. It is one thing to be a soldier going to battle; another to be a sacrifice going to altar. Alrin has always been punished for being more dragon than human. I am guilty of being one of those punishers." Telmé always had a sad air about him, but for a moment, the lines in his face seemed to cut deeper than usual, the shadows in his eyes heavier. "He has always been one of the best soldiers in the Legion, even from a young age. When all the rest of us had given up on Håkon, he believed Kristof and defied us to help him rescue Håkon. I feel a bastard for returning that faith by sending him to his death. I hope at least he was happy in his final night."

Raffé remembered every kiss, every whispered word, every emotion that had passed over Alrin's face. "As happy as he could be, I think," he said quietly.

"Good." Telmé stepped in closer and cupped Raffé's face. Raffé startled, almost jerking away before he caught himself.

"Highness?"

Telmé laughed. "How are you, that aside? You have been a Prince of the Blood several months, but for the most part, you have not gone through the more aggressive changes. You are remarkably controlled. Usually I'd have had to beat them back into their humanity at least once. Even I needed several stern reminders before I truly got control of it."

"I'm not controlled," Raffé muttered, dropping his gaze, intimidated by the way Telmé always, *always* seemed to see everything. "It wasn't my place to yell at them."

"Yes, it was," Telmé said sharply. "No one else did. Several were thinking it—and should have said it as well—but you were the only one who did."

Raffé frowned at that. "Dalibor would have. Håkon would have. Why did they not?" He looked up, brow furrowed—and caught the flicker of a pleased smile glancing across Telmé's mouth. "They stayed silent on purpose. Why?"

"They are as invested in your training as I," Telmé said.

"What's so special about my training?" Raffé asked. Was he doing poorly? Was he slower to learn? "Am I doing something wrong?"

Telmé's smile widened as he slid a hand up to ruffle Raffé's hair. Raffé stared, stunned. Telmé laughed ever so faintly and dropped his hands. "Every

Prince has his strengths, and they all possess many fine qualities, but even Håkon and Dalibor and Athanasi are not suited to someday take my place. I am forty-two years old; I have been a Prince—and Commander of the Legion—for twenty-six years. It is long past time I had an heir. You must be the only one in the castle who has not noticed I am grooming you for the role."

"Me. Replace you." Raffé shook his head. "Have you lost your mind?"

Laughing, Telmé ruffled his hair one last time. "Yes, but I lost it a long time ago. Everyone is accustomed to my madness by now. But I'm not mad in this matter. All the skills and abilities are there. They need only honing. Your confidence is chief amongst those. Get it through your fool head that you are here, you have the right to be here, and you have proven that time and again." His levity faded away into somberness as he continued. "You will hurt yourself and others by continuing to disbelieve that fact. You're smart. You're tough. You do not need someone else to remind you of your humanity. One day I will not be here. I do not aim for that day to come to pass any time soon, but we seldom have a choice in the matter. Everyone will look to you for guidance when that day comes. Start accepting that."

Raffé swallowed. "Yes, Highness."

"Good. Now you must listen. Whatever happens, whatever it takes, do not let our foe open the Entrance. It will ultimately take the Ninth Seal and the Master Key. Alrin has gone to secure the Master Key. We are to defend the last seal and the location with our lives. The Entrance must be opened at the Altar of the Breaking in Zyke Lorn Fall. If something goes wrong, that is what you must protect. We have tried to keep the location a secret for as long as possible, to give the Paladins time to get there to secure it and set up defenses, but the unhappy truth is that it was probably never a secret at all. Be on guard at all times."

"Yes, Highness," Raffé said quietly. "You think something will go wrong."

Telmé sighed and looked away, glance sliding over the great hall as though looking at something that was no longer there. A memory? Raffé only sort of knew Telmé's history. Everyone had heard the bare bones of the story, but the truth of the matter had always been kept quiet.

All he knew was that twenty-some years ago nearly all the Legion had been slain, including all of the Princes of the Blood save one: Telmé, who had only been a boy at the time.

"I have learned that with a problem like this, the source of it is always somebody you trust. We try hard, time and again, to build a true circle of trust—but there is always somebody who has decided that something else is more important than the circle. I have not been able to figure out who, but they will reveal themselves soon. They won't have a choice. But I fear the power of a person who can hide right in the midst of us without drawing even a sliver of doubt toward their person. Be alert, be careful, and when they tip their hand ... be ruthless. Be *heartless*."

Raffé nodded. "I will."

Telmé gripped his shoulder, returned the nod, then let go and spun neatly around. "Let's go, then, before our teammates begin to drive the Tamers mad." Raffé followed him out the castle and across the bailey to the stable yards where Méo, Edvin, and Axel waited. Three griffons, saddled and with packs strapped to their bellies, fluttered and stamped restlessly. "Méo, ride with me," Telmé said. "Raffé, ride with Edvin. Axel, try to stay out of trouble—and stay close to Raffé."

"Yes, Highness," Axel replied and mounted up. Telmé swung up onto his griffon then helped Méo climb up behind him. They flew off, and once they were clear, Axel launched into the air, flying close but out of the way until Raffé and Edvin joined him.

Edvin's arms were tight around his waist, almost painfully so. Raffé let go of the reins with his left hand and covered Edvin's with it, squeezing lightly. He half-turned his head to shout, "It's all right. Nothing will happen to you." There was no reply, but Raffé felt Edvin nod against his shoulder.

Raffé had been little better his first time flying. Training had lasted three weeks; it had taken nearly that long for him to brave jumping *off* a griffon. Learning how to land properly had been an entirely new misery. He'd broken his leg four different times and his arm twice. None of the tales of Princes ever spoke of how much *pain* they endured, day after day after day.

Practice had certainly taken care of his fears, but flying never ceased to be strange. It was cold high up in the sky, and the wind made seeing difficult. At least he had no trouble breathing, which was something most of the rest of the Legion struggled with. Thankfully, for all his fears, Edvin seemed familiar enough by the way he moved or held still in accordance with how the griffon flew.

There was nothing like vanishing into the clouds and then rising above them, watching the world shrink, seeing what a rainstorm looked like from above. When the clouds were so numerous that they blocked all view below, it was like being in another world entirely, and Raffé felt bereft when they slipped back through the clouds to return to the brutal world to which they belonged.

It was easy, for a few minutes, to forget that all that waited for them when they landed was confusion, fear, violence, and death. Far too easy to let his mind slip to thoughts of Alrin. His chest gave a sharp, painful twist, the ache of it lingering, and with a rough noise Raffé tried to put his mind elsewhere.

The clouds broke and off in the distance he could see the unmistakable stretch of black that was Zyke Lorn Fall. History had no precise record of what exactly had finally destroyed Zyke Lorn Fall. Too much of everything was the accepted answer. Zyke Lorn Fall was where everything had most gone wrong. Though Alwyn was lost as well, it was a tragedy, not a terror.

Nothing good ever happened when Zyke Lorn Fall was involved. Méo's brief history lesson rolled through his mind, and Raffé shook his head, unable to reconcile that such a terrible place had been the foundation of what eventually became the Temples of the Sacred Heart and the Sacred Three.

They passed over clouds again and the long patch of misty black vanished from sight, leaving Raffé with a knot of dread in his stomach and entirely too much time to allow it to grow.

But his mind had nowhere else to turn—nowhere pleasant anyway. He could think of Alrin going off to die at a location Raffé did not know, accompanied only by the High Priest. He could think about all that Telmé had just told him, but the idea that he was meant to someday take Telmé's place just set the ball of dread in his stomach to churning. He wasn't fit for it, he couldn't—

The smell of blood caught his nose, sharp, sweet, brief. Familiar blood—Telmé's blood, the first Raffé had tasted after waking as a Prince. Raffé looked ahead to where Telmé flew well in the distance, mostly hidden by flapping winds and Méo's slighter form.

He turned to look at Axel, who was looking down at the ground and did not seem to have noticed. Perhaps he had only imagined it.

The clouds parted again, and Telmé began to fly downward, slowly descending as they drew closer to the Lass Province, part of the Reach of the West alongside Zyke Lorn Fall and Krimkoryn. Raffé had not expected the western side of the country to look so different, but it seemed rougher, harder, darker. It all seemed so much heavier and denser, though he could not entirely say why. The trees were different, the mountains more jagged. Perhaps it was just that the weight of Zyke Lorn Fall had a presence that spread out rather than confining its gloom the way Alwyn did.

Raffé smelled blood again, as though a wound was being healed as quickly as it was inflicted. Perhaps something had cut Telmé mid-flight. It had happened before. He did not seem alarmed, at any rate. Raffé was simply taking his words to be cautious a little too far.

The smell of evergreen trees was bright and sharp on the cool evening air. They landed in a field of blue and yellow flowers that smelled like perfume. Well, the perfume likely smelled like the flowers but whatever. The griffons cawed as they settled, flexing their wings before folding them neatly on their backs.

Stretching with a loud groan, Raffé made certain Edvin was well before he turned toward Telmé's griffon. He froze as he watched Telmé sink to his knees, eyes a brilliant flame blue but dull, vacant. Fear coiled through Raffé. "What ..."

"Down!" Axel roared, and Raffé barely ducked in time as arrows flew at—

At Méo.

Angel

Raffé drew his sword, readied his magic, not quite believing his own eyes as he stared at Méo. His eyes were the same brilliant blue as Telmé's, but they were glowing so brightly they hurt to look at. "Go!" he snarled at Edvin, throwing him on the griffon and ordering it back into the air.

He turned back as a second flurry of arrows sent Méo flying back. Raffé shunted his questions aside for later and lunged for Telmé, scooping him up, throwing him over one shoulder, and scrabbling onto the griffon close to Méo.

It screeched as he ordered it into the air, climbing swiftly. Raffé held tightly to Telmé, sword still in his other hand, balance precarious as he used his legs to hold fast to the griffon. He felt Telmé shift and grunt, but the words that tumbled out were incomprehensible.

The griffon screamed again right as blinding blue-white light flashed, and the smell of blood was so strong that Raffé's mouth watered, nostrils flaring and his fangs aching to drop. Then the griffon gave a soft sigh, shuddered, and died. They fell far faster than they had risen, and Raffé screamed as he heaved Telmé as far away as he could before throwing himself from the griffon moments before they hit the ground.

He rolled as he hit the ground, barely keeping hold of his sword and clambering clumsily to his feet and whipping around—only to be thrown back as something planted in his chest, cutting through layers of fabric and leather and metal as though they weren't even there. Raffé landed heavily on his back, choking on his own blood as he struggled to pull whatever was in his chest out but drew back immediately, fingers blistered and bloody.

It was like a solid shaft of blue light, some strange magic of holy origins. Biting down on his cheeks against screaming, Raffé gripped the damned thing and slowly, agonizingly, pulled it from his chest with burned, bloody fingers.

Tossing it as far away as he could, Raffé rolled over and got to his knees. His right hand was nigh useless, and showed no signs of healing. Neither did the gaping hole in his chest. Fuck, he couldn't *breathe.* Every breath burned, struggled. Raffé grit his teeth, grabbed his sword with his left hand, and forced himself to his feet.

He turned, stopping when he saw that all of the griffons were dead … as was Edvin. Raffé swallowed bile as he saw Méo take a bite from the severed arm he held, crunching and chewing through it as though he were eating a piece of crusty bread. The sounds … Raffé shivered as the snap and smack and wet chewing raked over his ears.

Telmé was nearby, his eyes still that strange blue color. Of Axel, there was no sign. Raffé looked at Méo. "What are you?"

Méo laughed; the sound was like metal scraping over stone. He ate another bite of Edvin's arm, smacking his lips. He had far more teeth than any human should possess, each one pointed and wet with blood. "The only thing a demon truly has to fear."

OF LAST RESORT

Holding his injured hand to the hole in his chest, hoping the way that it felt like they were healing in the barest increments was not self-delusion. "A backstabbing Priest with sharp teeth?" They reminded Raffé of the minion that had shredded his arm.

"An angel," Méo said, voice rumbling, deepening, and yet somehow softening at the same time, as though he were being careful to keep his voice low for fear of what might happen if he spoke loudly. He began to glow with blue light, as though he was the heart of some terrible flame. "An angel of holy wrath, called down by the abused to visit justice on the foul demons and would-be demons bent on destroying the Goddesses' beloved lands."

Raffé tried to remember all he knew about angels, but there was woefully little past knowing that he should be terrified:

> *Angels possess ultimate holy power. The life force of an angel can sustain any living creature.*
>
> *Angels are servants; they must be ordered to do something, but they will carry out their given task no matter the obstacles.*
>
> *Angels are weapons; it is not theirs to determine where they fall and what they strike.*
>
> *Angels may only be summoned by the High Priest, and only when he has*

the agreement of the Commander of the Legion and the approval of the king.

But Korin wasn't behind this, because the only other thing he remembered about angels was that they always inhabited the body of the Summoner. Méo had summoned the angel. "Why?" Raffé finally asked.

Méo—the angel—Angel-Méo laughed in a way that said the pain of others was the best possible entertainment. "Why, what? Why an angel? Why am I here? Why am I visiting holy wrath upon you pathetic things?" He shoved the last wet, dripping clump of Edvin's arms into his blood-caked mouth, chewing it loudly before swallowing and wiping the blood from his face with the back of his hand, only smearing it further. "You should be asking '*Why haven't you killed me yet?*'"

That was one of the many thoughts flitting through Raffé's mind, but his real concern was making a more successful attempt at escape. *Distract. Escape. Plan.* Where had Axel gone? "I was going to ask, 'why are you eating him?' actually," Raffé replied.

"Everyone knows that angels can sustain everything. But what does an angel need for sustenance?"

Raffé licked his chapped lips. "Angels are made of holy power and the will of the Goddesses."

Angel-Méo laughed. "Perhaps in my true, unbound form. But I have been called down, confined to this body, and it erodes quickly. Why do you think you stupid Princes drink blood? You are too powerful for the feeble bodies you're stuck with."

"Drinking blood is not the same as *eating* people," Raffé snarled. "You're—" The words choked off with a stuttered whimper as Angel-Méo moved, *fast*, and was suddenly right up against him, claws sunk into his throat. Raffé could feel the blood dripping warm and sticky down his neck, slipping beneath his armor to drip down his chest, soak into his quilted undertunic.

Angel-Méo's breath was rank, wafted demonsbane and holy power over Raffé, making him dizzy. "I'm an *angel*. The Angel Umah, Most Holy Servant of Wrath and Vengeance. Demons are fallen angels, cast out for their unworthiness. Pale imitations, piddling foot soldiers meant for slaughter while true warriors do all the work. I am much more than a demon, little prince. I require far more susten—"

He stood stunned, as though frozen. Raffé stared wide-eyed at the arrow point jutting out of his forehead.

Distract. Escape.
Escape. Escape. Escape.

Raffé turned to mist, passed around and over Angel-Méo, shifted back, and heaved Telmé up over his shoulder. Then he ran.

He ran until everything hurt and the effort of continuing anyway would have made him cry if he could spare the energy. Until it was well past sunset and the night was so cold his lungs felt as if they were filled with thousands of scalding needles.

His foot caught on something, his shin gave an ominous crack, and he went down with a cry, Telmé tumbling away. Tears pricked his eyes as everything hit him at once. Raffé examined his broken left leg, clenching his jaw as he forced himself to shove the bones back into place so that everything would heal properly. He felt like vomiting as the healing process began, sluggish and agonizing. His chest still ached from where he had been stabbed, though it had finally closed up. He curled fingers around his throat, felt the lingering bruises where Angel-Méo's claws had dug in.

Exhaustion, pain, and helplessness washed over him. Damn it, they needed to start moving again. The longer he held still, the likelier Angel-Méo was to catch them again, but Raffé could not go anywhere until his stupid leg healed, and he had already spent so much energy healing from a wound inflicted by holy magic. That he had survived was not reassuring—it meant Angel-Méo needed them alive.

Gritting his teeth, Raffé forced himself up, stumbling and wavering, almost toppling, but finally gaining footing before he hobble-hopped over to Telmé. Slowly sinking to the ground again, he pulled Telmé into his lap and felt for his pulse. He pried open one eye, relieved to see there was no longer any sign of a blue glow. Perhaps he had wrenched free of Angel-Méo's hold, then. Hopefully there were no long-term effects.

Raffé looked up at the stars to get his bearings. They were close to Zyke Lorn Fall. Now that he was paying attention he could smell the sulfur and rot.

"You ... lost your sword ... again ..." The words were weak, raspy, but Raffé silently cheered as he stared down at Telmé, who stared back through half-open, groggy eyes.

"Are you all right?" Raffé asked.

"W-weak," Telmé replied. "What happened after we landed?" He struggled to sit up, and Raffé helped him, keeping a steady arm looped around his back.

"Your eyes were holy blue. Méo had you."

"Tried to control me," Telmé replied. "I remember. Thought to control all the Princes through me, but that's not how it works."

"Axel tried to kill him. I grabbed you and escaped, or thought I had, but Méo brought the griffons down. By the time I'd recovered …" He closed his eyes, reliving moments he would give anything to forget. "I was too late to save Edvin. I should have tried harder, done *something*. But I was more concerned with getting you to safety than him. He—the angel—Méo—he was *eating* him. I thought only necromancers did that."

"They both do it for the same reason," Telmé said, voice weak, a trifle shaky. "Necromancers are humans using a power they're not meant to have. Shades, Shadowmarch, and Dredknights are *granted* their powers, so while it taxes them, it does not poison them. They survive purely through interacting with people; just being in a crowded room sustains them, though, of course, the more intimate the contact the better the sustenance."

He paused to lick his lips, and Raffé's offered up his wrist. Telmé grimaced at the necessity, but accepted, taking a few swallows of blood. Raffé tried to encourage to keep going when he stopped, but Telmé firmly pushed his wrist away.

Telmé slumped against Raffé, closing his eyes, but resumed talking, slow and soft. "Necromancers are a type of living dead. They sustain themselves by eating humans healthy in body and strong in spiritual or earthly energy. Angels are … fire trapped in ice. Constantly melting it. They consume human flesh to restore the ice. The Princes are a less extreme version of that." He shook his head. "An angel. I cannot believe Méo summoned an angel—he should not have had enough power to do that."

He seemed to sway unsteadily. Raffé held him tightly, swallowing when Telmé fell inward to rest his head on Raffé's shoulder. Was his commander supposed to look so fragile? "What do we do?"

"We need to get to the Altar of the Breaking," Telmé said, eyes sliding shut, face pinched. "That is exactly where Méo wants us to go, but there's no help for it. The Paladins are strong enough to hold him off until they can reach Korin, who will have the power and skill to banish an angel, especially with the Paladins to back him up." He slowly opened his eyes again. "Help me up. I'm still weak, but we have to move. Hopefully my strength will recover sufficiently as we travel."

Raffé nodded and slowly rose, testing his leg and sighing in relief when it held. Stooping, he hauled Telmé up, keeping an arm around his waist as they started walking until Telmé gave a nod and pulled away. "You need to stop losing your sword. I have never in my life known a soldier so careless about retaining his weapon."

"I'm better with magic, anyway," Raffé replied.

"That's no excuse, and right now you are still drawing pretty even. You will be more of a mage someday, that I agree with. Until then, stop losing your sword." He lapsed into silence, and Raffé had no inclination to break it as they continued trudging on.

The night had just begun to fade when they crested a hill and looked down at the clear demarcation between Lass and Zyke Lorn Fall: a sharp divide between the healthy, alive Lass and the brown-black, parched, barren earth of Zyke Lorn Fall. A putrid stain that birthed only dead-walkers, wraiths, and revenants, serving as nothing more than a reminder that the division between earth and hell had become far too blurry.

Raffé shivered as they left Lass behind, body thrumming, aching slightly as the corrupted land began to sink into his skin. "I hate this place already."

"It only gets worse," Telmé said with a grimace. "Ideally we will travel in peace. The denizens will be drawn to us because of our hellish powers, but I can feel the residue of holy might, which will repel them. By the time they decide we're more appealing than the holy presence is revolting, we will be close enough to the Paladins that they'll have no choice but to stay away. I hope, anyway. I fear we have not the strength to fight off a horde of dead-walkers, and I dread encountering revenants."

Telmé started moving more quickly, ending the conversation again, and Raffé hastened after him, letting his claws out so he was prepared should something happen. Their footsteps and panting breaths were the only sounds in the dry, sulfur-laden air save for the occasional dry crackle or hollow rattle. Petrified trees littered the landscape along with boulders and the last, crumbled remains of buildings. Dried bones were scattered about, and here and there a still-rotting, half-eaten corpse lay waiting for the environment to finish destroying it. There were barren hills and plains of cracked earth, rocky dips and canyons where streams and rivers had once been. Though the sky was cloudless, the sunlight that shone down was faint, dull, as though even it could not live in such a place. It was still enough to make Raffé completely miserable. Sunlight might not affect him as badly as when he had first become a Prince, but he vastly preferred working at night.

He wiped sweat from his brow, wishing fervently for something to drink, even water, for all the good it would really do him. He dared not think about blood. His jaw ached, throat working to swallow something it would not have for hours yet—assuming they reached the Paladins at all.

Telmé sighed and tilted his head up to look at the sky. "I cannot believe we never realized it was Méo."

"I don't understand why it *is* Méo."

"Jehan," Telmé said softly. "I suspect this is all because of Jehan. I remember being surprised that Méo … accepted his death without more anger. Korin and I decided he was unusually strong and the rest could be attributed to his training." He sighed, face suddenly etched deep with his forty-odd years of age. "Méo came to the castle as a little boy, about five years old, I suppose. Two years after he arrived, a man joined the Legion as a general foot soldier. He brought a wife and two children with him, and the son proved to be a candidate for the Blooding. He and Méo became best friends. Korin and I thought they would marry well, and they were informally betrothed until they were old enough to decide if that was what they really wanted.

"Jehan became a Prince at age twenty. He proved to be a great Prince, but a powerful demon was accidentally loosed by an amateur necromancer and devastated a village. We caught up to it halfway to another village, but by then it had acquired more power. One of its minions took Jehan by surprise, tore his head off. We were all distraught, but Méo far more than the rest of us. There was no consoling him for days; we thought he would ask to leave ... but then he seemed to bolster. He spoke privately with Korin, and that seemed to be the end of it. He has faithfully assisted the Princes ever since. Apparently he was just biding his time and getting all of his pieces into place." Telmé slammed a fist on his thigh. "Damn him." He raked a hand through his hair. "Damn me for not noticing."

Raffé reached out and covered Telmé's hand with one of his own. "He was an angel hiding in the Temple of the Sacred Three. Even the High Priest did not notice. If they are the only beings more powerful than him, it sounds as though sensing him before he wanted would have been impossible."

Telmé nodded but did not look reassured. "Korin is the only real threat to him—well, Korin and Prince Kristof. He is the epitome of a Paladin and was raised well by his mother. He is a fearsome force, all the more with the Paladins at his back. It worries me Méo has not already killed them when he clearly could have done so at any time."

"I thought Korin was needed to access the Master Key?" Raffé said. "Or would an angel be able to blaze past that requirement?"

"I don't know," Telmé said quietly. "Let us hope it does require Korin." He shoved to his feet. "Come, we've held still as long as we dare."

Raffé stifled a groan and stood, wincing with every step until his stiff muscles eased with movement. He rubbed a hand over his still-sore chest, swallowed against the aching need for blood. Soon. They just had to make it to the Altar of the Breaking.

His mind grayed out as they walked, falling into a rhythm of step-step-step as they trudged on, too consumed by pain to focus on anything else. Fear gnawed at the back of his mind, a hyper-awareness that at any moment an angel could be upon them and they were not strong enough to escape a second time—and Méo had made it clear that death was not the worst that would happen to them.

The light—what little there had ever been of it—faded all too quickly. There must have been some, however, because he could still see as they walked, but it seemed as though they traveled through perfect dark. The smell grew more pungent, set his head to throbbing.

A soft, rattling sound penetrated the dull fog filling his mind. In front of him, Telmé's steps slowed ... stopped, a hand going to his sword and resting there lightly, ready to draw in a moment. "Something is coming," he said softly.

Raffé nodded, calling up his magic, hating himself all over again for losing his sword. He stepped in closer to Telmé and turned so they stood back to back, eyes surveying the darkness—

"There," he hissed, staring hard at a distant, hazy red light. It bobbed like a torch being held by someone walking slowly. "Revenant."

"Damn," Telmé replied softly, tensing as it drew closer and became more visible. Its single glowing eye was filled with bobbing red light, bones rattling softly in the dried, flapping flesh that clung to it, hung from it like tattered clothing. Sulfur and rot rolled off its body, making Raffé gag. It hissed softly, single flaming eye glowing brighter as it began to let loose its terrible, draining magic.

Normally Raffé would rush it, take it head on. That was somewhat more difficult to do when he was weak and weaponless. But he still had a better chance than Telmé. "Give me your sword."

"Don't lose it," Telmé said, a hint of a smile in his voice as he flipped the sword to Raffé.

"I shall do my best to keep it this time," Raffé said, hefting the sword. It fit well in his hand. The leather-wrapped grip was soft from use, warm from Telmé's hand, and it thrummed with residual magic from years of being used by a mage—a hellish mage, which made it that much more suited to Raffé's grip.

The icy, spider-creep of the revenant's power grew stronger, the chill wind of its soul-sucking breath. His body thrummed with heat as he brought up his magic, pulsing, rushing as it snaked through him to gather in his empty hand.

Raffé waited. Waited.

When the revenant screeched and began to *suck* in earnest, he bellowed and lunged, calling up hellish fire and bathing the blade with it. He brought the blade slashing down, cutting the revenant open from right shoulder to left hip, shifted, and did it again from the left shoulder.

He stumbled back, gasping and struggling to stay upright, clenching the sword even more tightly so he did not drop it. He watched as the revenant writhed and twisted and tried to scream, movements fading, far too slowly. At last it held still, and the magic and menace that had held it together and spawned its sickening semblance of life dripped from its bones and rotted flesh to be absorbed by the parched earth.

"I thought the revenants would stay away from us longer," Raffé said, turning and holding out the sword.

Telmé shook his head. "Keep it for now. I'm in no shape to use it, not really. Something must have them stirred up, though we should feel it too …" He sighed and shook his head again. "I don't know. Best to press on harder than ever. We should be close. The presence of holy magic on the air is growing stronger. Come." He headed off, slower than before despite his efforts but with the determination Raffé knew so well and greatly admired.

He could not fathom ever being good enough a Prince—a person—to replace Telmé. Raffé's hand tightened on the sword he held, which fit so *rightly* in his grip even as keeping it felt wrong. He would not lose it, damn it. Never again would he lose his sword.

The silence was broken some indeterminate length of time later by the raspy groans, dry shuffle, and rattling bones of dead-walkers. Seventy-nine of them.

Raffé turned and saw that thirty-one of the bastards had been slowly creeping up behind them for a while. Probably since he killed the revenant. He and Telmé must have been even more drained than he realized if they had not noticed they were being stalked by an entire horde of dead-walkers. "We're in trouble," he said softly.

Telmé just gave a sad, tired laugh as he turned around to face them. He raised a hand, hellish fire flickering—then pitched forward, collapsing on the ground. Raffé stared at him but jerked his head up at the raspy, almost crunching sound of laughing coming from the dead-walkers. They should not have been so aware, which meant they were strong, strong enough to become something even worse.

What was he supposed to do? How could he have escaped an *angel* only to die at the hands of bloody dead-walkers.

OF LAST RESORT

He was meant to have been an accountant—

Anger boiled up. No. He had never been meant for anything. No one had given him a chance—himself included. The only people to ever say he *could* be something were the Princes. He would not turn into a whining coward now.

But he wasn't stupid enough to think he could fight off so many dead-walkers in his weakened state, not when he also had to protect Telmé. Sheathing his sword, Raffé once more heaved Telmé into his arms, turned, and ran as fast as he was able, which was pathetically little, but faster than the dead-walkers would be able to catch up to easily. He hoped.

His vision began to fade after perhaps a hundred paces, entire body trembling—shaking—with the effort of carrying Telmé and running.

When he tripped, Raffé could not even be surprised. Tears of frustration pricked his eyes as he stared down at the unconscious Telmé. Blood dripped down onto Telmé's chest; Raffé pressed a trembling hand to his own chest and realized the wound inflicted by Méo had opened up again, which meant it had never even healed properly to begin with. Damn.

Raffé drew in a ragged breath, and then froze, realizing he could taste, and now feel, holy magic on the air. Stronger than it had been before when Telmé had mentioned it. Were the Paladins close, then? Close enough to hear?

The rasp and rattle came behind him, and Raffé turned to see the number of dead-walkers had increased. They thrummed with faint red light, which Raffé had never seen before. Something hellish was granting them more power. Or an angel with access to demonic power. Damn.

Pushing slowly, agonizingly to his feet, Raffé drew his sword again. He filled his lungs with air, then bellowed with all his might, "Paladins! We need you!" Hefting his sword, Raffé braced himself against attack as the dead-walkers came at him.

He only managed to cut down three of them before he was knocked off his feet, landing awkwardly to sprawl over Telmé. Dead-walkers. He gave a tear-filled laugh. Fucking dead-walkers would be what killed him and Telmé.

Rotted fingers pawed at him—

And a war-cry rent the air, filled with so much power the world seemed to shake. Blinding blue-white light flooded the space between Raffé and the dead-walkers, and they screamed before holy light burned them, drove them back.

Then Raffé was surrounded by gleaming armor and blue tunics. Feeling nauseous at the abrupt inundation of holy power, he let the world gray out.

He stirred to the sound of someone calling his name, felt the weight and strength of a heavy arm wrapped around him. Blood. He whimpered at the bright, sharp, sweet smell of pure human blood and dragged his eyes open to see Kristof staring down at him in concern. "Drink, Highness."

Raffé needed no further urging, wrapping his mouth around the wrist offered to him, sinking his fangs through soft, sweat-flavored skin, and sucking desperately at the warm blood that filled his mouth. Hard, so hard not to drink it all, swallow every last drop. With a frustrated cry he tore his mouth away, sealed the wound, and looked up into Kristof's slightly-paled face.

"Are you all right?"

Kristof huffed a soft laugh. "I am fine, Highness. You are the source of much concern, not I. Are *you* all right?"

Raffé closed his eyes and focused on the fresh blood filling up all the cracks and crevices, patching up the broken places. It burned, sharp and bright, as it worked to finally heal the wound in his chest. "I am not better yet, but thanks to you I will be. How is Prince Telmé?"

"It's taken five men to feed him so far," Kristof said, voice low, heavy with worry. "That has not happened … in longer than I care to think about. What happened?" He immediately shook his head and held up a hand. "Nevermind. Wait until we are safely back at camp."

Not giving him a chance to reply, Kristof stood, carrying Raffé as though he weighed little more than a child. Raffé started to protest, but it was so much easier to fall asleep. "Look out for Méo," he mumbled as unconsciousness rushed over him. "If you see him, kill him."

The Ninth Seal

Raffé woke to dull light and the smells of dusty earth, old tents, metal and smoke and a crush of people. He stared up at the top of the tent for a moment, then slowly sat up and looked around. It was empty, though there was another cot on the opposite end, a discarded red tunic lying across the unmade blankets, and the broken remains of a familiar bow. Axel had made it?

Relief coursed through him but could not entirely grab hold. His head felt heavy, thick. He could not seem to entirely wake. Every part of him was stiff and sore from healing, with a deep, dull ache that said there was more to heal but not quite enough blood to do it—though he hazily remembered Kristof offering his wrist. How long had he been asleep? Where were the others? He could hear the bustle of the camp, could count the exact number out there, but he could not pick out if Telmé and Kristof were among them.

At least the bustle of a camp making preparations meant nothing had yet happened. The knot in his stomach eased slightly and his mind drifted back to the need for blood, jaw aching with it.

The jangle of spurs drew his attention to the tent flap just as Kristof pulled it aside and stepped in, followed by two Priests. "Greetings, Highness," Kristof said, nodding in greeting. "It's good to see you are awake. I knew you would need more blood, so I brought along men on the chance you might be awake.

After you've fed, we've much to discuss." He motioned the Priests forward. "They've not fed anyone yet, so they've plenty of blood to offer. From the looks of that wound on your chest, you need all you can get."

Raffé grunted an acknowledgement, hunger, pain, and exhaustion making words entirely too difficult to bother with. He shoved away the blankets covering him and hauled the nearer of the two Priests in as they stepped up to his cot, sinking fangs into his neck and drinking greedily. It was not quite as rich and sweet as Kristof's blood, but it was sufficient. Shoving the first Priest away, Raffé reeled in the second, pushed him into the bedding, and buried his face in the man's throat. The Priest made a sound that might have been cut off laughter or a sigh, hands falling heavy on Raffé's shoulders to steady him, thumbs stroking soothingly over his skin. He thought he heard someone say something, and Kristof reply laughingly, but the details of the exchange held no interest. All he wanted was blood.

When he was done feeding, Raffé pressed a soft kiss to the second Priest's cheek and moved so he could stand. He thanked both Priests, who then departed. When they had gone, Raffé crouched on the ground, dizzy and hot from feeding so quickly, so ravenously.

With the hunger quenched, the grogginess faded off to be replaced by anger. By a hunger far more dangerous. He wanted the angel, wanted to tear its limbs off, crack its head open, drink its blood and devour it bone by bone.

He snarled as heavy hands dropped on his shoulders, looked up and shoved—

Stopped. Raffé drew heavy, panting breaths, braced his fists on the ground and bowed his head. "What's wrong with me?"

Kristof's voice was quiet, steadying, as he replied, "You traveled hard, fighting and running, for at least two days. When we reached you, you were nearly dead; Telmé is little better. Your demon nature is taking over, determined to live at all costs. Just breathe. Focus on memories of being human. Think—think of Alrin, if you can."

Hearing Alrin's name hurt, but the knife of pain, the stab of longing, helped calm him down. The demonic urges stood no chance against the very human love that Alrin inspired. Raffé breathed, slow and steady, for several minutes. When he began to feel more like himself, he looked up at Kristof, who watched him with a slight frown, brows draw down tight. "I'm sorry. Thank you. Are the Priests all right?"

"They're well-trained and long accustomed to hungry Princes," Kristof said with a faint smile. "If I had thought they were in danger I would have handled it, but you never gave me even a moment of alarm. You have admirable control. Are you well?"

"I will be," Raffé said and accepted the hand Kristof held out, letting Kristof haul him to his feet. "How long have I been asleep? What has happened? Did Axel return?"

Kristof offered another faint, wry smile. "You've only been asleep a few hours. Whatever demon gave you its blood, it was not one to be trifled with. Telmé is still asleep, but he seems to have suffered more. Axel returned, in far worse shape than you." Kristof flicked his gaze to the empty cot, face clouding. "We thought we had stabilized him, but he faltered again about an hour ago and the Priests took him to their tents. He will make it, I think, but it will take time."

Raffé's mouth twisted. "I was sure he was dead. Méo nearly killed all of us. He came far too close with Telmé. I still do not know what he did. Telmé's eyes glowed holy blue, and he stood there like a statue, responding to nothing, completely helpless. I managed to break him out of it, but I could not begin to tell you how."

"Méo ... that is the second time you have said Méo is responsible for this," Kristof said. "Axel said his name as well, but he's been too weak to talk to us. What is going on?"

Blowing out a frustrated breath as he recalled all that had transpired since they had landed in Lass, Raffé said, "Méo summoned the angel Umah, and he has been working toward exacting vengeance upon the Legion all these years." Kristof hissed, and by the time Raffé had recounted the tale, he practically crackled with anger and magic.

"He is not the only one to have lost someone! He is not the only one to suffer. How bloody fucking *dare he*—" Kristof spun away, slammed his fists down on a nearby table, sending papers scattering and dishes tumbling off to clang or shatter on the ground. "I will tear him limb from limb myself. Does he understand what he has done in unleashing an angel? And not just any angel—no that fucking *fool* had to call down one of the most dangerous. Umah is the Angel of Wrath and Vengeance, the living embodiment of the Goddesses' displeasure. His sole purpose is to bring terrible justice wherever he is ordered. There are very good reasons only the High Priest may call forth angels."

Raffé did not think there was anything worse than watching men who normally seemed unafraid of anything fall prey to terror. To think he had once been afraid of attending a *dinner party*. "We'll stop him. Goddesses know how, but that is our purpose and we shall not fail."

Kristof sighed and nodded. "No, we shall not. As to that … walk with me. There is something I want to show you."

"As you wish. Are there—" he broke off as Kristof pointed to a pile of clean clothes. "Thank you." Raffé pulled on the fresh hose, undertunic, and tunic before picking up the … "This is Telmé's sword belt. Why is it here?"

"You had his sword and seemed pretty intent on keeping it—even unconscious you would not let go of it until we were in camp and had you in bed. Telmé will not miss it anytime soon." Kristof shrugged. "Figured you may as well use it."

Raffé frowned but buckled it into place. He had only borrowed it while he and Telmé struggled to reach safety. He had no desire to keep it, no matter how well it fit his hand. "I lost mine escaping Méo. Telmé gave it to me because he was too weak to use it against the revenants that came after us. But I should not be using it anymore; there are plenty of other swords I can use."

"It belonged to Prince Tunç," Kristof said quietly. "His mentor and the previous Commander of the Legion. It's his most precious possession after the necklace that Korin gave him."

"I …" Raffé shook his head, at a loss. It was necessity alone that had provoked his taking it, which seemed wrong. "I definitely should not have it then."

"Telmé trusted it to you, and as I said, even unconscious you would not be parted from it. I think Telmé would want you to retain it while he recovers."

"If you say so," Raffé said. He curled his fingers around the hilt reflexively, unable to deny it still felt warm and right in his hand. He would keep it only until Telmé woke. "Lead the way, Highness."

Snorting, Kristof spun around and strode from the tent. He led Raffé through camp, nodding and calling to various men but not pausing. Raffé kept his eyes on Kristof's back, not in the mood to face the stares he could feel on his skin—at a loss as to why everyone was staring so hard.

He breathed a soft sigh when they finally left the camp behind, though the rankness of the air grew more acute and made him sneeze. Their boots crunched on broken shards of dusty, fragile rock and dried bones as Kristof wended through a maze of towering boulders and a crumbling mountainside. "What is this place?" Raffé asked softly.

"All that remains of a once powerful place," Kristof replied. "I've only read of it in old books that were poor copies of books long rotted with age. I never thought to see it." They turned a corner and Raffé drew to a halt, startled and struck with an unexpected sadness as he stared at the ruins before him. The stone was faded, a pale, dusty red-brown. He had seen such stone before when it was still a rich, dark crimson. Bloodstone it was called, a remarkably uncreative name that had always made him roll his eyes.

Kristof made the sign of the Goddesses, whispering a soft prayer. "All that remains of the Temple of Spilled Blood, the origin of the Temples of the Sacred Heart and the Sacred Three. It was here that a man or woman was declared the first Priest of the Broken Heart." He smiled faintly at Raffé's puzzled look. "That's the original name of the High Priests. A bit … much, which is why the title is practically never used."

Raffé wrinkled his nose but made no comment. Kristof resumed walking, picking his way carefully through and around the ruins until he stopped in what seemed to be the approximate center of them. The space was wide, long, and reminded Raffé passingly of the sanctuary of the Temple of the Sacred Three.

They stood on large marble tiles—almost more like panels, really—that seemed impressively intact. Three of them were set in a neat row, covered with deep-carved runes that Raffé could not read. Håkon had been teaching him to read magic, but it was a skill that took mages years to master.

"They're too perfectly intact to be anything but magically protected," Kristof said, clutching the edge of his heavy, dark blue cloak in one hand, the other hand resting lightly on the hilt of his sword. "I can't read much of it. This sort of thing would take a Priest or a Sorcerer. But I know that accessing whatever is sealed here requires a sacrifice."

"Doesn't all of it," Raffé said bitterly. "What's the point of all of this if everything we do requires someone to die or risk death. What's the point of protecting life if we can only do that with death?"

Kristof rubbed at his face with one hand and sighed. "I asked my mother that once, back when I was still a boy in training. The Reach of the North has a long, bloody history of sacrifice, more than the rest of the country. It's something we wish would quietly go away, but the bloodstains are always there. My mother is quite knowledgeable on the subject because she believes it's stupid to be ignorant of such an important part of our history, and the more terrible it is the more important it is to know. At the time, I thought she was wrong, because I was young and cocky and thought bad things were best forgotten. But I asked her why, if it was so bloody important that we keep everyone alive, did we keep demanding that people die to do it? Was that not counterproductive? And she said the most powerful and dangerous things were locked up behind doors of death with keys of pain in the hopes that people would realize life was far too precious and the power was not worth the price. That when that proves to be true, we will truly begin to drive back this hell we've brought to earth."

"Your mother sounds … fierce." Her words certainly made Raffé stop and think, and feel small for not having thought of that himself.

"She is," Kristof said softly. "It is not an easy calling to be High Priestess of the Sacred Heart. I wish I had listened to her more often than I did. Without her I would never have found Håkon again. If I had listened to her from the start …" He shrugged and gestured to the tiles. "I can tell that whatever these seal away, it requires a sacrifice to open. I am fairly certain it says something about a *willing* sacrifice by … something or someone, I cannot quite tell. A powerful position, I know that much, but those runes are not for the High Priest, which are the only ones I recognize easily."

Sacrifice. Even if they were as much a necessary evil as the Princes, he was damned tired of the word. No one truly wanted to die, least of all to purposefully throw their lives away on the uncertain chance others might live. Even on a certain chance. He remembered exactly how he had felt when he had offered himself for his parents, and *willing* was not what he'd felt at all. "I cannot fathom that anyone willingly sacrifices themselves for something like this."

Kristof laughed. Raffé raised his brows. Chuckling fading off, Kristof said, "Funny words coming from you, Highness, when you very willingly sacrificed yourself for your family."

"I don't think it's willing when it feels like there is little choice in the matter, when the motive is inherently selfish," Raffé said with a grimace. "I hated myself, but I had no real drive to change me or my circumstance. My family was a bunch of bastards, but I do not know that I was all that better. It seemed the right thing to do, but it was also an escape. That's not a willing sacrifice."

"Many scholars would agree with you," Kristof replied. He lightly scuffed across the runes with one boot, frowning pensively at them. "A true sacrifice is something precious surrendered freely without the burdens of duress and desperation. As no one resorts to such methods unless it is a dire situation, the idea of sacrifice is itself inherently flawed. They work, but only because if you throw enough force at a door it is bound to break open eventually. It is not the same as using a key. But this …" He touched the stone with his boot again. "This does require a true sacrifice, and it's old magic that has survived centuries. Given what has brought us to this location …" He looked back up at Raffé. "I believe this is the Ninth Seal, meant to be opened by the Master Key. But I think, like the other Seals, that it must be brought out first. Something must be sacrificed to retrieve the Ninth Seal, and only then can all the Seals be brought together with the

Master Key to open the Entrance. Only supposition of course, but it makes sense."

Raffé nodded. "That's not why you brought me all the way out here, though. Something about the sacrifice, past that it must be truly willing, troubles you."

"Willing is troubling enough." Kristof jabbed at the stone again. "A true sacrifice is committed via *suicide*. Someone must kill themselves on these stones to bring forth the Ninth Seal, if all my supposition is correct. And it must be someone of power, but I cannot tell if it is a specific someone or merely *anyone* of power. If it must be the king, or any royal, or even someone like me or Telmé—leaders of our respective units, and of course, Telmé is Commander of the entire Legion. After the king and high Priest, he is the most powerful figure in the land." Kristof gave him a long look. "Though, if he is incapable, the passing of the sword formally marks you his heir and therefore suitable to take his place."

"I knew there was more to the sword than you were telling me, back in the tent," Raffé groused.

Kristof smiled fleetingly. "I, of course, am next after him. I do not know what any of this means, or what will come to pass, but I thought you should be aware of what it might all come to."

"Hopefully we are able to stop Méo before anything comes to pass in this place," Raffé said quietly. "Thank you for telling me. I am sorry I am not Telmé, or even suitably trained to be his heir. I should not have his sword."

Kristof spread his arms. "The Goddesses spilled Their Blood that we might walk our own paths, but Their Touch still falls where They think it must. Hold fast to the sword, Highness, and a legacy of Princes will hold fast to you and lend their strength." Distant voices carried on the wind, breaking the strange private world in which they had been standing. Kristof clapped him on the shoulder. "Come, we should return to the others so I can explain what has happened and we can figure out what to do next."

Raffé followed him back through the ruins and the winding path between the rocks and mountain, back into camp where the familiar smells of people, burning fires, and roasting meat filled the air, dampening the fetid, rotting smell of Zyke Lorn Fall.

"Why does everyone keep staring at me?" Raffé asked in a low voice, fighting an urge to hunch in, make himself as small and uninteresting as possible.

Kristof shot him a brief grin. "Until now, it was an unspoken thing between a small group of us that you would become the next Commander. But now you carry Telmé's sword, which as I said, makes it official. Even if he takes it back when he wakes, the declaration has been made: You are Telmé's heir."

"I have not even been a Prince of the Blood a year," Raffé said. "It seems a rash decision."

Kristof shrugged. "Prince Telmé was declared the Commander's heir the very day he was born. When he was only sixteen, most of the castle was felled by poison, including all of the Princes. He became a Prince a few days later and had to rebuild the Princes of the Blood more or less alone. Believe me, you are already far more prepared than he ever was; he would be the first to tell you. Come." He led the way into a large tent close to the center of camp, but they both whipped around when the sentries gave a sudden cry.

Turning in the direction they signaled, Raffé stared in surprise at the beautiful black griffons flying toward them—the black griffons of the king. Behind him came several other gold griffons, and one of them flew the banners of the king and the Princes.

Raffé ran ahead of Kristof to the landing field, going straight to Håkon and Yrian. "You're all safe."

"Barely," Håkon said. He started to say something else but froze when his gaze landed on the sword at Raffé's left hip. He hissed, eyes flaring hell-red, and surged forward to yank Raffé close by the front of his tunic and snarled, "Where in the hell is Telmé?"

"Resting," Raffé said quietly. "Méo almost killed him. He's still recovering."

Kristof stepped in and settled his heavy hands on Håkon's shoulders, gently tugging him away. Turning him around, Kristof gently traced the lines of Håkon's cheek with his fingertips. "Be a little kinder to the one who kept Telmé alive long enough for us to save him."

Grunting softly, Håkon turned his head and pressed a brief kiss to Kristof's fingers before pulling away and turning to face Raffé once more. "I'm glad you're both well. You— Did you say Méo?"

"Yes," Raffé said as King Waldemar, Prince Birgir, and all the Princes of the Blood gathered around him. Beyond their small circle everyone from the camp gathered, and Raffé pitched his voice to reach them all as he told his tale one more time.

By the end of it he felt drained, and did not protest when Yrian curled a hand around his upper arm, guided him back to camp, and pushed him down onto a bedroll before a campfire. Raffé stared across the flames and saw King Waldemar sit down. "Majesty, my apolo—"

"Forget it," Waldemar said. "Thank you for performing so well. If not for you and Axel, our situation would be far worse."

Raffé swallowed. "I take it that since all of you are gathered here, the last seals were taken?"

"Yes," Yrian said sourly, scowling at the dirt, letting go of the Priest he still held when the man winced in pain. "Sorry." He motioned for the Priest to go, murmuring another apology. Once all the Princes had been fed and the Priests had departed, leaving only the Princes and the two royals, Yrian added, "It was an angel—a piece of an angel, rather, that came upon us. We tried to fight it, but we were no match. I think it *let* us get away. We returned to the castle, and not too soon after, so did the others. His Majesty said we must all come here." He looked to Waldemar.

"Though I had hoped to avoid having to make this last stand, I fear that is what it has come to," Waldemar replied. "I never would have guessed Méo, however." His eyes glimmered ever so briefly, and Raffé wondered if it was Waldemar or Satrina who spoke. He supposed there was little difference. "Méo will bring the eight seals here. He lacks only the Master Key, which is beyond his complete control now, and the Ninth Seal, which I will now also take from his control."

"That will make it impossible for him to open the Entrance?" Premisl asked.

Waldemar shook his head. "No, the possibility is still there, but ... it puts in place an impediment that he cannot overcome. Not easily, anyway. That is all I am saying on the matter for now. I suggest you all get rest while you can. He will be here far sooner than any of us likes, and I suspect Korin and Alrin will be arriving shortly as well."

Raffé's felt like he'd been struck by holy light. "What? Alrin is dead by now."

"The sacrifice of the Master Key is split in half," Waldemar said quietly. "Half his life given to become the key, the other half to use it."

Rage—hate—turned Raffé's vision hell-red. He stood up and stormed from the fire before he did something stupid, like plunge through the flames to slit the king's throat.

It had been bad enough to watch Alrin leave, to be forced to watch him head off toward his death. But to learn that Alrin was not quite dead yet, and Raffé would have to watch him die? If this was how he was meant to spend the rest of his life, in a constant state of fear and anger and despair, always a knot of dread in his stomach for what terrible thing might happen next …

His anger went out like a snuffed candle, the last bits of it curling and fading away in the air. He was Legion; that was their lot. If he was to someday lead them he had best become better at enduring—handling—it.

All the same, he was grateful that no one chased after him. Bad enough to lose Cambord, then Alrin … must Raffé lose him again? How many times must he watch Alrin vanish from his life and be helpless to stop it.

The air seemed restless all around him, more of a breeze blowing about than he could recall ever feeling while he and Telmé fled across Zyke Lorn Fall. He could not wait to leave the damnable place, scrub it from his skin, and bury the memories of it deep in the recesses of his mind.

A short distance away he could hear as the camp grew livelier while they ate supper and quiet again as everyone bedded down or settled into their sentry posts. The lingering scent of smoke and cooked meat wafted over him, but he was still so gorged on blood all he felt was an ache for company. All that did was remind him afresh of Alrin and further blacken his mood.

The jangle of spurs drew him from his brooding, and he looked up to see Waldemar, Birgir, and Kristof walking toward him. Straightening, pushing away from the boulder he'd been leaning against, Raffé waited for them to reach him. "What's wrong?"

"Come with us," Waldemar said.

Raffé was not surprised that Waldemar led them back through the boulders and into the ruins. It was impossible, in the distorted air of Zyke Lorn Fall, to tell the time of day, but sunlight or moonlight seemed to make the rune-covered tiles glow faintly. Waldemar stood in the center of them and turned to face Raffé, Birgir, and Kristof. Looking at Raffé, he said, "Kristof has already told you what he deduced of this place."

"Yes, Majesty," Raffé replied.

"Then I will tell you that he was correct. This is the Ninth Seal. It does require a sacrifice—mine."

"Majesty—"

Waldemar held up a hand. "These protections were laid by the first of the Guldbrandsen line, and we would never ask of our people what we would not ask of ourselves. The Ninth Seal is my responsibility, and it's already done."

"Already ...?" Raffé asked.

"Poison," Waldemar said, smile wan. "It nearly killed me once, and it shall succeed this second time, but it is of my choosing and freely taken." The smile faded. "However, once freed, the Ninth Seal is yours to take, Prince Raffé—yours to become."

Raffé nodded, although he had absolutely no idea what he was agreeing to. "Why me? I am not the only who must be thinking I am too new, too inexperienced, to bear such an important responsibility."

"Telmé and Korin can no longer do it. Events I did not anticipate, could not prevent, warped them. For better and for worse. I've gone all these years hoping it would not matter, but my decision has endangered all of us. You're what we have."

"A last resort," Raffé said, recalling the fear he had felt, tasted, when he had told this man he would take his brother's place in the Blooding. "I can do that."

"A last hope," Waldemar corrected, his voice the gentlest Raffé had ever heard it. He abruptly coughed and dropped to his knees, body jerking, seizing.

"Father!" Birgir strode up to him, kneeling and draping an arm over his father's shoulders, holding him close. Waldemar held fast to his second hand, face curling into Birgir's shoulder as he endured the poison. Birgir's voice was softer, shakier, as he repeated, "Father."

Raffé looked away, feeling like an intruder. Kristof caught his eye, expression saying he felt much the same. They half-turned, close by in case something happened but offering as much privacy as they could. The pain and love in Birgir's voice, a love clearly returned by the king, was such a stark contrast to Raffé's last night with his family.

"You'll be a good king," Waldemar whispered. "And you'll always have Satrina to guide you." Waldemar lifted and turned his head just enough to look at Raffé, who turned back to face him directly. "You have forged a nigh-unbreakable bond. Use it. The Ninth Seal is …"

Waldemar went lax and still in Birgir's arms. Tears fell down Birgir's face as he laid his father's body down, gently folding his arms across his chest. Only then did Raffé notice that he already wore the royal ring. Slowly standing, Birgir stepped away as the marble tiles began to glow increasingly bright. The light consumed Waldemar's body, seemed to absorb it. Raffé covered his eyes as the light brightened to the point of pain—

And then all seemed dark. He slowly lowered his hand and realized he stood in … nothing. Dark, endless nothing. "What …" his voice seemed to echo softly. "Where is everyone?"

Grimacing at the echo, he stopped speaking. What was going on?

Blood of Manon.

Raffé whipped around. Nothing.

Something brushed along the back of his neck. "Who's there?" he demanded and flinched at the loud echo.

You are of the blood of Manon.

"What …" Raffé paused as realization dawned. "Manon is a demon."

Was a demon. Summoned to the mortal world, lost there. You are his get. Child-demon of riches. Of greed. Tempter of men to need more and more and more.

"I don't know what that means except that I'm good with numbers."

OF LAST RESORT

The wispy voice seemed to laugh, and something like cold fingers trailed over his skin again.

"Are you the Ninth Seal?"

I am a minor demon like you, long before they were given fancy titles and duties. Sacrificed to make a last protection against those who would destroy the world. If you are granted access to me, my Mistress has deemed you worthy and a queen is dead.

"King, actually. There's not been a queen for three generations."

A pity. I think queens better suited to leading countries. Are you to be the Ninth Seal? Do you want to be?

"I think I have no choice," Raffé said quietly. "And I am tired of playing your games. There are people waiting for me. Make me the Ninth Seal or kill me, but stop playing."

Are you so eager to rush into the arms of death, then, child-demon?

Raffé closed his eyes, not even remotely surprised that Waldemar had failed to mention being the Ninth Seal would mean dying. Of course it did. "Death?" he asked anyway.

The eight seals can only be woken when they are brought together at the entrance and united by the Ninth Seal. That forms the door. To open that door, open the Entrance, the Master Key must break—kill— the Ninth Seal.

Not certain how else to react, Raffé began to laugh. It was a jagged, sharp-edged sound, dripping with the tears that streamed down his cheeks. "Do it," he said. "If Alrin is to be the Master Key, then I shall be the Ninth Seal and damn them all to the depths of hell."

So be it.

Raffé gasped as something reminiscent of arms wrapped around him, like being embraced by a being made of ice. Winter-cold lips pressed against his and a freezing heat filled his body. He tried to scream but couldn't. Tried to breathe but only struggled in a silent, frozen panic—

And then he gasped, stared wide-eyed and lost at Kristof and Birgir. "What happened?" he finally said, shivering from the remnants of cold.

"I-I could not say," Kristof said, shaking his head. "You stood there, eyes blank, and then suddenly they were not blank. Are you all right?"

"Fine," Raffé said. "I feel strange, but I'm fine. I think."

"Your skin looks strange," Birgir said. "Like ... it's been tattooed with white ink."

Raffé lifted his hands, pushed back the long sleeves of his undertunic, and saw what Birgir meant. They were so faint they were barely visible, but the marks were there. "I've become the Ninth Seal. The other eight cannot wake without me to bind them."

Kristof looked him over several times, brow drawn down. "I ... thought you would be different. Something else."

"I am," Raffé said, closing his eyes as a cold, wispy voice seemed to giggle in his ear before it was lost on the wind. The longer he stood there, the more firmly he returned to the real world—the mortal world—the more aware he became of all the changes. "I am the blood of Manon, demon prince of wealth and greed. I know the number of coins in your purse from the way they jingle. I know the number of men in the camp from the sounds they make. I can hear the shuffle and groan of five thousand and thirty-seven dead-walkers slowly approaching this camp. Counting is a trifling thing." His mouth curved as he opened his eyes. He felt powerful. Alive in a way that made humanity an amusing attempt at living. Why would anyone want to be human when they could be a demon? "I know how to measure the want of every man. I know how to determine the price each is willing to pay to obtain what he thinks he needs." He knew how to convince them to pay that price, how to make them happy to suffer if only it meant they got what they thought they wanted.

Kristof rested a hand lightly on the hilt of his sword, eyes shimmering with banked holy magic. "Are you dangerous?"

Raffé shook his head. "Extremely, but not to the Legion, not to the kingdom. I have my own greeds. The seal makes me stronger to protect it. Should I turn against that, the seal will turn against me. I'll be locked away again, and it will take another sacrificed king or queen to bring me back out." He closed his eyes, feeling out more of what he had become. "I am only for the Master Key. Any other will be killed, and should I be killed by another anyway, I will be sealed away again." He opened his eyes again, stared at them. "I am the Ninth Seal and meant only for that purpose."

Birgir shook his head. "You are far removed from the man whose voice trembled as he told the king he would die in his brother's place."

"Merely awakened. Human fears are as nothing to me," Raffé replied, suddenly feeling hungry. "We should return to camp." He looked at Birgir, who was barely holding back his grief, face tight, hands trembling slightly, and his hunger—his new eagerness, new power—calmed as he was reminded abruptly of what it was like to be human. How much it had hurt to say goodbye to Alrin, who shortly would try to kill him. Perhaps humanity was still something to him after all. "I am sorry."

Birgir nodded stiffly. "We all have our duties. We all make sacrifices. My father always knew his life might end this way. He has long been at peace with it."

"Peace," Kristof muttered but said nothing further, only swept ahead of them to lead the way back to camp.

BOND

Telmé was awake when they returned. He stood in the center of a cluster of Paladins so excited to see him awake and looking well they had forgotten propriety to clap him on the shoulder and back, squeeze his arm and shake his hands. They all slowly went still, however, when they saw Raffé and the others return—and noticed that Waldemar was missing.

Striding over to a barrel, Kristof leapt neatly up onto it. A nearby sentry blew his horn, gathering the whole of the camp. When everyone had fallen silent, Kristof bellowed, "The king is dead." Real silence fell then, as even fidgeting and fussing and murmuring faded off. A cluster of Priests, standing close to Kristof, began softly to sing a mourning hymn. The soldiers nearest them joined in, and quickly the song spread through the camp.

When it faded off several minutes later, Kristof recited a prayer that was echoed by the camp. As those words too faded away, he spread his arms. In front of the barrel, Birgir lifted his bowed head, sad but determined as Kristof bellowed out, "Long live the King!"

"Long live the King!" the camp shouted back, so loud the high canyon walls around them seemed to shake with it.

Birgir nodded to all of them, murmured something to the men nearest him as they bowed, then turned and vanished into his tent.

The crowd around Telmé slowly dispersed, and he walked over to them, face lined with sadness but not surprise. He looked Raffé carefully up and down before finally meeting his eyes. "I am sorry this burden fell to you."

Raffé shrugged, looking out over the camp, mentally counting and cataloguing. The hyper-counting had always been there, ready to be used, but now he couldn't *stop.* Coins. Links of armor. Swords. People. Dogs. Griffons. Tents. Boots. On and on and on. Wants and desires came to him in the way people moved, what they said, the things they carried and the quantities of certain items they possessed. His skin prickled with an urge to tempt them, see how far they would go to be given what they wanted, to take all that they carelessly threw away for the chance of some superficial gain. Greed was the easiest weakness to prey upon.

Hands fell heavy on his shoulders. He startled, stared blankly before he comprehended Telmé. "Sorry."

"Don't be sorry. There's no need," Telmé said quietly. "Breathe. Focus on me. Focus on … on Alrin. He, I think, most keeps you human." A faint, sad smile twisted his mouth. "You look as you do when numbers fill your head but worsened, as though you are trying to count every stone on the mountain."

"I could," Raffé said, fighting an urge to do precisely that now the idea had been put there. "Every stone, every shard, every boulder and rock and pebble. The only things I cannot count are the stars in the sky, for they are the domain of another and nothing to do with avarice." He jerked away from Telmé, covered his eyes with the heel of his hand, and breathed slow and deep as he tried to remember the feel of Alrin's skin, the press of his mouth. The sound of his laughter, the warmth of his eyes. "I do not like this. I want to find the weakness of every person here and use it to break them. I want to laugh as they surrender true wealth for trivial. I want to lap up their pain as they realize their mistake."

Raffé froze in shock when Telmé *hugged* him. He smelled faintly ill, as though not quite as recovered as he wanted everyone think. His breathing was unsteady, his heart half a beat slower than usual. He smelled of sweat, blood, wool, and the metal tang of his lined leather armor. Not certain what else to do, Raffé raised stiff arms to return the embrace.

"Hold strong," Telmé murmured. "Remember how to be human. It will be over …" he trailed off as the sentries all cried out, and the Paladins throughout the camp pointed at something in the sky.

Telmé drew back and turned, staring wide-eyed at the creature flying toward them. Two somethings, actually. The one with wings carried another in his arms. His skin prickled as he watched their rapid approach. The man flying … something … the wings were beautiful, the dark purple-blue-black of a bruise, gleaming where dulled sunlight managed to catch them. His hair was the same color, falling to just past his ears in jagged edges as though poorly—

"It's Alrin," Raffé burst out. "Goddesses, it's Alrin."

He rushed to the landing field as the winged figure gracefully dove and landed in a crouch on the ground. The four enormous wings on his back fluttered, flexed, then folded in.

"Korin," Telmé breathed as they all saw who it was that Alrin held cradled in his arms. Making a soft, pained noise, Telmé ran up to him and took Korin away, sinking to his knees with a soft sob that Raffé doubted any but the Princes could hear. "What—what—"

Alrin dipped his head low in apology. "An angel's minion came after us. Korin destroyed it, but that combined with breaking the seal on the Master Key ... his aura was nearly depleted. He rests. I do not know..."

Raffé reeled back as Telmé screamed, a high, angry, anguished sound that provoked tears so abruptly he did not at first realize he was crying. Holding Korin close, Telmé stood, turned, and strode from the clearing. The crowd gathered around Alrin parted for him, heads bowed low, the only sound in the sudden silence the occasional sniffle or jangle of armor and spurs.

When he was gone, Raffé slowly turned back to Alrin, who was watching him intently, the wings on his back twitching. "I ..." Raffé shook his head, unable to look away from the man he had thought he'd already lost forever. "You look different." His legs were stiff as he forced them to work, slowly walking over to Alrin. He stared at the strange tattoo of the Sacred Heart in the space over Alrin's heart. "What happened?"

"I'm not entirely sure," Alrin replied. "I was unconscious for most of it. But I'm not a dragon anymore. That was the first half of the sacrifice. Stripped of my strength, my power, left only human, then given this ... form, I suppose, to protect myself."

"I don't see how this is better protection than a dragon," Raffé said, finally surrendering to the impulse, the need, to touch—

And reared back with a cry when light sparked between them, jolting through him with a crackle-burn. Alrin's wings snapped out as he stepped back even further, tensed as though to spring into the air. His eyes glowed red-blue-purple, chest heaving, jaw clenched. "Don't—don't come near me."

"You need to kill me," Raffé said quietly. "You're the Master Key. I'm the seal you have to break."

"I don't—why would they do this?" Alrin demanded, voice cracking. "I do. I want to tear you apart, feel your blood pour over my hands." Tears streamed down his face, and he clutched at his head as his drive to kill warred with his desire to protect.

Raffé did not know what to say or do. The longer he stood there, the harder it was to be close to Alrin. He could feel the Master's Key need to kill him. Felt his own impulse to surrender—to be the Ninth Seal and open the way to hell. He needed to get away before they both fell prey to their new purposes.

All the words on his tongue were bitter, angry, and would help nothing. Around him, the other Princes gathered protectively, and Raffé protested only briefly before he let Dalibor drag him away. "This isn't right."

"Neither is an entire army of monsters led by blood-drinking demons," Dalibor replied. "But it's the world we made, and we can only fight with what we're given."

"Che," Raffé said but let the matter drop. He turned to look over his shoulder and could just barely see the top of Alrin's head where he had been surrounded by Priests and Paladins. He looked up, their eyes caught—and Raffé turned away, depressed. Cambord was there but all dark where he had been fair, close but beyond reach, a lover turned killer.

You have forged a nigh-unbreakable bond, Waldemar had said. Raffé had thought he'd meant Alrin, but that bond was quite obviously severed. The eyes that had glowed emerald-bright as they stared at him had turned the color of a fresh bruise, sharp with a magic-rooted need to kill him. An obsessive desire to keep him had turned into an obsessive desire to kill. If his bond with a dragon had been their last resort ...

What do we do now?" Raffé asked.

"We wait," Dalibor said.

Raffé made a face. "I'm tired of waiting."

"Aren't we all," Håkon replied, coming up on Raffé's left. "But we are not strong enough to kill an angel. The Princes of the Blood are good for much, and we have always been the slight advantage the Legion needs to hold back hell on earth, but we are still minor demons and cannot hope to kill a being made to slaughter us. Our only hope is this last stand, to use the seals against it. Though I couldn't fucking tell you how. Hopefully the Priests know." He sighed and looked toward Telmé's tent. "I hope Telmé has something to offer."

"Leave him," came Athanasi's voice from behind them. They all stopped and turned. Athanasi's expression was sad but touched with pride and affection as he stared at Telmé's tent. "Those two have done enough, and they've done it longer than anyone who came before them. We will solve this problem."

Raffé nodded. "So we wait for Méo. I don't like it."

"It feels as though we stand at a cliff and can hear footsteps coming behind us but are helpless to keep from being pushed off the edge," Håkon said.

Dalibor narrowed his eyes at him. "I will cut your tongue out if you do not still it."

OF LAST RESORT

Håkon gestured crudely.

"Dead-walkers!" A sentry called out. "Thousands of them!" He began to furiously ring a bell that echoed deafeningly throughout the camp, shaking the fragile walls of mountain that surrounded them.

Kristof burst from his tent, looked to the sentry, then climbed up on the barrel he had used earlier and looked out beyond the camp. Swearing loudly, a haze of power around him, eye glowing briefly, he bellowed out, "Paladins prepare for battle!" Leaping down, he vanished into his tent again, followed by three men.

Only a short time later he re-emerged in full plate armor, hair braided back, pulling his helmet on and settling it in place before accepting the reins of his horse. He mounted easily, his warhorse, outfitted in its own armor, seemingly untroubled by all the weight it carried.

Raffé drew his own sword and raced out of camp, the other three close behind. The rest of the Princes joined them, forming a long line. "Five thousand one hundred and eighty-six. The number has increased since I last counted them," Raffé said, skimming over the army of dead-walkers. "Still more come from further afield to lend their numbers. Something is strange about them."

"They're threaded," Håkon said, eyes glowing bright yellow. "Something summoned them from across Zyke Lorn Fall, brought them together, is keeping them bound, and ordered them to kill us at all costs. But … this is a paltry attack. The Paladins don't even need us for this."

"You think it's a distraction," Raffé said.

Håkon nodded. "Yes."

"Agreed," Athanasi added and up and down the line the other Princes nodded or voiced agreement.

Silence fell. They waited for him. It wasn't fucking *fair*. He had been a prince for mere months. He wasn't fit to make such decisions. He tried to think of what Telmé would do—but it was the demon part of him that rose up, amused and impatient, lazily counting and marking and making a decision that seemed suddenly obvious. "Leave two of us here on the battlefield in case there is something amiss we've not yet noticed. The rest return to camp, where we are most likely to be needed."

"I'll stay," Dalibor declared. "Lassē, remain with me." The two Princes stepped forward out of line and plunged straight into the fight as the Paladins came thundering up and past.

Raffé withdrew, the other Princes around and behind him, and headed back toward camp—

And screamed as the world burst with holy blue light.

Something hot-scalding-searing wrapped around his throat and limbs, lifting him off his feet. He tried to scream again, feeling blood pouring out wherever the hot *things* touched his skin, burning through fabric and armor as though they were paper. He could not draw breath, could not do anything but endure the smell of blood and burning flesh, the screams and sobs of pain that surrounded him. "Wh—?"

He was dropped abruptly, grunting as he slammed to the ground, whimpering as all his fresh wounds protested the abrasive treatment. He could feel them trying to heal, but like the wound in his chest, the fact they were caused by holy magic made them far more difficult to heal.

OF LAST RESORT

Raffé managed to get to his knees, but when he looked up, all he saw was light and smoke, glimpses of dangling bodies, snatches of blinding blue light that flashed in and out.

A muffled thumping sound, like someone—several someones—pounding against a hard, padded surface. Coughing hoarsely, lungs and throat burning, he forced himself to his feet and stumbled through the smoke trying to find the source of the sound.

He ran into it so hard he was thrown to the ground again. He blinked, shook his head, and stared at the way Paladins and three Princes pounded on *air* as though there was an invisible wall there. He could hear the pounding, but all their screaming and shouting made no sound at all. Slowly standing again, Raffé reached out and flattened his hand against the invisible barrier. Goddesses damn it.

A familiar form appeared in front of him, and he looked up to meet Kristof's eyes. He splayed his hands across the barrier, cocked his head. Kristof shook his head. He couldn't break it, damn. Raffé nodded, then turned away, drawing his sword as he vanished back into the swirl of acrid blue-white smoke, following the sound of screams and the smell of blood not quite buried by the smoke.

When he stumbled unexpectedly through the smoke, he froze, too horrified to move as he took in the devastation of the camp. Everything was gone, destroyed, burned to ash and smeared across the dry, cracked ground. Bodies of those who had remained in camp lay scattered about, many of them burned, the rest likely to end that way soon.

In the very center of the destruction, a circle of runes had been scorched into the earth, glowing blue-white, lurid against the blackened earth. Eight bodies had been placed in regular intervals around the circle, pinned there with swords through their arms, legs, or torsos: Athanasi, Tollak, Håkon, Premisl, Yrian, Göker, Božidar, and Axel. Half of them were unconscious; the rest looked at him with despair. And Raffé realized his mistake—he had listened too much to his demon self, forgotten he was the Ninth Seal and wanted to be opened. He had ordered most of the princes remain in camp, ensuring disaster. Damn it. No one ever should have trusted him.

Looking beyond the circle, he saw the bodies of the other Princes. Two were definitely dead, their heads removed and lying nearby—Magnus and Cemal. Raffé made a low, rough noise.

Where were Telmé and Korin? They had never needed the Commander and High Priest so badly—where the hell were they?

Before he could figure it out, movement caught his eye. Raffé stared at the chains dangling from the smoke in the center. They seemed covered ... no, the chains seemed to be *made* from blue and silver fire. As he watched, the chains flicked out, striking the trapped Princes before slowly withdrawing into the smoke. Raffé watched as the smoke slowly began to dissipate, breath freezing in his lungs at the *thing* was revealed. It seemed to be composed entirely of those chains of fire, or they were wrapped so tightly around whatever was beneath them that they gave the thing some vague, human shape. Only the head-like portion remained uncovered, though it was a head only in the barest sense of the word, the vague shape of it. Every bit of space was covered in eyes that glowed from palest silver to a blue so dark it nearly seemed black.

They blinked randomly, something about the out-of-sync nature of it unsettling Raffé further.

The chains dripped down like tentacles, undulating, jerking, swinging out to inflict more pain, as alive as the octopuses Raffé was fleetingly reminded of. He sheathed his sword with shaking hands, then made himself take a step forward. Another step. Chains shot out toward him.

Raffé flinched. But the chains froze just short of touching him, the heat of them burning and blistering his skin. He slowly looked up and saw that most of the eerie eyes were focused on him, burning brilliant blue. There was so much holy power in the air that Raffé could feel his own power slowly leeching away.

Why had they ever thought they could defeat an angel?

The Ninth Seal. The Master Seal. The blood of the Prince of Avarice boils in you. Come closer, child-demon. Come and open the Entrance. You know you stand no chance now.

Raffé considered resisting, but he was the only one who would *not* be hurt for defiance. If they stood any chance of coming out of the mess, the only way was to blaze through it. Jaw clenched, he batted the chains away and stepped forward, refusing to react to the way they darted out to leave pockmarks of burns all over his body. They withdrew only as he stepped between Göker and Božidar and into the circle. "I'm here. Why did you kill Magnus and Cemal? I thought you wanted them alive."

Only until I knew which eight were best suited to take the seals. The rest can perish, return to hell where they belong.

"A hell you are opening to destroy earth," Raffé said.

Mine is to obey.

Raffé said nothing, gaze sweeping over the Princes who watched him and those who had fallen unconscious. He could feel their anger, their hate over the unfairness of it all. But more than anything, he could feel their desire to live.

Stronger than everything he could feel—taste—Méo's rage. Umah's rage. He let it wash over him, fill him, stir the demon in him. He would not accomplish anything right then by behaving like a human. Looking up into the angel's hundreds of eyes, he said, "Angel Umah, you are in danger of Falling. There is already a Prince of Rage. He will not tolerate your attempt to usurp him."

I am not so weak as to Fall. I was summoned by a Priest. I do holy work. There is no sparing this land. Better to see it destroyed. When there is nothing left, let something new and precious worthy of Their love grow. That is the reason I was summoned, the order I was given, and so shall it be.

"Be careful the orders you obey," Raffé drawled in reply, power curling through him, senses thrumming at the taste of blinding hunger on his tongue. The angel practically dripped with it, like a boy eager to have his wet cock sucked. Raffé laughed, low and rough. "You might find the master you follow is nothing but a stripling, and your true master waits to thrash you."

Umah hissed, the sound a searing echo in Raffé's mind. *I have no interest in the words of Manon's watered-down get.*

"Not so watered down as that," Raffé replied, power speaking with him, over him, rising up from deep within him as the pale marks of the seal burned so hot they felt cold. "Be careful the demons with which you play, little angel. I am not the only one here who would haply crack you open and feast on your innards like sweets."

You are nothing more than cast outs. Failures. You failed to serve and now you will die failing to defy. You are mine, and I tire of your words. In the name of the Holy One, long ago sundered into the Sacred Three. In the name of Heaven, of Earth, of Hell, I call to waking the Eight Seals of the Entrance. Pointing at each of the trapped Princes, he cast out balls of light to hover over each of them. The seals taken from around the kingdom. *Ture, Seal of Earth.* Athanasi screamed as the first seal consumed him. *Ari, Seal of Air.* Tollak. *Molec, Seal of Fire.* Axel. *Raab, Seal of Water.* Håkon glared hatefully before he was overtaken. *Haris, Seal of Birth.* Yrian. *Doum, Seal of Death.* Göker. *Seir, Seal of Heaven.* Premisl. *Belza, Seal of Hell.* Božidar.

Each seal shot out a beam of light. Raffé braced himself as they all struck him, dropping to one knee and panting raggedly as it burned, woke the magic sealed in the marks covering his body. He thrummed with the power of the Entrance. He was the door. He was the lock. *"None shall pass who do not command the Key. Those who fail to command what they have brought forth, fail to open the door they have summoned, shall find themselves imprisoned by it. Do you hear and understand?"*

I hear and understand, Umah replied.

"Who seeks to open the Entrance?"

Umah, Angel of the Wrath and the Vengeance.

"Command you the Key?"

I command the Key, Umah replied. Crackling chains pulled from the smoke that still hovered above, and the power of the Ninth Seal fractured for a moment as Raffé stared in horror at the broken, burnt, and bloody form of Alrin as he was dropped to the ground. His wings were broken and wet with blood, feathers falling to scatter around him. *Open the Entrance.*

Alrin stood up slowly, seemingly oblivious to his own pain, eyes black as he limped toward Raffé, leaving a trail of bloody footprints behind him.

Raffé's awareness wavered—fell, rose, fell again as his skin burned with the presence of the Master Key. *"I am the Master Seal, meant for the Key that will make of us the Entrance."*

"I am the Key," Alrin replied. *"Meant for the Master Seal that will make of us the Entrance."* He glowed with holy power, crackling like lightning along his skin, waiting to strike, and destroy them both—destroy everything. He reached up and wrapped one hand around Raffé's throat, the very tips of his claws, not yet extended to their long, deadly lengths, pricking Raffé's skin. The other he rested lightly against Raffé's back, and his claws threatened there too.

Around them the world darkened, Zyke Lorn Fall succumbing to the fresh poison polluting what little had remained of it. Darker and darker it grew until only the burn of chains and the crackling power skating over Alrin's skin offered light. The smoke, the influx of so much power, the searing brightness of those sharp, too-bright sources of light, blurred Raffé's eyes, and he was forced to close them.

Alrin's breath was hot against his skin as he laughed, taunting and cruel, a sick parody of …

"Cambord," Raffé breathed.

The hands on him jerked, tearing skin, then withdrew. Raffé opened his eyes to see Alrin's power had dulled slightly, the black of his eyes fading to reveal eyes that Raffé knew so much better even if they were no longer green. "What ... "

Umah snarled above them, undulated closer—and snarled again as light flared around them.

"I am the Key," Alrin said, looking hurt. "Why would you deny me? We are meant, were always meant, to be together! And now we can be. Why would you deny us our last chance?"

And Raffé understood why Waldemar had said that Telmé and Korin could not have been the Master Key and Ninth Seal. "I love you. I want to stand by you as long as we both live. But I don't want to die to be with you. That's not a triumph. You don't want that either. That's why you hated being a dragon. Do you think this is any better? That's not the bond we made, Cambord. We've learned how to love and let go. Do that now. Let go."

No! Umah screamed in fury, the sound so shattering that Raffé dropped to his knees, covering his ears and bowing his head in a futile effort to escape it. Power burned through him, seemed to burn through his skin from the inside, and he added his screams to Umah's.

No, no, no. I command the Key. I command the Entrance. You will open for me! Damn you, Defiants!

Raffé dared to look up, felt something dripping, and reached up to try and staunch the blood coming from his nose. He tried to stand as Umah came at them, burning with silver-blue fire, clogging the air with hate.

Alrin turned, spread his arms, and Umah shattered into pieces of light as they collided, falling into a pile of glittering shards that began to melt, turn black, and were slowly absorbed by the rune-riddled ground.

For a moment, for an eternity, the world was a familiar black void. Raffé felt something like a kiss on the back of his neck, a squeeze around his waist, and a soft sigh as something seemed to pull away from him like a cloak being removed. He looked down and saw the white marks were gone. The power that had simmered hot since they'd appeared was gone, and he felt mostly like the Prince he usually was.

"Raffé."

He looked up and saw Alrin, whose hair remained black and his eyes a dark blue-purple. The mark over his heart had become a faded scar ... but it was Alrin. His Cambord. "I thought we would die."

"I think ... I think that price was paid by Umah because he could not make me kill you," Alrin said, lightly touching his own chest, as if confused it was there—that he was there. "I feel different. I think the dragon part of me is gone forever."

"You smell human," Raffé murmured. "You smell as good as Kristof—his blood, I mean." He smiled faintly. "You always smelled good to me."

Alrin smiled, bright and shy and sweet. It broke whatever paralysis had been holding Raffé in place. He surged forward, threw himself into Alrin's arms, and kissed him. Alrin's lips were dry and cracked, and he tasted like smoke and old blood, but Raffé did not fucking care. He loosened his arms just enough to cup Alrin's face, his thumbs wiping through tears.

When he finally drew back, panting softly, the world had returned—or they had returned to the world. He could hear people calling his name, reflexively counted the voices he could hear, silently tallying the living and the dead. "I don't want to let you go." He wanted to stay right there, forever, never let Alrin go again.

"You said yourself we can, though," Alrin said quietly, turning his head to press a soft kiss to Raffé's palm. "The others need you right now, Commander-in-Waiting. Go."

Raffé nodded, withdrew, and spun away to start seeing what needed to be done. One of the trapped Princes groaned. Relief stung Raffé's eyes as he realized they weren't dead. Striding to the nearest, Božidar, Raffé yanked the sword from his thigh and pressed Božidar's cloak to the wound. "Will you be all right?" he asked.

"Nothing a Priest and a bit of rest won't fix," Božidar replied with a weak attempt at a leer. "Thank you."

"Nothing to thank me for," Raffé murmured and moved on to the next. When all the Princes were free, he looked to where, through curling traces of lingering smoke, the barrier still held. "How is it still in place? Should it not have died with Méo?"

"He killed Priests to make it," Håkon replied, groaning as he heaved himself to his feet and hobbled over to Raffé. He stumbled at the last, barely catching Raffé's shoulder in time to avoid falling again. Raffé looped an arm around his waist. "It's not as strong now without him to feed additional power into it, but it will still take some effort to break. Take me to it."

Raffé obeyed, helping Håkon over to where Kristof stood looking at them through the barrier. Håkon shook Raffé off with a grunt of thanks, then drew a dagger from his belt and slit his left palm. Dipping a finger in the blood that pooled, he began to write swiftly on the barrier. The words burned away almost as fast as he wrote them, but Kristof's expression brightened with comprehension. He spun away and plunged into the crowd.

"What's going on?"

"Kristof needs Priests and Princes to break it, and thankfully he has both on that side—unless, of course, Dalibor and Lassē are dead, but I doubt it." His face clouded, and Raffé knew he was thinking of Magnus and Cemal. Swearing softly, shaking himself, Håkon said, "Come on. We have to find his Majesty. Where the hell is Telmé?"

"Safe," Alrin called out. "I managed to get his Majesty, Telmé, and the High Priest to safety before the barrier closed. That's why Méo was able to grab me." He gestured to all his cuts and bruises and burns. "I'll go retrieve them once it's down. It looks like everyone else within the camp is dead. I'm sorry."

Raffé sighed. "Me too." He looked over the camp, the fallen, feeling tired. "Once the barrier is down, we'll collect the dead and burn them properly, purify this place as best we can." He looked at Håkon and the others as they slowly joined them. They all nodded; a few said, "Yes, Highness."

"If you're able, start gathering the dead. Everyone else, rest until the Priests can help. Do not push yourselves too hard. We don't need anyone else dying. Focus on recovering, on granting peace to the dead, and on getting home."

This time, all the Princes chorused, "Yes, Highness."

OF LAST RESORT

Disconcerted, Raffé nodded at them then turned to watch as Kristof, three Priests, and Dalibor and Lassē began to work on the barrier. Håkon stood beside him, and not too far off behind him, Raffé could hear the soft rumble of Alrin's voice. The urge to turn and look at him was strong, but Raffé resisted, focusing on those who needed him. Alrin was there; that was enough.

EPILOGUE

The gates of the inner ward slammed down behind Raffé and the men who had ridden with him, the guards blowing the horn to signal that all were accounted for and the gates were closed for the night. Raffé dismounted and handed his horse off to the Tamer who came running up.

"Excellent work," Raffé murmured to the Wolves of the Moon as they came up to him, grinning in their toothy way, still thrumming with the energy of a successful mission. "Go wreak some minor havoc, just not too much of it."

Growling, the Wolves nudged against him, clapping him on the shoulder before bolting off into the depths of the castle, no doubt intent on first food, then fucking. A familiar large, looming figure stepped out of the shadows of the castle, and the wolf at the head of the group bolted toward the man, and Dalibor's booming laugh briefly filled the ward.

"I take it you successfully addressed the demon?" Håkon asked, striding up to him, torchlight gleaming in his pale hair and sinking into his blood red tunic.

Raffé nodded. "Yes. Were there any problems south?"

"None at all, Highness," Håkon replied, falling into step beside him as they headed across the ward and into the bright, boisterous warmth of the great hall. It was filled with men recently come off a late watch and enjoying the second round of supper. At the front of the hall, Birgir sat with his wives and three eldest children, enjoying a rare evening quiet enough he could dine with his Legion. He saw Raffé and lifted a hand in greeting. Raffé returned it then resumed skimming the hall. "Telmé is with Korin?"

"Yes." Håkon's voice was soft, threaded with worry. They all worried. Since returning from Zyke Lorn Fall seven months ago, Telmé had barely left Korin's bedside in the Temple. With Korin's heir a four year old girl, everyone worried what would happen if he did not wake. Kristof had taken up most of the High Priest's duties, but everyone waited to see if Korin would ever wake—and what would happen if he did not.

Making a note to go see him later, Raffé asked, "Where is Alrin?"

"I only returned a couple of hours ago and have not seen him." Håkon smirked faintly.

Raffé snorted. "I guess that explains Kristof's absence." He clapped Håkon on the shoulder. "If you will pardon me, then, I am going to seek out my husband."

Leering, Håkon said, "Enjoy your seeking."

Rolling his eyes and cuffing him lightly, Raffé abandoned Håkon and the nearby Paladins who had overheard the conversation to their sniggering and left the great hall. He wended his way through the castle up to the top of the second level where his suite was located. It was a different room than what he'd had before because formally being declared Telmé's second gained him a suite comprised of a bedchamber, study, and receiving room.

It smelled like fresh bread and honey when he stepped in. A servant tidying the place looked up and smiled upon seeing him. Bustling over, the man helped Raffé out of his cloak, armor, and weapons. "He's in the study, Highness."

"Thank you," Raffé said, and handed over his gloves. He smiled faintly as his eyes caught the mark on the back of his right hand: a Sacred Heart surrounded by thorns and feathers, the marriage mark he and Alrin had designed.

He waited until the servant was gone before walking across the room to push open the door to the study. Witchlights bobbed around the small room, filling it with plenty of light by which to read in a windowless room.

Alrin sat at the large desk that took up much of the room, the shelves behind and beside him taking up much of the rest of the space, leaving room only for a smaller work table and extra chair. A thick, colorful rug covered the floor and kept back part of the chill, which was further mitigated by a small fireplace on the only wall lacking bookshelves. Alrin was bent over a large book, delicately turning beautifully illuminated pages filled with words of sorcery. With his draconic nature stripped away, being the Key had left behind magical abilities that a pure human would not normally possess; Alrin spent most of his time reading or practicing with the Master of Magic, learning how to be a Sorcerer instead of a Dragoon. His black hair had grown to just past his shoulders and was currently pulled back in a loose tail that would slip free the moment he moved. The gold rims of his reading glasses gleamed in the witchlights, and the fragrant smell of spiced tea mingled with the sweet, sharp anise scent that was entirely Alrin.

Looking up, hearing or sensing movement, Alrin broke into a warm smile when he saw Raffé. He stood, discarding his reading glasses, hair sliding free of the thong barely holding it as he moved around the desk and strode across the room to hug Raffé tightly. "Welcome home," he said gruffly and drew back just enough to press a long, thorough kiss to Raffé's mouth. He tasted heavily of spiced tea, lips warm and soft as they pressed against Raffé's, their mouths fitting together as though long worn to a perfect fit. His hand was heavy, almost hot, as it combed gently through Raffé's cold hair. "I did not think you would be back until tomorrow at best. I do like a pleasant surprise." His mouth slid along Raffé's again as he took a slight step forward, just enough to lightly press Raffé against the wall. When he eventually drew back, his voice was husky, lips swollen and wet, so red Raffé's jaw ached as much as his cock. "How was your trip?"

"I don't give a bloody damn about my trip," Raffé replied, tugging playfully at Alrin's hair. "I want you, now."

"Yes, Highness." Mouth curving in a grin, Alrin leaned in to quickly nip Raffé's bottom lip, dancing away before Raffé could retaliate. Alrin held a hand up, murmuring softly as he curled his fingers into a fist. The witchlights dimmed, leaving only a spectral glow behind. "Come to bed, Prince," Alrin said softly and led the way from the room.

FIN

MEGAN DERP
WITH PRIDE
PRINCES OF THE BLOOD

When his sister falls ill, Kristof is ordered to assume a duty never meant for him: become the Duke of Stehlmore and marry a notorious Prince of the Blood. It is one of the oldest honors and duties undertaken by his family, but Kristof feels only resentment that he must leave behind all he knows to serve an arrogant half-demon his mother's reach has never needed.

Prince Håkon Vinter is an exceptional Prince of the Blood: respected, feared, and unstoppable. He has no need of an arrogant, cowardly Paladin who clearly wants nothing to do with him. Once they figure out how to stop the demons suddenly plaguing the kingdom and whoever is orchestrating the attacks, he'll figure out how to free himself of his worthless fiancé as well.

About the Author

Megan is a long time resident of queer romance, and keeps herself busy reading, writing, and publishing it. She is often accused of fluff and nonsense. When she's not involved in writing, she likes to cook, harass her wife and cats, or watch movies. She loves to hear from readers, and can be found all over the internet.

meganderr.com
patreon.com/meganderr
pillowfort.io/maderr
meganderr.blogspot.com
facebook.com/meganaprilderr
meganaderr@gmail.com
@meganaderr

Printed in Great Britain
by Amazon